NEW EROTICA 4

In the following pages you'll find some of the finest erotic writing available anywhere. The Nexus imprint has continued to grow and change to reflect the more sophisticated demands of our readers, and now features tales dealing with the most bizarre extremes of sexual activity. We plan to carry on bringing you the best in contemporary erotic fiction, with the most stylish covers and the kinkiest stories you can find.

T0314672

Other titles in the series:

NEW EROTICA
4

Extracts from the best of Nexus

This book is a work of fiction.
In real life, make sure you practise safe sex.

First published in 1998 by
Nexus
Thames Wharf Studios
Rainville Road, London W6 9HT

Extracts from the following works:

The Black Room	© Lisette Ashton
Penny in Harness	© Penny Birch
The Mistress of Sternwood Grange	© Arabella Knight
Amanda in the Private House	© Esme Ombreux
Citadel of Servitude	© Aran Ashe
Agony Aunt	© G. C. Scott
Annie and the Countess	© Evelyn Culber
The Training of Fallen Angels	© Kendal Grahame
The Schooling of Stella	© Yolanda Celbridge
Bound to Submit	© Amanda Ware
Chains of Shame	© Brigitte Markham
Sisters of Severcy	© Jean Aveline

Typeset by SetSystems Ltd, Saffron Walden, Essex

ISBN 978 0 753 539040 0

The Random House Group Limited supports The Forest Stewardship
Council (FSC®), the leading international forest certification organisation.
Our books carrying the FSC label are printed on FSC® certified paper.
FSC is the only forest certification scheme endorsed by the leading
environmental organisations, including Greenpeace. Our
paper procurement policy can be found at
www.randomhouse.co.uk/environment

MIX
Paper | Supporting
responsible forestry
FSC® C018179

Printed and bound in Great Britain by Clays Ltd, St Ives PLC

CONTENTS

INTRODUCTION

The Nexus imprint is the largest collection of erotic fiction published in Britain. The list is as diverse as it is erotic, boasting a wide variety of themes and settings – from classic Victorian erotica to contemporary and cutting-edge SM fiction – while ensuring that only the finest and most arousing stories are published. With two new titles every month and an extensive backlist, readers new to erotica – or those wishing to reacquaint themselves with this fascinating genre – might find the choice available a little daunting.

With *New Erotica 4*, the latest in a series of anthologies, we hope to give the reader a taste for the variety of the imprint – from Aran Ashe's obsessively detailed fantasy world to Penny Birch's naughty pony-girl antics. Virtually every erotic activity imaginable – from bondage to watersports via depilation and orgies – is featured, and described in the most explicit detail.

We hope you enjoy the collection as much as we enjoyed putting it – and all the other Nexus titles – together. Have fun!

THE BLACK ROOM

Lisette Ashton

Lisette Ashton is one of the most talented new authors of erotic fiction in the field. Her novels always have unusual and contemporary settings – one is set on the Amazon (*Amazon Slave*), while her forthcoming novel (*Fairground Attractions*, to be published in December 1998) is set in a fairground. Her characters are always absolutely credible, something of a rarity in erotic fiction, and she demonstrates an unashamed enthusiasm for the perverse worlds of domination and submission.

The following extract is taken from the *The Black Room*, Lisette's first novel for Nexus. This novel marks the debut of Jo Valentine – a private investigator with some unusually rude interests – who also appears in a subsequent adventure, *The Black Garter*. When she is assigned to infiltrate the Pentagon Agency, she is prepared to do anything to get results – but nothing can prepare her for what lies in the black room. The more she discovers about the agency, the more she learns of her passion for dark and bizarre sexual games that go beyond anything she has experienced before. In this extract a prospective trainee of the Pentagon Agency discovers, as she undergoes a lewd and intimate inspection, that there is more to her further education than she'd previously bargained for.

K elly sat nervously in the waiting room, trying not to think about what she had done.

It was a clean, pleasant room with sunlight glinting through the louvre blinds at the windows. The walls were plastered with a wide array of posters, warning against the dangers of smoking and unprotected sex, in cheerful, primary colours. Dozens of the eye-catching images covered the entire room but Kelly, lost in her own solemn reverie, could not be bothered to look at them. She ignored her surroundings just as she ignored the untidy pile of glossy magazines on the seat next to her. Her fingers played nervously with the clasp of her bag and her head was tilted downward, as though she was totally absorbed by this fascinating spectacle.

Sitting alone in a discreet corner of the room, she looked like a woman trying to hide from the world.

Her thoughts were fully occupied by the big step she had taken and the greater ones that stretched ahead of her. In spite of her fiery mane of red hair and enigmatic good looks, Kelly was not a confident woman. Every decision she made was invariably dogged by grave doubt and deep misgivings. This latest one was no exception. Admittedly she had been left with no other choice but Kelly still fretted at the boldness of her own actions. This was not simply a giant step she had taken: it was a desperate leap into the unknown.

The waiting-room door crashed open. The sound was so sudden and unexpected it jolted Kelly abruptly from

7

her thoughts. She glanced up to see a young woman burst into the waiting room.

Long golden curls bounced over the girl's narrow shoulders as she ran. The hair hid her face from view as she glanced back at her pursuer. The blonde was closely followed by a brunette, taller and blessed with a muscular, athletic build. Both women were breathing heavily, as though the chase had been an arduous one.

Before the blonde could reach the room's only other door, the darker woman grabbed her by the shoulder. She pushed her heavily to the wall, pinning her there.

'One more stunt like that, Helen, and I'll see you in the black room,' the brunette said breathlessly.

Kelly considered the pair uneasily.

Helen, the woman being pressed against the wall, was a good-looking Nordic blonde. She had a haughty expression and a severe, arrogant line to her jaw. Under other circumstances, Kelly guessed the woman would have looked intimidating or austere. She had the innate self-possesion of a Valkyrie warrior-maiden. Now, as the blonde stared timidly at her captor, she did not look remotely imposing. Her terrified expression hovered somewhere between desperate defiance and outright fear.

'I . . . I . . . didn't . . . didn't do anything, Mistress Stacey,' she stammered hurriedly. Her eyes were wide with trepidation. 'I . . .' She got no further.

'Don't give me that crap,' Stacey growled fiercely. She pulled Helen forward then shoved her roughly against the wall again. Swiftly, she raised a hand and slapped the blonde hard across the face. The sound echoed around the waiting room like a pistol shot.

Kelly muttered a small cry of surprise. She was briefly thankful that her own shocked whimper was drowned out by the blonde's startled gasp.

Mistress Stacey was a formidable figure, not only taller, but also broader than the younger woman. Her powerful athletic body was clad in a loose blouse and skirt but this did not detract her from obvious physical capability. She moved her hand away from Helen's cheek – revealing the angry red blush her blow had caused.

'You're this far away from spending a day in the black room,' she whispered furiously, holding her index finger and thumb slightly apart. Her teeth were clenched together as she spoke, reinforcing her barely concealed fury. 'Why don't you just come clean and make it easier on yourself?' She paused for a moment, studiously watching Helen's face for a response. When Helen made no reply, Stacey acted swiftly. She released the girl's shoulder and made to grab at the front of her blouse.

'No!' Helen gasped. She half-heartedly put her hands in front of herself for protection.

The commanding brunette slapped Helen's hands away and then brought her knuckles across the blonde's strong Nordic jaw. Helen moaned, a low, guttural sound, and raised a hand to the side of her face where she had been struck. She began to sob as Stacey placed both hands on her blouse and effortlessly ripped the garment open.

From her unnoticed seat Kelly tried fervently not to look at Helen's breasts. She had been brought up to believe in the virtues of modesty and chastity. Even though she was a reluctant witness, the scene being played out before her made Kelly feel like a depraved Peeping Tom. She employed a huge effort of willpower trying not to look at Helen's body. However, the sight drew her gaze like a magnet.

Helen's full, round orbs were barely concealed in a white lacy bra. The dark circles of her areolas were clearly visible through the skimpy fabric of her underwear. There was also a noticeable rise and fall of her chest, as though she was very excited; the hard nubs of her nipples strained urgently against their confines. Her laboured breathing had deepened into low gasps of obvious pleasure. The sultry pout of her lips, and the shine of excitement in her eyes, made it clear that Helen was not Mistress Stacey's unwilling victim.

Stacey fondled Helen's breasts with a careless disregard that bordered on brutality. Her fingers roughly massaged the girl's pliant flesh through the fabric of her underwear, pressing mercilessly into the soft, sensitive skin. She paid particular attention to the taut buds of Helen's nipples, extracting a series of responses from her victim that sounded simultaneously pained and pleasured.

'We could have sorted this out a lot quicker in my chamber,' Stacey said dourly. 'Don't tell me you didn't enjoy my little game with the tawse last week?' she whispered.

Helen groaned softly, as though she were enduring the special delights of a half-forgotten memory. She closed her eyes and pressed her head back against the wall. Her bottom lip pushed forward unconsciously and she sighed happily beneath Stacey's rough handling.

'Tell me where it is, Helen, and we can overlook this little matter,' Stacey growled softly. She squeezed one of the blonde's nipples between her thumb and forefinger. Her grin widened as Helen tried unscucessfully to stifle a gasp of pain. 'Speak up,' Stacey hissed in a threatening tone. 'You don't want me to play rough, do you?'

Before Helen could reply, Stacey was already acting. Continuing to hold Helen's erect nipple, she kept the blonde pressed securely against the wall. With her other hand she reached downwards and traced her fingers up one of Helen's stocking-clad legs.

'No, mistress!' Helen whispered. She breathed the words in a dark, husky murmur that sounded more like encouragement than refusal.

Stacey stared menacingly into the blonde's face while her hand continued its slow journey upward. Helen wore a short, flared skirt and the hem was raised by Stacey's wrist as her hand went higher. The skirt lifted to reveal the dark tops of Helen's stockings, beneath the creamy expanse of her milky-white thighs. Helen's hem continued to rise until the white triangle of her knickers was on full view.

Stacey's fingers paused at the gusset of Helen's panties. She traced the outline of Helen's pouting labia through the thin cotton fabric. Then she drew her fingertips along the warm skin next to the elasticated band of her knickers. Each movement was slow, yet decisive, designed to arouse Helen without letting her forget who was in charge.

Helen moaned softly, the sound coming from some dark, delightful place situated between agony and ecstasy. With her eyes still closed, she licked her lips avariciously, savouring the pleasure of the moment.

Stacey continued to study Helen's face. A tight, twisted smile curled her lips, as though she was enjoying the blonde's discomfort and unhappiness. She used her fingers adeptly and shifted the gusset of Helen's panties to one side revealing the tender pink lips of the blonde's shaved pussy. With the tip of her index finger she traced a slow line back and forth along the length of Helen's crease.

Helen sighed softly. Lost in the elation of the moment she seemed to have forgotten the danger that threatened her. Unconsciously, she rubbed the tops of her exposed thighs with the palms of her hands. Her fingers were splayed wide apart as though she were in the throes of unprecedented ecstasy. Her soft sighs slowly became deeper as Stacey continued to tease the sensitive pink flesh of Helen's hole.

Stacey's cruel smile tightened as she watched Helen. She continued to squeeze one nipple, rolling it carefully between her tightly pressed fingers. Her other hand was occupied in the warm cleft between the blonde's legs, rubbing the tactile lips of her pussy with slow deliberation. Deftly, she used her index and ring fingers to part the blonde's labia, then slowly slid her middle finger deep into the heated wetness of Helen's sex.

The blonde cried out in shocked surprise, her eyes opening wide.

Kelly watched as the middle finger slid deeper and deeper into the depths of Helen's moist hole. She had never seen two women sharing such intimacy before and as her initial feelings of revulsion dissipated, they were replaced by an unbidden thrill of excitement.

She had been holding her breath from the moment the

11

two women burst into the room. Initially she had been wary of disturbing the pair and suffering their retribution. Now she was fearful of alerting them to her presence and interrupting the erotic scene. Watching Stacey fondle Helen with such brutal disregard had been intensely stimulating, as had the sight of the brunette fingering the blonde's vagina. The heat of Kelly's excitement had brought with it a delightful moistness she had not anticipated. She was determined to see how the spectacle progressed.

Along with the middle finger, Stacey thrust her index finger upward, deep into the welcoming warmth of Helen's pussy lips. The blonde released a long sultry moan of ecstasy. Stacey twisted her hand slightly to one side, then pushed both fingers deep inside Helen's cleft as far as they would go.

'N– . . . No, Mistress Stacey, I . . .' Helen's cheeks were furiously red with the warm glow of her mounting excitement. Her refusals and denials were half-hearted in the extreme. The enjoyment she was receiving from the mistress's unorthodox body search clearly exceeded her embarrassment and discomfort. One nipple pressed fiercely against the confines of her bra, the other stood rigidly between the tips of Stacey's merciless fingers. Each breath was a short, ragged exclamation of her arousal.

Stacey squeezed cruelly hard on Helen's nipple, inspiring a sharp cry of surprised pain. At the same time she tugged her fingers swiftly from Helen's pussy, making the movement viciously harsh and lacking in intimacy.

Helen gasped as though she had been slapped.

The fingers slid easily from Helen's warmth, bringing with them a small plastic-wrapped package that she had secreted in the most intimate of hiding places. Both fingers, and the package, were glistening slickly with the creamy moisture of Helen's excitement. Stacey held the bag between her index finger and thumb, then swayed it hypnotically to and fro in front of Helen's face.

'Money, Helen?' she enquired knowingly. A pantomime frown of maternal disapproval stretched her lips. The charade did not mask her true feelings at making this discovery, nor did her austere tone. The fact she was delighted with this result was blatantly obvious. 'Quite a lot of money, it would seem. You know the rules about having so much cash in the hostel, don't you, Helen?' Stacey sneered. 'Have you been stealing again?'

Helen stifled a sob, closed her eyes and turned away from Mistress Stacey. A pained expression strained her features. Helen placed a hand to her groin, and was rubbing her fingers purposefully against the swell of her exposed lips. Her manicured nails deftly stroked the dark-pink flesh. Spreading the folds wide open she eased a finger inside herself, moistening the pad with the creamy juice of her arousal. Suitably lubricated, she began to draw impatient circles over the hood of her clitoris. The bead of erectile tissue was slowly teased to the brink of climax with a wicked combination of skill and urgency. Oblivious to her audience, Helen furiously caressed herself to the pinnacle of pleasure. Her colour darkened and a broad smile of elated satisfaction crossed the blonde's face. She groaned happily with a climactic shiver of pleasure that coursed through her entire body.

As the waves of happiness receded she stood quietly for a moment in a state of delighted rapture. When she opened her eyes, they were shining with excitement. The expression was only a fleeting one, disappearing the instant she found her gaze focusing on Kelly. A shocked expression replaced the look of satisfaction she had been wearing. Modestly, she tugged her skirt down and coughed back a surprised exclamation.

Aware of the sudden change in Helen's mood, Stacey turned and saw Kelly for the first time. She sucked in her breath angrily, treating Kelly to a glare of the darkest venom. Acting with the instinctive alacrity of a wild animal, Mistress Stacey walked over to Kelly and pointed a menacing finger in her face. 'You didn't see anything, do you understand!' she hissed threateningly.

In her hurry to agree, Kelly found herself on the point of stammering just as Helen had done. She swallowed nervously and closed her eyes, trying to compose her thoughts before replying.

'You didn't see anything,' Mistress Stacey repeated.

Her finger was so close to Kelly's nose she could sense the fragrance of Helen's musky pussy juices that still lingered there. It was a sweet scent that filled her nostrils and unwittingly triggered the memory of her earlier arousal. Wilfully dismissing this notion, Kelly nodded her head in furious agreement. 'I didn't see anything,' she repeated. 'Nothing at all. I'm sorry,' she added unnecessarily.

Stacey appeared not to have heard anything else. She turned her attention back to Helen and graced her with a look of the darkest fury. 'We'll finish this in your dormitory,' she said in a tone of barely tempered rage. 'Wait for me there, you little thief.'

Dismissed, Helen fled from the room casting a meaningful glare at Kelly. The defiant expression only flickered in her eyes for a moment. It was not there long enough for Mistress Stacey to notice but it was sufficient for Kelly to know she had just made an enemy. A very dangerous enemy.

As the waiting-room door closed on Helen, Kelly realised she was alone with Stacey. It was an unsettling realisation and Kelly swallowed nervously, aware that her heart was beating an alarmed tattoo in her chest. She stared up at the woman uncertainly, wishing she did not feel so intimidated. 'I didn't see anything,' she repeated earnestly. 'Honestly I . . .'

Mistress Stacey reached out and stroked a finger across Kelly's lips, silencing her panicked babble. It was a gesture that should have felt unpleasant or threatening. Instead, Kelly found the careful caress was curiously stimulating. The delicate touch rekindled the deep warmth of her earlier arousal. Her finger traced its way gently along the length of Kelly's pouting lower lip, provoking a shiver of excitement that travelled from the base of her neck to the tip of her spine.

She was startled by an unexpected pang of urgency that

14

seemed to emanate from her nipples. With an inward sigh of disdain she realised she was suffering the unexpected symptoms of pure sexual arousal. It had been so long since she had experienced such feelings, Kelly wondered if her memory was playing tricks on her. However, when the inner walls of her pussy began to throb with their own hungry desire, Kelly knew she had not been mistaken. She stared into the mysterious depths of the mistress's ebony eyes, wondering if she too had sensed that electric tingle of sexual attraction.

'Is this your first day at the hostel?' Stacey asked softly, stroking her finger along Kelly's cheek.

Kelly swallowed nervously again and nodded, not trusting herself to speak. She felt torn between conflicting emotions, not knowing whether to trust her desires or her fear. Stacey had been brutal and domineering in her treatment of Helen, and Kelly considered the woman to be utterly terrifying. However, she had never before felt stimulated or aroused by the presence of another woman and the sensation was so unfamiliar it piqued her curiosity. Struggling valiantly with her inner turmoil, Kelly suppressed a shiver and stared helplessly into Stacey's face.

The mistress's smile was not an unkind one. 'If it's your first day at the hostel, then I'm sure you won't be making waves, will you?'

Kelly shook her head, amazed that she felt so eager to please this callous, antagonistic woman. Her treatment of Helen had been cold and barbaric. Yet without knowing why, Kelly felt anxious to meet with Stacey's approval. Worse than that, Kelly thought unhappily, she felt a strong desire for Stacey to touch her as she had been touching Helen.

'I guess I'll be seeing you around,' Mistress Stacey said quietly. She allowed her fingers to caress Kelly's cheek one final time, and moved her mouth close to Kelly's. The two women were on the point of kissing. Their faces were so close, Kelly knew she would only have to move forward slightly and her mouth would be pressed against Stacey's. The warmth of the brunette's breath tickled her top lip and Kelly wondered bewilderedly if she should be making that first move.

'I guess I'll be seeing you around,' Mistress Stacey said again, moving her head away from Kelly before she could make up her mind. She dropped one eyelid in a solemn wink and then left the waiting room without another word.

Kelly shivered and released the pent-up sigh of relief that had been welling inside her.

Simultaneously she felt hot and cold and more than a little confused by her reaction to Mistress Stacey. Before she had a chance to analyse her thoughts and feelings, the door to the examination room opened. Wasting no time on pleasantries, a petite, dark-haired girl curtly summoned Kelly into the doctor's office.

'I'm running a little behind schedule today,' the doctor declared, as Kelly entered the small room.

Her accusatory tone made Kelly feel guilty, as though she was in some way responsible for the doctor's problems.

'It will speed things along if you strip and answer questions at the same time.'

Kelly looked uncertainly at the doctor, wondering if she had heard the woman correctly. She was sitting behind a meticulously tidy desk, with Dr A. McMahon written in gold on the wooden desk-plaque. She had a proud head of long raven locks spilling over her shoulders and Kelly guessed she was in her early thirties. The doctor did not look as formidable as Mistress Stacey but the crispness of her voice made it clear she was not the sort of person who tolerated fools.

'You want me to undress?' Kelly asked nervously.

Doctor McMahon glanced up from the papers she was studying and graced Kelly with a despondent frown. Her eyes were the same ultra-black jet as her hair, contrasting starkly with her sallow complexion. The only thing that stopped her from looking incredibly attractive was the contemptuous curl of her upper lip. 'I haven't yet perfected the art of doing clothed examinations,' she said with icy sarcasm. 'So, I'm afraid you'll have to tolerate my lack of skill and just undress as I asked.' This said, the doctor turned her attention back to the notes on her desk.

Kelly cast a nervous glace around the small examination room. There was an examination trolley resting by the wall behind her and a chair facing the doctor's desk. Aside from these pieces of furniture, the room was bare, save for one full-length mirror and a rack of bookshelves filled with important-looking leather-bound volumes. The petite nurse who had escorted Kelly into the room was bent over a clinically sterile sink busying herself by washing her hands. Directing her question at the doctor, Kelly asked uncertainly, 'Do I just undress here?'

Doctor McMahon drew a sharp intake of breath. She raised her head from the papers and glared impatiently at Kelly. 'Undress here if you want,' she said, speaking tightly. 'If you like, you can leave the building now and undress on the front fucking step. Just take your clothes off so I can begin the examination.'

Left with no doubt as to what was expected of her, Kelly began to undress.

'Your name is Kelly Rogers?'

Unfastening her blouse, Kelly nodded. Then, realising the doctor was not looking at her, she quickly answered, 'Yes. That's right.'

'Twenty-four years old?'

'Yes.'

'And you've been with the Pentagon Temp Agency for a month now?'

'That's right,' Kelly said quickly. 'Mr Peterson at the Agency said I'd been doing really well and suggested I should do this course and consider becoming a professional temp.'

'A simple yes would have been sufficient,' Doctor McMahon said dryly.

Blushing furiously at the other woman's cold disregard, Kelly shrugged herself out of her blouse. She folded it neatly and placed it next to her handbag, on the chair facing the doctor.

'You're qualified as a medical and legal secretary,'

Doctor McMahon continued briskly. 'And you have a degree in business management.'

'Yes,' Kelly said simply, knowing that no other response was required.

She responded with one-word answers to a string of questions the doctor fired at her. They concerned a wide range of topics including the medical history of herself and her family. Her ability to answer them concisely helped Kelly to feel a little more relaxed. As the questions went on, she was almost beginning to feel comfortable about the examination, in spite of the doctor's brusqueness and the distinct lack of privacy.

Doctor McMahon paused in her questioning and glanced up from the notes she was looking at. 'It says here that you're married.'

Kelly paused in the act of stepping out of her skirt. 'Separated,' she said quietly. She realised the doctor was staring at her and continued to step out of the skirt with a contrived air of feigned nonchalance.

'How long have you been separated?'

'Is that important?' Kelly replied.

Doctor McMahon shrugged, studying Kelly's half-naked body with a wry smile on her lips. 'I suppose not,' she replied. 'I was just interested, that's all.'

'It's not something I care to talk about,' Kelly said with soft defiance.

Standing in front of the doctor, clad only in her bra, pants, stockings and suspender belt, she did not feel defiant. Being totally honest with herself, Kelly felt distinctly vulnerable standing half-naked before this antagonistic stranger. Her marriage and subsequent separation were topics she still felt uncomfortable with. However, the thorny subject of her failed marriage was not something she wanted to discuss and she was determined not to be pushed on the issue.

From the corner of her eye she glimpsed her reflection in the full-length mirror and was surprised by the image of an attractive woman she saw there. Blazing red hair cascaded over her shoulders and down her back in a torrent of fiery, warm, orange and scarlet shades. The glossy satin sheen of the emerald-green underwear she wore complemented her whey-coloured complexion perfectly. The frilly green suspender belt went down into a V at her waist, accentuating the pronounced slenderness of her smooth, flat stomach. Her seamed stockings were still in place, and the heels she wore emphasised the length and firmness of her long, coltish legs. She wished she felt as glamorous and confident as the woman in the mirror looked but she knew such an ambition went far beyond her dreams.

'Are you practising sex with a partner at the moment?' Doctor McMahon asked briskly.

Kelly's blush deepened. 'Do I have to answer that one?' she asked.

'I'd prefer it if you answered all my questions,' the doctor replied crisply. Glancing disdainfully up at Kelly she seemed to notice the woman's underwear for the first time. 'According to my reference books, undressed usually means taking all your clothes off. Now, are you currently, practising sex with a partner?'

'No,' Kelly said, reaching awkwardly behind herself for the clasp of her bra. She unfastened it and slid the garment off, placing it carefully on the pile of neatly folded clothes she had created on the chair. She could feel her blush darkening to a furious degree as she displayed her bared breasts to the doctor. Her cheeks felt as though they were smouldering with the heat of her embarrassment. Not daring to disobey the doctor's instruction, Kelly unfastened the clasp of her suspender belt and, after stepping out of her shoes, began to unroll the stockings from her legs.

'When you've finished undressing, lie down on the trolley,' Doctor McMahon said simply. Without taking a breath she asked, 'Have you ever been involved in a sub–dom or sadomasochistic relationship?'

Kelly stopped unrolling her stockings and stared at the doctor with an expression of genuine bewilderment. 'I don't know what that means,' she replied innocently.

The doctor rolled her eyes. 'During your marriage, did you ever punish your husband physically, or mentally, for sexual gratification?'

'Of course not!' Kelly declared, shocked by the suggestion.

'Did your husband ever do that to you?' Doctor McMahon persisted.

'I told you, I don't want to talk about my marriage,' Kelly said, turning her gaze away from the doctor's. She busied herself with one stocking, unwilling to meet the other woman's angry expression.

The doctor's sign of exasperation was clearly audible in the quiet confines of the room. 'All right,' she said stiffly, making obvious attempts to control her dissipating patience. 'Have you ever been involved with anyone in a relationship like the one I've just described?'

'No!' Kelly said firmly.

'You don't know what you're missing!' a small voice whispered behind her.

Kelly had almost forgotten about the nurse until she added her wry contribution to the question-and-answer session.

'I thought you'd already learnt not to speak until spoken to,' the doctor snapped.

Placing a horrified hand over her mouth, the girl whispered her heartfelt apology. 'Please, Doctor McMahon. I'm sorry. I spoke without thinking, I . . .'

Doctor McMahon waved a dismissive hand, silencing the apologetic girl. Fixing her attention on Kelly she glanced unhappily at the skimpy pair of green satin panties she wore. 'When you eventually get around to taking your knickers off, you can lie on the couch and I can start my examination.'

Mortified by her own feeling of vulnerability, Kelly stepped quickly out of the pants and placed them with the rest of her clothes. She had never felt comfortable with her own nudity. This sensation was heightened by the close proximity of the doctor and her nurse. Staring meekly at the floor, she walked swiftly to the trolley and eased herself on to the uncomfortable, paper-covered mattress. There was no pillow or raised end and she found herself staring miserably at the ceiling, her hands folded demurely over her stomach. She could not see Doctor McMahon or the nurse from her position and, in that moment, Kelly grasped a brief moment of relief, imagining herself alone. It was only a small reprieve, the illusion of solitude being broken by the sound of a chair moving and the doctor's whispered command to her aide.

Then Doctor McMahon was standing beside her. She had removed the white three-quarter-length physician's coat she sported earlier and Kelly now saw her as a young attractive woman in a plain white T-shirt. 'Relax a little,' the doctor said, placing a reassuring hand on Kelly's shoulder. It was the first time she had spoken to Kelly without a note of vicious contempt inflecting her words. 'This won't be so bad if you ease up a little.'

Kelly tried to return the doctor's comforting smile but found her gaze was drawn to the tight white T-shirt the doctor was wearing. She noticed the woman was not wearing a bra beneath the garment and from Kelly's prone position she was close enough to see the hard nubs of the doctor's erect nipples. The sight made her swallow nervously and she was about to say something when she felt the doctor's hand gently caress her breast.

The sensation was electric. She had never had a woman touch her so intimately and the feeling was exhilarating. Remembering her responsiveness in the waiting room when Stacey had stroked a finger along her lip, Kelly wondered if she was developing some sort of mental illness. She had never been sexually attracted to women before, yet within the last ten minutes she had come close to kissing one woman and was now allowing another to nonchalantly stroke her breasts. The fact that she was enjoying these encounters added fuel to her fear of insanity. Her heart began to race and she could not tell if it was hurried by apprehension or excitement.

The doctor's fingers traced slow circles on the soft flesh of Kelly's orbs, gently stimulating the tactile skin with her

21

subtle caress. Her smile, although not unkind, was predatory enough to make Kelly feel acutely vulnerable. 'Relax a little,' the doctor encouraged once again. 'You're going to enjoy this. Trust me.'

Laid on the trolley, having witnessed Mistress Stacey's punishment of Helen and then endured the doctor's harsh, invasive questioning, Kelly did not feel relaxed enough to enjoy anything. All she wanted was to get the physical aspect of the examination over and done with, regardless of what it entailed. Afterwards she could shut herself in the confines of her own room and try to analyse the bizarre attraction she was feeling for other women. She glanced downwards, trying to convince herself that the doctor's touch had only been accidental. Seeing the woman's fingers casually caressing her right breast, tracing circles around the darkening areola, Kelly realised the touch had been no accident. She took a sharp intake of breath. 'You're tou . . . touching me,' she said awkwardly.

The doctor smiled easily. 'Yes,' she admitted, not moving her hand away. 'You do like it, don't you?'

Unsure of her opinions and her body's mutinous responses, Kelly did not trust herself to respond to the question. 'Is this part of the examination?' she asked, struggling to sound indignant and failing miserably.

'Sort of,' Doctor McMahon said. She placed a finger on either side of Kelly's nipple and tweaked it playfully.

Unwittingly, Kelly found herself enjoying a thrill of pleasure she had not anticipated. The sensation was so intense a shiver coursed through her entire body. She stared at the doctor, unsure of how to respond. Without knowing when it had started, Kelly realised her breathing had deepened.

'The best part of the examination is still to come,' Doctor McMahon said softly, rolling the nipple playfully between her fingers. Her hand cupped Kelly's breast and caressed the sensitive flesh with a measured degree of care. Her fingers were cool against Kelly's warm skin but the silky touch of the doctor's palms created a friction that was intense enough to generate its own heat.

Kelly heard herself moan softly in appreciation. Whatever the reason for her sudden loss of inhibitions, she knew that now was not the time to contemplate it. The pleasure she was receiving from the doctor's touch was something so exciting anad new she was prepared to enjoy it now and think about it later. She glanced nervously at the doctor and was surprised to see the petite nurse peering lecherously over her shoulder.

Noticing Kelly's attention was distracted, the doctor moved her hand away and turned to the nurse. 'Is that what you found?' she asked crisply.

'Yes, doctor,' the nurse replied timidly.

Kelly cound not see what they were talking about but she felt an unsettling thrill of trepidation at the doctor's curt tone. A tiny butterfly fluttered nervously in the pit of of her stomach, enhancing the darkly erotic flavour of her arousal. She tried to surreptitiously shift her position and see what the pair were discussing.

'You've done well,' the doctor told the nurse stiffly. Turning to Kelly, she said, 'This was found in your handbag. Would you mind telling me why you have it?'

Kelly felt her face darken with embarrassment as she stared at the small phallus in the doctor's hand. She did not need an explanation to know that it was the same one she kept in her handbag. At the back of her mind she knew she should have been outraged by the unauthorised search. However, her inner confusion and a wave of mortified shame seemed to cloud all other thoughts. 'I didn't know I wasn't allowed to have one,' she said quietly. 'I . . .'

'That doesn't answer my question,' Doctor McMahon snapped. She reached across Kelly's prone, naked body and carelessly teased her left nipple. Her touch was deft and Kelly's response was an instantaneous sigh of delight. 'Why do you have it?' Doctor McMahon repeated.

'I use it sometimes,' Kelly replied meekly, unable to meet the doctor's gaze as she spoke.

'You use it,' the doctor repeated. She stroked her hand over the flat, smooth expanse of Kelly's stomach. The tactile stimulation was incredibly erotic and Kelly felt herself trembling with anticipation. 'Show me how you use it,' the doctor said, whispering the words softly into Kelly's ear. 'Show me.' She placed the dildo in Kelly's hand and tried to wrap her fingers around it.

'What if I refuse?' Kelly asked.

'You won't,' the doctor replied confidently. She placed her fingers under Kelly's chin and tilted her head so the two women were able to enjoy eye contact. 'During your induction Mr Smith will have told you that disobedient and recalcitrant behaviour is not tolerated here at the hostel.'

Staring into the unfathomable depths of the doctor's jet-black eyes, Kelly remembered Mr Smith's austere introduction to the hostel earlier that morning. She suddenly felt cold as she realised how gravely she had misunderstood his words about the hostel's strict regime and its disciplined environment.

'I don't know if you've already heard of the black room,' the doctor continued easily. 'But it's the sort of last resort that I don't think you want to experience just yet.'

Kelly remembered Stacey's whispered threat to Helen in the waiting room. The woman had only mentioned the black room to her and Helen had trembled with fear. Whatever the black room was, Kelly had already decided she did not want to encounter it. Reluctantly, she allowed her fingers to accept the dildo.

'That's better,' Doctor McMahon enthused cheerfully, allowing her hand to work casually down to the neatly trimmed triangle of wiry orange hairs around Kelly's pubic mound. 'Now, I'm sure you know what to do with it,' she encouraged.

Feeling her face burn crimson with shame, Kelly closed her eyes and took the dildo in both hands. She felt the familiar modest length and girth with her fingers, trying not to think of what she was doing. Deftly, she twisted the hard plastic base all the way around. The dildo buzzed wickedly. The sound reverberated deafeningly in the quiet confines of the doctor's room. Feeling more exposed than

24

she had ever felt before, Kelly directed the vibrator between her legs. Normally, before pressing the instrument into herself she would have spread the lips of her vagina apart. This time, before she had a chance to open herself, she felt a pair of fingers doing that task for her. The feeling was so sudden and unexpected she opened her eyes and stared down between her legs.

Doctor McMahon graced Kelly with a knowing smile, then turned her concentration back to the hand she had in Kelly's lap.

The feeling of the woman's fingers pressed against her vulva was an unprecedented stimulation. Whilst Kelly still felt embarrassed to be performing such an intimate act in front of a complete stranger, the doctor's gentle touch was disturbingly arousing. As she slid the merrily buzzing dildo into the open folds of her labia Kelly was poignantly aware of her heightened arousal. The plastic tingled on her exposed flesh in a wave of stimulation that felt delicious. She paused before pushing it any further inside, enjoying the myriad delightful prickles of pleasure to their fullest. She found herself staring into the doctor's face as the first wave of pleasure rolled through her. It seemed unreal to be focusing on the face of another woman whilst she was masturbating but Kelly realised she had not just come to terms with the situation; she was actually loving it.

The first orgasm coursed through her body as she plunged the buzzing dildo deep within the warm folds of her moist pussy lips. She had enjoyed stronger orgasms in the past but because of the bizarre circumstances surrounding this one she did not think she would ever have one as memorable. Gasping breathlessly at the ease of her own climax, she stared into the doctor's smiling face.

'Please – continue, Kelly,' Doctor McMahon insisted. She allowed her fingers to playfully stroke around Kelly's hole before moving her hand beneath the vibrator. Kelly was startled to feel one of the doctor's fingers slide rudely between the cheeks of her buttocks and into the forbidden warmth of her anus.

'Relax,' Doctor McMahon whispered coolly, allowing

her tongue to tickle the sensitive flesh of Kelly's neck. 'You'll enjoy it so much more if you relax.'

Wordlessly, Kelly tried to follow the doctor's instructions as she slid the length of plastic slowly in and out of herself. The whirring sound in the room intensified and then muted as the dildo was pulled out and then pushed into the tight depths of her hole. Kelly felt the tingling increase as the vibrator filled her, sparking a wealth of dizzying pleasure. On its own, she knew the dildo would have been enough to make her climax again. Coupled with the delightfully taboo sensation of the doctor's fingers playing in her anus, Kelly felt herself rushing towards another orgasm with unnerving alacrity.

As the rush of pleasure filled every pore of her body, Kelly's back arched upward. She pushed the dildo so deep into her pussy she could feel the tip tingling perfectly on the neck of her womb. The doctor slid her finger slowly in and out of Kelly's anus, creating a frisson of unimagined delight. She was perversely aware of feeling fuller than she had ever felt before and as the doctor slid a second finger alongside the first, Kelly groaned blissfully.

With her other hand, the doctor was attending to Kelly's breasts, alternating between careful caresses and punishingly playful pinches. The contrary sensations were infuriatingly well timed, hastening Kelly's ascent to the brink of orgasm.

When the orgasm struck, she shrieked ecstatically. Her pelvis bucked forward, as though her crevice was greedily trying to accept even more of the dildo. She felt the inner muscles of her pussy squeezing on the phallus with a familiar, furious tightening. A hazy red mist of joy clouded her vision and with a groan of agonised pleasure, Kelly collapsed limply on the trolley.

Several moments passed before she dared to open her eyes. When she did, Kelly found herself staring into the knowing smile of Doctor McMahon. She wondered briefly if she had passed out with the intensity of her climax. The doctor was now wearing her lab coat once again and Kelly could not recall feeling the woman remove the two fingers she had been employing so skilfully.

Hestitantly, she raised her eyes to meet the doctor's, warily anticipating a look of staunch disapproval. She was surprised to see the woman smiling indulgently down at her. Her surprise increased when the doctor reached between Kelly's legs and slowly withdrew the dildo. It was still buzzing and she quickly unscrewed the switch with well-practised ease. Kelly felt her embarrassment return as she realised the vibrator was slick with the remnants of her glistening love juice. It did not temper her unease when she watched the doctor slowly lick pussy juice from the implement.

The broad grin she graced Kelly with was wanton and avaricious. Her dark eyes sparkled merrily. 'Welcome to the Pentagon Agency, Kelly.' Doctor McMahon smiled easily. 'I do believe you're just the sort of woman we're looking for.'

Kelly closed her eyes and sighed, hoping fervently that she was doing the right thing.

PENNY IN HARNESS

Penny Birch

Penny Birch is a very naughty girl. Not only does she shamelessly reveal her love of the bizarre world of pony-girl carting in her first novel for Nexus, *Penny in Harness*, but she also reveals dark secrets about her best friend in *A Taste of Amber* (to be published in November 1998) and tells us everything we ever wanted to know about her cheeky activities in *Bad Penny* (to be published in February 1999). Fans of Penny's enthusiastic writing and encyclopaedic knowledge of perversion will know that these books really are treats to look forward to. Penny is, moreover, a founding member of one of the UK's first pony-girl carting clubs – everything you are about to read is based on real experiences.

The following extract is taken from *Penny in Harness*. Penny has by now been welcomed into the fold of pony-girl enthusiasts, and has enjoyed exploring ever-stranger extremes of sexual fantasy with some truly lewd individuals. Here, in front of all her friends, she plans to turn the tables on the snooty and dominant Anna Vale – by engineering a pony-girl race with a difference.

From the onset, there was an atmosphere of suppressed excitement. Not so suppressed in Ginny's case, as she could barely keep still. The six of us sat round the table, balancing out the details until nearly one in the morning, then retired, each satisfied that she or he would be getting plenty out of the next day's events.

Personally, I knew that I could rely on the others to give me all the attention and sensation I needed, both as a pony-girl and in the way of punishment. My aim was rather different: to have Amber and Anna Vale as my pony-girls.

The morning was a bustle of activity, with everybody trying to sort themselves out. The weather was firmly on our side, sunny with few clouds and a moderate breeze – perfect for pony-carting. Henry Gresham arrived at ten, Anderson and Vicky somewhat afterwards, and by ten-thirty we were driving up to the old park in a convoy of cars and one horsebox.

I felt light-hearted, excited and keen to play, a mood echoed by the others as we set up the three carts and Vicky and Anderson's carriage. Amber had also filled the horsebox with paraphernalia: a pillory, a whipping stool, various punishment implements and a great pile of spare tack. When we were finished, the yard was a true pervert's paradise. Three pony-carts stood at one end, the carriage behind them. To the side, the whipping stool and pillory stood ready, next to a table laid out with devices for just about every sexual curiosity imaginable.

All we needed to start was Anna and Poppy, on whose arrival Amber intended to read out the order of events and kick off the meet. The first spectacle was to be my long-awaited punishment of Ginny, a prospect that I was looking forward to with relish. She was already giving me nervous, excited glances as I stood admiring the selection of goodies that were spread out on the table. I was just trying to choose between cane and strap when Amber hailed us from on top of the carriage.

'It looks like they've chickened out,' she announced, 'so let's start. I think all the introductions have been done. I will be leading the ceremonies and would like to thank you for your support for the post. As referee, we have Mr Henry Gresham, my godfather and a man who trained his first pony-girl before most of us were born. His knowledge is extensive and his decision final, so we'll have no arguments about tactics, Michael Scott.

'In between pony-girl events, there will be a number of spectacles designed to correct the behaviour of some of our number. The first of these will be the punishment of Mrs Virginia Scott by Miss Penelope Birch. Penny, you may proceed.'

'Thank you, Amber,' I called out to her, then turned back to the table. Ginny was a strapping girl and used to Michael, so I didn't really need to hold back. On the other hand, I had no idea if she had any particular favourites. She was waiting with Michael, dressed in a simple white dress, naked underneath but for her panties so that she could quickly become a pony-girl. I walked over to them, smiling cheerfully at both and getting a nervous grin back from Ginny.

'What does she like best?' I asked Michael boldly.

He gave me the cool, amused smile I'd always enjoyed and put his chin in his hand. 'Hmm, let me see,' he said evenly. 'It's more a question of what she doesn't like. You could try giving her an enema.'

'Michael!' Ginny protested, the first genuine objection I'd ever heard her make.

'A dose of the strap usually keeps her in line,' he continued casually.

'I'll strap her, then,' I replied. 'Does she ever come without her clit being played with?'

'Not really,' Michael told me. 'In fact, no; never.'

'Good,' I answered, 'then I have an ideal punishment for a girl like her; fat-bottomed, that is. Come on, Ginny.'

I took her by the hand and she followed me meekly across the yard, the others making themselves comfortable to watch her being punished. In practice, I wanted to make it spectacular and effective but I didn't want to make her too sore to be spanked and whipped later, as she undoubtedly would be.

The pillory was my chosen piece of equipment, a solid wooden affair designed not to be upset by a victim's struggles. Amber had built it deliberately low so that, instead of the conventional position, the offender's bottom would be higher than their head.

Ginny looked at it apprehensively but bent down to put her head in the central hole submissively enough. I cleared her long golden hair from her neck so that it fell around her face, running my nails gently along the exposed nape before shutting the pillory and clipping the catch into place. A leg-spreading pole completed her position and there were murmurs of appreciation from the onlookers as I threw up her dress to expose her for punishment. I walked around her, admiring my handiwork. She did look beautiful, her eyes big and moist, her mouth set in a sullen pout, hair cascading down around her face. Her big bottom looked great, raised up with her pale blue panties stretched taut across her seat, the shape of her pussy showing because her legs were as wide apart as they would go.

'You should have had her take her knickers off before you put the leg-pole on,' Anderson pointed out from the crowd.

'Not at all,' I answered. 'You'll all see plenty of her pussy later, but for now her panties have a function.'

I pulled them down as far as they would go anyway,

leaving Ginny's bum bare with the panties in a taut line just below her cheeks. It also seemed a pity not to show her tits off, so I adjusted the dress to leave them swinging bare beneath her, on full view for everybody. She now looked even better, so I signalled to Henry over to take a few photographs while I went to choose from the table. Ginny squirmed and pretended embarrassment at being photographed in such a position, but also made an effort to stick her bum further out and turn to give a suitably remorseful look to the camera.

It was Anderson's treatment of us as pony-girls that had inspired my idea for Ginny's punishment. The difference was that I intended to beat her while the vibrator was actually in her pussy. With a skinny girl, it wouldn't be safe, because you might catch the base of the vibrator with the strap. On Ginny's big firm bottom, there would be plenty of flesh to cushion the smacks. The purpose of leaving her panties on was to hold the vibrator in place, otherwise her wriggles were bound to push it out.

I chose a thick cock-shaped vibrator made of rubber. It also had a rubber prong above the main shaft, designed either to tickle a girl's clit or fit into her bum-hole, a feature that real cocks would certainly be improved by. For a strap, I chose a genuine Lochgelly tawse, a heavy leather implement made for use on Scott and Amber's pride and joy. I had felt it across my own bottom and knew how much it stung, and there was a satisfying weight to the smacks that was a particular turn-on.

Ginny watched me as I walked back to her, looking uncertainly at the vibrator and tawse. Once behind her I laid the tawse across the crest of her bottom and pulled her panties open to get at her pussy. I made sure the crowd got a good view of her full sex lips and moist, pink vulva. I sucked a finger and slid it into her, making her groan as the flesh of her pussy tightened on the intruding digit. Amber was never that keen on being fingered, and the sensation of having my finger in another woman's vagina was still unfamiliar enough to make me want to explore for a bit. Ginny moaned again as I wriggled it inside her; I was enjoying the sensation as the tight wet tube of flesh clamped around my finger.

When I had finished opening her, the vibrator slid in easily enough, only needing to be pulled back a couple of times until it was deep inside her. I couldn't resist a quick lick of her anus to help the little probe in; Amber and, I think, Anderson laughed at my readiness to lick a bottom. Lastly, I tweaked the panties back into place, the taut elastic holding the vibrator well in her pussy while there was perhaps an inch and a half of finger-width rubber probe in her bottom hole. I turned it on, immediately drawing a sigh of pleasure from Ginny.

'Could you just take a couple of close-ups of that for my album?' I asked Henry, a suggestion that made Ginny squirm until I told her to keep still.

As he backed away, I hefted the tawse over her naked, vulnerable bottom, then brought it around in a full arc to land across her seat with a meaty smack. She jumped and squealed, her bum bouncing and wobbling prettily. The tawse had left a broad red mark across her bum, which I inspected before standing back for the second stroke. The onlookers were quiet, concentrating on Ginny's beating, each taking their own pleasure in the spectacle.

After the second stroke, Ginny was panting faintly from the beating and beginning to pull herself back in and tense her buttocks rhythmically from the effect of the vibrator. I knew how she felt: exposed, punished and teased all at once but unable to come, an exquisite torment that would put her on a sexual high for the rest of the day.

As the third stroke smacked down on Ginny's plump posterior, there was the sound of a car horn from the direction of the gate. I stopped, waiting while Michael went to investigate and then returned with Anna Vale and Poppy. This meant that Ginny had five minutes just stuck there with the vibrator running and, by the time they had got out of the car, she was writhing her bottom from side to side and begging to be allowed to come.

I ignored her, greeting Anna with a peck on each cheek and Poppy with a kiss on the lips. Anna was in a uniform:

WRAF, I think, from about 1940. This was very neat and bore an officer's insignia, giving her a cool, commanding look. Poppy wore a light summer dress that showed her legs in the bright sunlight. For an instant the wind blew it against her bottom, showing an outline that told me she was pantyless underneath. Anna smiled to the women and gave the men formal nods as she walked across the yard, Poppy following.

Of course, the scene was exactly what Anna would have expected to see. The ultra-dominant Amber Oakley strapping some remorseful female across the bare bottom while the others looked on respectfully. The real Amber had agreed to maintain the deception until lunch, so that was how long I had to seduce Anna into submission. After lunch, I was due a punishment that would destroy any illusions she had about me being untouchably dominant.

Strapping Ginny was a good start and, as I returned my attention to her bottom, I noticed that Anna took care to stand where she got a view directly between Ginny's legs. It takes concentration to apply a tawse properly, so I gave Ginny her fourth smack and then went round to talk to her and stroke her cheek. I know how good it feels to have the person who's punishing you come and soothe you in between strokes, and that was mainly what I was doing. It also gave me a chance to watch Anna. She looked cool and poised, an officer observing a just and necessary punishment, but in my mind I was already rolling the tight skirt up to inspect her underwear.

I gave Ginny two more, both hard enough to make her bottom wobble and draw a gasp from her lips. I then took her around the waist and fucked her with the vibrator until she was once more begging for her orgasm. It was nice watching it slide in and out. Her pussy was soaking and took the thick shaft easily, while the little probe forced her bum-hole open with each push. The little ring would tense, then open to the pressure and reluctantly admit the rubber finger.

I was considering trying to fit the main shaft in her anus when she started to call 'Amber' and I realised that I really had taken her to her limit. I turned the vibrator off and pulled it gently out, then hurried round to talk to her. I knew she was all right when she gave me a big happy smile, so I kissed her and offered her the vibrator to suck. She took it, savouring her own juices with her eyes shut as I fed it in and out.

That was it; I had no intention of letting her come, but instead took the vibrator away and unclipped the stocks. She had to wait while I released her from the leg-spreading pole, but got a lovely warm hug when she was free. Everyone clapped when we started to kiss, with Ginny's leg up so that her hot pussy was against my thigh. I broke away and sent her to Michael with a smack on the bottom, bowing to the crowd as she snuggled into his arms.

Our little show had put everyone in just the right mood, myself included. Whether anybody else was scheming quite as much as I was, I doubted. From her previous behaviour when she'd been really turned on, I knew Anna would enjoy submitting to me, if she could only justify the act in her own mind. Once she made that all-important initial gesture I was sure she'd be mine, and if the intensity of Amber's passion in similar conditions was anything to go by, the results should be spectacular. Then again I could always cheat . . .

As Amber announced that Henry was now taking challenges for racing, I sidled over to where Vicky was getting into her pony-girl gear. Anderson was across the yard, talking to Michael and Ginny, so Vicky asked me to help her.

She was already naked, and I kissed her and squeezed one firm buttock before starting to lace the waist belt of her harness.

'I'd like to make a deal,' I whispered. 'Are you willing to lose a race?'

'Maybe,' she answered doubtfully.

'How about a nice bribe?' I offered.

Her mouth broke into a mischievous grin, telling me that a bribe was exactly what she wanted.

'A piggy-girl to play with?' I suggested.

Her eyes lit up. I'd known she liked the fantasy for some time.

'Maybe two, if I can pull it off,' I offered. 'Look, throw out a challenge that anyone who can beat you on a single lap – with the driver of your choice – can punish both you and the driver. Make it girls-only and ask Anna Vale to drive you, then add a heavy punishment for the challenging driver if she loses. Lose, and I'll do the rest.'

She nodded, glancing over to Anna who was standing rather aloofly, admiring the carriage. I helped Vicky with the rest of her tack, leaving only her bridle off so that she wasn't technically in role. She then walked over to Anderson, who in turn spoke to Henry Gresham to arrange to challenge. I strolled away nonchalantly heading for where Catherine, Matthew and Amber were standing.

As I reached them, I saw Anderson slip Vicky's bit into her mouth and give her reins to Henry. Both men then made for the centre of the yard; Vicky, now 'Hippolyta', paced behind them.

'Ladies and gentlemen,' he announced, 'we have our first challenge. Mr Anderson Croom challenges any all-female team to beat his pony-girl Hippolyta over a single lap. Mr Croom will not be driving and would like to offer his seat to Miss Anna Vale by special request from Hippolyta. Miss Vale?'

I glanced over to Anna. She was clearly flattered, as anyone would be if a beautiful pony-girl wanted to be driven by them.

'And the prize?' she demanded haughtily but not without real curiosity.

'The prize,' Henry continued, 'should you win, is the submission of both pony-girl and driver of the losing team to your desire, subject only to stop words. The stops words incidentally, are "yellow" for slow and "red" for stop. Should you lose, the winning driver will have the right to spank you and to drive Hippolyta herself.'

That wasn't quite what I had said, but the offer was good and surely had to tempt Anna. She got to drive Vicky anyway, and if she won she would have the submission of two other women. I saw her glance cautiously around, and I wondered if it were too obvious a trap. She was lighter than everybody else except myself and Poppy, and maybe Catherine. Also, among the girls, only Ginny and Amber had anything like Vicky's muscle and neither were built as sprinters. Anyone who accepted the challenge was clearly going to end up as her plaything. It occurred to me that she might have seen me speak to Vicky, but if she had, it might have seemed that I was manufacturing an excuse to submit to her myself. I shot her a coy glance to reinforce that theory in her mind. She responded with a knowing look and I knew I had her.

'I accept the challenge,' I announced.

'A challenge from Miss Amber Oakley!' Henry responded, fortunately getting the names the right way around. 'Who, then, will be your pony-girl?'

'Honey, of course,' I answered, reaching out to stroke Amber's head. I hadn't explained to her what I was up to and she shot me the most wonderful 'I'm going to get you later' look. The expression on Henry's face was spendid, too, as he evidently hasn't expected to see his one time protégée as a pony-girl.

Amber was a good sport and began to strip immediately. As I helped her harness up, I saw Anderson buckling Vicky into place and wondered if they might not have decided to pull a double bluff on me. It seemed unlikely, as Vicky would then lose her piggy-girls, and anyway, there were worse fates than being Anna Vale's plaything.

A naked Amber was a rare sight for most of the men and she had no shortage of admirers as I put her into harness. I had dressed in riding gear as part of my deception, and I like to think that when we were finished we made an exceptionally fine turnout.

'We're going to win, Honey,' I whispered as I pulled a bridle over her head.

'Are we?' she answered doubtfully.

'Yes,' I assured her, slipping the bit into her mouth and cutting off communication.

I had my beautiful Honey in harness as I had wanted,

and there was a good chance I'd soon be naming Anna as I strapped her in alongside. Everything was going perfectly, but there was one other detail that I couldn't do without.

'Aren't we racing with tails?' I asked loudly as if the idea had only just occurred to me.

'We don't, usually,' Michael pointed out. 'It slows you down.'

'Referee?' I queried.

Ask a fifty-year-old pony-girl enthusiast if he'd like to see two girls wearing plug-in tails and the answer is not going to be no.

'Yes, tails it is, I think,' Henry said, as if on cue.

Amber gave me another of her looks. I smiled and kissed her.

'Is poor little Honey going to have a tail up her bottom?' I teased her, letting my hand slide down over the curve of her bottom to prod meaningfully between her cheeks.

I had her kneel and stick her bum out while I fetched Ginny's tail and pulled a condom over the plug. A well-greased finger opened Amber's bum-hole.

'Come and watch,' I announced as I put the plug to her anus.

A little crowd gathered around us and Amber hung her head as the plug popped in and her bottom-hole closed around the shaft. She looked really sweet and I promised myself to make sure she made herself a tail for regular use. Vicky was served the same way but with less ceremony, accepting the tail without fuss.

Anna lacked the experience to know how much a tail was going to slow her pony-girl down. Vicky did, but she was now Hippolyta and so not allowed to say anything even if she'd wanted to. Both pony-girls would be slowed, but the race was now more even, especially as we had more experience over the course.

I climbed into the cart and ordered Anna to rise. She was now Honey, and was my pony-girl, sleek and strong and beautiful. I know I'd got my wish rather sneakily, and the setting was erotic more than romantic, but at that moment I loved her more than ever.

A rush of adrenalin overcame my momentary sentimentality as I steered her in a wide arc to bring the cart to rest beside our rivals. Vicky looked lovely, with her long black tail hanging down over her neat little bottom. So did Anna, haughty and confident enough to make me want to submit to her, but not until I'd had my pleasure.

Henry took his place to our side, raising a handkerchief of the most startling vermilion silk as a flag. I tensed, then yelled to Honey as he brought the handkerchief down. We set off fast but they had a lead before we reached the carriage sweep in front of the ruined house, and we came into the wood a good ten yards behind.

Racing is very different from ordinary pony-carting. Normally you can sit back, admire the view, hold the reins in one hand and the whip in the other. You are in complete control of your pony-girl, who can be commanded at leisure. When racing, the best thing you can do is take a tight grip on the cart and pray your pony knows what she's doing. The lower the seat of the cart, the better, but minor potholes and stones in the path still become terrifying obstacles.

As Honey belted after our rivals, I was sure I was going to be thrown at any moment. I had only gone so fast once before, with Chris Ford, and his weight and strength had made the cart much more stable. It must have been worse still for Anna, in a higher-seated cart and close to equal in weight to Hippolyta.

At the low point of the track, we were twenty or so yards behind, but the rise was ahead and that would be to our advantage. We started to gain and I saw Anna take a smack at Hippolyta's rump. The unexpected sting of the whip only broke her stride and helped us.

I know Hippolyta could have kept her pace up and beaten us fairly, even with an inexperienced driver. As it was, she was brave enough to become more fretful with each smack of the whip on her bottom, so that we had managed to pull up right to their rear when we reached the big nettle patch.

The path was tight but we just had room to overtake, only Anna started to steer Hippolyta in a weave, blocking our path.

'Give way!' I shouted, not really expecting Anna to take any notice. We could actually see the stable-yard gate and, for a moment, I thought I might have been betrayed. Then their wheel struck the edge of what had once been the lawn. Hippolyta stumbled, slowed and then righted herself. It looked real to me and made Anna clutch the cart to avoid being pitched out.

Honey dashed forward, her thigh brushing the nettles back as she overtook, but never losing speed. They were still trying to regain full speed and we had five yards on them before Hippolyta began to gain on the last stretch of flat path. It was too late and we came through the gate with the best part of a length to spare.

I drew Honey to a stop in the centre of the yard, feeling absolutely elated as Henry gave me his arm and then held my hand up as the winner. Behind us, the other cart came to a halt, Anna ordering Hippolyta to kneel and then climbing out.

She looked seriously discomfited and I thought she would back out, but instead, she stood to her full height and put her head up with absolute dignity.

'I have lost and I accept your right to punish me,' she announced, addressing me. 'However, I must ask that no one watch, especially men.'

'I can respect that,' I answered coolly, although inside I felt like skipping. Anna Vale was actually going to submit to me; to accept her virgin spanking over my lap; to allow me, little, submissive Penny, to chastise and humiliate her.

I was prepared to spank her alone, but not to take my moment of triumph completely without an audience. Marching briskly up to her, I took her by the ear and led her out of the yard behind me. I knew that at the back of the stables was a fallen tree, and it was to this that I led her. Tangled rhododendrons and overgrown holly bushes screened the location effectively, creating a nicely private atmosphere for us. She had made no protest at my rough treatment and so I pulled her smartly across my knee and tucked an arm round her waist to keep her in place. Her bottom made an inviting ball under the material of her skirt, ready for spanking.

Having her across my knee felt absolutely glorious. Spanking Catherine or Ginny, even Amber, had been a blend of sex and the pleasure of accepting their submission. This had all of that, but also a sense of achievement and of having been a sneaky little brat to get my way. I knew it wouldn't last long but, for now, I had Anna Vale as my plaything and I intended to get the most out of the experience.

'Right, Anna,' I told her, 'now I'm going to spank you. Have you ever been spanked before?'

'No, Miss Oakley,' she answered in a meek, penitent voice, far different from her normal tones.

'You've done it to plenty of other girls, though, haven't you?' I continued.

'Yes, Miss Oakley.'

'Well, now you're going to find out how it feels. First I think we'll have this pretty bottom bare . . .'

She hung her head as I said that, obligingly going up on her toes so that I could get the tight skirt fully over her hips. There was no reluctance, but genuine submission. I pulled her skirt up slowly, savouring the exposure of stocking tops, then the soft, creamy skin of her thighs and finally the seat of her panties. Her bum was sheathed in tight ivory silk, clinging to the swell of her bottom and fringed with lace, very feminine and just the sort of garment I would have expected her to wear.

'Think of all the girls who've lain over your knee with their panties as their last shred of modesty,' I told her. 'Did you ever think how they felt, as their bums were stripped? How do you think Poppy feels, as you ease her pants down over her chubby little pear of a bottom? Well, you're about to find out, because yours are coming down right now, Miss Fancy-pants.'

She gave a little gasp as I took hold of her waistband, but stopped with only the first inch of her bottom crease showing. Her whole body was trembling and I knew I was really getting to her.

'Actually,' I continued, 'I think you are getting off rather lightly. Let's make a few adjustments.'

I began with her hair, fishing for hairpins in order to take the little hat off, then release the full bulk of it. It was long, straight and a lustrous brown, faintly scented with some perfume I didn't recognise. She let out a little sob as it cascaded down around her head, falling to the earth and leaves beneath her. I hadn't been expecting such a strong reaction to this relatively minor humiliation and I paused for an instant, in case she wanted me to slow. When nothing was said, I slid my hand under her chest and started to undo the buttons of her blouse. Her trembling increased as the first one popped open and she sobbed again as my arm brushed the tip of a breast.

'I think bare breasts add a certain something to a girl's punishment, don't you?' I asked. 'No one will see, not even me, but you'll know they're bare, won't you, Anna?'

I continued to fiddle with her blouse, opening it and then tugging her bra up to free her breasts. I caught one, heavier and fuller than I'd expected, the nipple small and hard as I rubbed at it with my palm.

'On second thoughts,' I added, 'stand up and put your hands on your head.'

She obeyed instantly, standing as I had directed, her fine breasts stuck out for my inspection. She looked exquisite. The bra matched her panties, big and old-fashioned but very feminine. With her skirt up and her blouse open and strands of hair falling across her naked breasts, she made a fine picture of dishevelment. Her tummy was showing, too, a gentle bulge of flesh, with her tummy button a neat dimple in the middle. My slight disarrangement of her panties had also left a wisp of dark pubic hair showing at the front, with a tell-tale damp patch lower down. Best of all was her face. Her eyes were wide and moist, her mouth slightly open, the lower lip pouted and trembling, her tongue moving nervously inside.

'You are pretty,' I told her, which was true. The disarrangement of her hair and the stripping of her breasts and belly had softened the lines of her face and body, which I had thought a touch too austere to be called pretty. 'Come back across my knee, now, and we'd better have those panties down.'

She obeyed and I made myself comfortable with one arm tight around her waist. I grabbed a handful of her panties and tugged them unceremoniously down over her bum, then inverted them neatly around her thighs. As she was exposed, I again caught a hint of the same unusual perfume, but mixed with the musky smell of her sex.

'There we are,' I said, 'that feels better, doesn't it?'

'Yes,' she sobbed.

She had started to sob quite hard, which was disturbing me. Her naked bottom and trembling flesh had me really turned on and, I have to admit, so did the sobs. I reasoned that she had a perfectly good stop word if she wanted to use it and placed my palm against the crest of her bottom. Her skin was soft and lightly downed with tiny hairs, the flesh yielding underneath. Virgin, I thought: a virgin bottom, so beautiful and all mine.

'Here goes, Anna darling,' I told her and lifted my hand, bringing it down hard across her seat, then again, and again, spanking her with the pace and firmness that leaves the victim kicking, squealing and utterly out of control.

I knew full well how it felt, and how a good spanking can leave a girl trembling in her lover's arms in an ecstasy that can only be achieved through punishment. This is the case for me, anyway, and I was sure it would be the same for Anna. She certainly squealed enough, and kicked too, but I was taken aback after about thirty smacks when she bursts into tears.

I stopped immediately, only to have her beg me to carry on. If she needed to cry while she was beaten, then that was up to her, so I started again, this time using my

47

fingertips to smack each cheek in turn. As she was slim and soft-bottomed, spanking her had quickly made my hand sore, and this was a technique Amber had taught me to use on less well-upholstered bottoms.

'Harder, Amber, like before,' she gasped, 'but right over my fanny.'

It would have been easy to exert my dominance and carry on as I liked, but there was a desperation in her voice that made me wonder if she wasn't actually going to come. I decided to compromise, planting a hard smack at the point where her buttocks and thighs met, even as I began to rebuke her.

'How dare you tell me how to spank you?' I demanded angrily. 'I'll spank you how I please, you snivelling little brat!'

I began to lay in with all my strength, each slap aimed so that my palm caught her pussy. She quickly burst into tears again, harder and mingled with choking sounds, then screamed and I knew that she was actually coming, just from being spanked. My palm stung like anything and my shoulder muscles were beginning to hurt, but this was no time to stop. The irony was not lost on me. She was the one being punished, but it was now me who was under her physical direction.

'Harder, Penny, I'm coming,' she screamed, then gave a yell that must have made the people in the stableyard wonder what we were doing.

I gave her one last resounding slap and then cupped her pussy in my hand and rubbed hard. She screamed once more and locked her thighs hard around my hand, grunting in abandoned ecstasy as her orgasm peaked again. She slipped from my lap, collapsing at my feet with her scarlet bottom raised and her fingers working the last drops of pleasure from her pussy.

To my surprise, the first thing she did when she rolled into a sitting position was pull her panties off her legs. She put them neatly to one side, then began to take off her stockings. I watched, happy to go along with whatever she was doing, but acutely conscious of one thing. At the very peak of her orgasm, when she was completely given over to her pleasure, she had called me Penny.

She stripped completely, never saying a word, then turned and knelt between my legs as if waiting for something. It was obvious that she wanted a cuddle, so I held my arms out and let her come into them, naked and trembling, her head pressed against my chest as I stroked her hair.

'Thank you,' she said, then, 'could I be your pony-girl now, please, mistress?'

It was an offer I was not going to resist and so I took her by the hand and led her back to the stables.

'What about the men?' I asked, stopping as we approached the gate.

She shrugged. I accepted this on face value, having given up trying to understand her. Most women I can empathise with, easily enough. Ginny was down to earth and playful, Amber complex but open with me, Catherine not dissimilar to myself. Anna was unreadable and often contradictory. She was fun, so I didn't mind so much, but there was one question I had to ask.

'You called me Penny, just now,' I said.

'Sorry, Miss Birch,' she answered. 'You can spank me again if it was presumptuous.'

'How long have you known?'

'Amber called your name when she came, that first day. I thought it odd and so I rang a few friends. They told me Amber Oakley was of average height with tawny curls and a fairly full figure, not petite and dark.'

'Why did you let me have you, then?'

'No one had ever had the courage to try and make me submit, before. I wanted to do it for you, even though you deceived me – maybe because of it.'

'And if you'd won the race?'

'I'd have had you and Amber both stripped and caned. Begging your pardon, mistress. Oh, and by the way, you are an exceptional spanker.'

'I've had plenty of practice,' I said pulling on her hand

to lead her into the stable yard. 'Most of it over the real Amber's lap.'

The others had been getting on fine without us. I'd obviously put Amber into a submissive mood, because she was still Honey pony-girl and was lead in a magnificent five-in-hand that was still having its system of traces attached. Or at least she soon would be, because Anderson and Michael were still arguing over how to set the carriage up.

'We did this last week,' Anderson was saying, 'only with three instead of five.'

'Make it six,' I called as we came into view.

It was wonderful. Everyone turned, including the pony-girls. The men in particular looked astonished to see me leading a naked Anna Vale by the hand, a shy smile on her face and her bottom cherry-red from spanking. The one I looked at was Poppy, expecting to see a satisfied smirk. Instead, she was looking directly at me, her eyes wide with surprise.

I smiled back, then turned to Anderson, who was holding a swingletree and a piece of rope.

'Could I drive that contraption?' I asked.

'Contraption?' he echoed. 'Yes, you can have a turn after me.'

'Fair enough,' I answered.

'What's the new pony's name, then?' he asked.

'I'm not sure,' I replied. 'Let me see.'

I took a step back from Anna and let go of her hand. She immediately put her hands on her head, standing for everyone's inspection.

'Quite beautiful,' Henry remarked.

It was tricky. Anna was tall and slender but she lacked the athleticism that made 'Hippolyta' suitable for Vicky. She had moderately full breasts, which her slim build accentuated. It should be a name that suited her, flattering yet subtly humiliating.

'Dumplings,' I said confidently, her immediate blush confirming that it was a good choice.

Anderson smiled as Henry nodded sagely.

I led her away, going to the table to look for spare tack. There was enough there to put her in full harness, mainly my own, which I put on her while she stood patiently by. I included my nipple bells and a bow of red ribbon in her pussy hair. When I had finished, one of the few bits of pony-girl tack left was my tail, which was a few shades darker than her own hair. I had tied her own locks into a long ponytail with a red ribbon and a set of hair rings.

Anderson was calling to me to hurry up but I ignored him, instead picking up a tube of lubricant and waving it meaningfully in front of her face. She gave me a startled look but turned her front to the others and stuck her bottom out. As I prepared the tail I noticed that Poppy already had her curly black tail in and I wondered who had put her in harness.

I had Anna pull her cheeks open and hold them as I slid a lubricated finger into her anus. She sighed as it went in and I wiggled it a bit before substituting it for the plug. She took it fairly easily, only squeaking slightly when the widest part went in, then standing upright and holding the tail while I attached the fishing-line belt.

She was finished, and looked gorgeous, the more so when harnessed into place beside Poppy on the left-hand swingletree. I then stood back to admire the formation, six girls, all naked but for their harness, four with tails, all with ribbons and bells and all looking good enough to eat.

'Exquisite,' Henry remarked as he fiddled with his camera, 'and I believe it to be a first. We must have a group photograph like this, mounted and with the names and so forth in silver ink, like a team photo. Actually, could you just run through the names please, Amber?'

'It's all right; you can call me Penny now,' I answered. 'Yes, Honey and Hippolyta are on the lead swingletree. Dumplings and Hazel to the left, to the right . . .'

I stopped, looking to Michael and Matthew. I didn't know Ginny's pony-girl name and I had no idea if Catherine had one at all.

'Venus,' Michael informed me.

'You choose; you seem to be good at it,' Matthew offered.

'OK,' I answered, trying to think fast but not disappoint my friend. 'Pepper will suit Katie, with her red hair.'

'Splendid,' Henry remarked. 'Now if we could have the three gentlemen standing by their seats I'll put this thing on automatic. Penny, perhaps you could stand at the front and take the reins in your hands. I'll come round to the back when I'm ready.'

He took that photograph and a couple more, then Honey stamped and I took her bit out to let her speak. As Amber, she asked for Henry and whispered something to him which I didn't hear, then went back to being Honey.

We spent the next hour playing with the six-in-hand, which was tricky to control but really the last word in pony-carting. Anderson took the first turn, with Michael and Matthew as passengers, a combined weight that said a lot for the engineering of the carriage. When my turn came I took them out onto a section of lawn that was still mostly grass and taught them to high-step in unison, a difficult task that gave me plenty of opportunity to apply my whip to their bottoms.

Only when I was satisfied with their performance did I relinquish my seat, ordering all six to kneel with their heads to the ground and their bums up before Michael took the driver's seat. I adjusted the four tails to leave six bare pussies showing, then asked Henry to take a close-up of each. I think the way a kneeling girl's pussy pouts out from between her thighs is particularly sweet, as well as humiliating when a man takes a photograph in which every single tuck and fold of her lips will show clearly. I half-expected Anna to object, but she never even flinched as he photographed her virgin pussy from no more than a foot away.

I was laughing and teasing them as the photos were taken, commenting on Poppy's curly tail and kissing Honey's bottom after her pussy picture had been taken. Henry had been working from left to right, and finished with Pepper. I remarked to Henry on how ginger her pussy was and leant down to stroke it, feeling wonderfully dominant and in control. It was the last dominant thing I was to do that day.

THE MISTRESS OF STERNWOOD GRANGE

Arabella Knight

Arabella Knight is one of our most popular authors, specialising in delightful tales of dominance and discipline. The judicious use of the cane and tawse abounds in her special correctional academies, as wayward young women are taught how to behave and soon develop something of an appetite for the pleasures of punishment. Her settings and themes have included an all-female community on a remote Hebridean island (*Candy in Captivity*); a specialist fashion house with a unique way of training students to be *corsetières* (*Susie in Servitude*); a wartime team of young Wrens using novel means to interrogate their quivering subjects (*Conduct Unbecoming*); a spoilt girl being sent by her despairing guardian to an education establishment with a difference to learn the penalties for disobedience (*The Academy*); and the heiress to a large mansion disguising herself as a maid to discern its true value, and discovering that beyond the oppressively strict regime lies a world of delicious torment (*The Mistress of Sternwood Grange*).

The following extract is taken from her most recent novel for Nexus, *The Mistress of Sternwood Grange*. Heiress Mandy has gathered the information she needs to prove that her inheritance is far larger than she'd originally thought, and has attempted unsuccessfully to escape from Sternwood Grange. Here she begins to receive her harsh but strangely sweet punishment for her recalcitrant disobedience.

'Follow me,' the cropped blonde commanded.

Conscious of her nakedness in contrast to Erica's fully clothed body, Mandy felt both vulnerable and humiliated. As if able to read her mind, Erica said that from now on, Mandy was to remain naked at all times.

'I can't – ' Mandy began to protest.

'Silence. You will remain naked at all times. You have broken the trust placed in you and going naked will be part of your punishment. And without clothes,' Erica laughed grimly, 'you won't get very far. This way.'

Part of your punishment. To remain naked was only part of her punishment. What else awaited her, Mandy wondered. Where was Erica taking her? They were not going upstairs to her bedroom.

'In,' came the curt command.

They entered the gym. Mandy saw Partridge standing over by the wall bars.

'Didn't believe me, did you?' Erica crowed. 'I told you she was dressed for an escape bid. Caught her in one of the Transits.'

The housekeeper turned her large, brown eyes upon Mandy in a sorrowful gaze.

'Up against the wall bars, girl,' Erica instructed, swiping Mandy's bare bottom with the crop. 'Partridge took you on here at Sternwood Grange and so she will administer the punishment.'

'The girl is tired,' Partridge reasoned. 'Cold and tired. Can we not see to her in the morning?' the gentle housekeeper remonstrated.

'If she's cold and tired then a taste of the cane should soon warm and wake her up. Twelve strokes, to begin with,' Erica laughed. 'Arms up and out against the wall bars.'

Mandy stretched up on tiptoe as she grasped the wooden bar above.

'Did you say strap or cane?' enquired Partridge.

'Cane her. Cane her bottom good and hard,' Erica rasped, standing alongside Mandy to appreciate the punishment at close quarters.

Mandy's knuckles whitened on the wall bar as she heard Partridge pace across the wooden floor of the gym, a bamboo cane gripped in her right hand. The cane-tip addressed Mandy's wet bottom almost tenderly, tapping off the undried pearls of water clinging to the swell of her rounded cheeks.

'Commence,' barked the cropped blonde impatiently.

Partridge took up her position and raised the cane aloft. Mandy closed her eyes and eased her breasts away from the wood which cushioned them. The first stroke swept across her naked cheeks, lashing them intimately and stripping them red. She grunted and jerked her nakedness into the wall bars, punishing her bosom on impact. The cane sliced once more, and then again, the two strokes coming unexpectedly in swift succession. Mandy squealed. Both strokes swiped her perfect peaches, leaving crimson kisses across their crowns.

'Harder. I want the bitch to suffer.' The voice of Erica curdled in the uncanny silence of the gym. 'She has caused me a lot of trouble tonight. She must learn her lesson. Learn, and suffer.'

Partridge planted her feet apart for the next six strokes. They were administered briskly and crisply, leaving Mandy's bare bottom ablaze. The housekeeper stepped forward, pressing the bottom with the length of the cane, and pretended to arrange Mandy's right arm at the wall bar.

'Nearly done,' she whispered. 'All over soon.'

Mandy nodded imperceptibly, acknowledging the whispered words of encouragement.

'Stand up straight. Bottom up,' Partridge barked, for Erica's benefit.

Mandy obeyed, presenting her striped cheeks for the remaining strokes.

'Wait,' Erica intervened. 'I'll finish the punishment. You may go.' She dismissed the housekeeper with a curt nod.

Partridge reluctantly surrendered the cane and departed. As the door of the gym closed behind her, a sense of dread stole into Mandy's mind. She was naked and alone – with the cropped blonde.

She heard but could not see Erica placing the bamboo cane down on the polished floor. She sensed the cropped blonde approach, then felt cruel hands gripping each of her caned buttocks and squeezing them, then spreading them apart. The hands of her tormentress squeezed again, bunching the buttocks tightly. Mandy's cleft became a thin crease as her soft cheeks bulged. Then the cupping hands taloned, dragging the cheeks apart, causing the cleft to yawn. Mandy whimpered.

'When the mistress comes down from London tomorrow, my girl, she will want a full explanation. She will want to know every detail. Why you decided to go, where you were heading for, what you proposed to do. So you had better have some good answers ready. She will of course be very disappointed in you. There will be many further punishments.'

Mandy clamped her thighs together and bowed her head.

Erica thumbed the hot cheeks and spread their softness painfully apart, bringing Mandy up on her toes in anguish.

'I am going to cane you now, then leave you to contemplate how foolish you have been. If, on my return, you

61

can convince me that you are truly sorry, I may omit to inform the mistress of your disloyalty and stupidity.'

The mistress: Mandy thought of the havoc the grey-eyed solicitor would wreak on her bare bottom with a flexed crop or bamboo cane.

'If you cooperate completely, I may decide to keep this unfortunate matter strictly between ourselves.'

Mandy twisted her head to see over her left shoulder. 'I'm sorry. I don't know what – '

'No,' Erica purred, sweeping her palm up across the naked, punished cheeks. 'Do not lie too hastily, girl. Let's have no sudden contrition. You planned the escape very carefully. The warm clothing, and the timing of the vans prove that much. I want to know the truth.' She cupped and squeezed the hot cheeks slowly. 'And only the truth. Now turn round and face the wall – and give me your bottom.'

Mandy stretched out her arms and, grasping the wall bars, braced herself for the concluding strokes of her prescribed punishment. Obediently up on tiptoe, she thrust her bare bottom up, her cheeks rounded and poised for their imminent stripes. They came in a sudden rush, swishing down across her bottom with a venom Partridge had not achieved. Mandy's toes curled up in anguish as she pressed her lips against a wall bar to smother her squeals. The concluding stroke sliced into her buttocks, searing them with a burning flame.

'Stay exactly where you are. I will return to hear your explanation within the hour,' Erica whispered, tapping the naked bottom with the tip of her cane.

Mandy unclenched her hands from the wall bars and soothed her ravished rump, skimming her palms across her reddened buttocks. Despite the caning, she felt relieved. Erica had caught her and had severely punished her, but no lasting harm to her ultimate plans had been done. Most importantly, her identity was intact – an identity which the mistress would soon unmask on close inspection. But Erica was not going to inform the mistress, if Mandy proved wholly cooperative. She decided to play into Erica's hands, and renew her bid to escape in a few days' time.

The caning had left her hot and sticky. She ached to touch herself but dared not risk being discovered playing with herself by the cropped blonde. She hated Erica: hated being naked before her, hated being at her mercy. Mandy also hated the knowledge Erica seemed to have of her weaknesses, cravings and desires. The cropped blonde seemed to unerringly know all of Mandy's lustful yearnings and secret wants. Mandy hated this because she knew it gave Erica erotic power and dominance over her – a dominance Erica might choose to exploit.

Mandy risked another furtive rub at her caned cheeks. She thought of the punishment, and how Partridge had been sweet, caning her just within the bearable limits of pleasure-pain. Mandy had almost relished that part of the punishment. Erica's stripes, on the other hand, had been cruel. She had swished the bamboo with savage intent and withering accuracy. The concluding strokes had been almost unbearable, turning Mandy in a moment from trembling desire to shivering dread.

Time passed slowly, achingly slowly. Erica would return. What then? Would Mandy be interrogated in depth tonight? It was already two – later, perhaps – and she felt exhausted. Mandy knew that she must remain alert and keep her mind razor-sharp. Her story must be sound, with no discrepancies or inconsistencies – easy enough perhaps in an ordinary grilling but, when naked and beneath the shadow of a cane, it would be all too easy to make a fatal slip. Above all, Mandy realised, even when being kiss-whipped by a crop, her identity and true purpose here at Sternwood Grange must remain her secret.

The door to the gym opened and Erica entered.

'I have decided not to bother the mistress with this matter, girl. You have much to thank me for. I hope you show your full appreciation.'

Saved from the close scrutiny of Celia Flaxstone, Mandy was prepared to be very appreciative. 'Thank you . . .' she started to gush warmly, then stopped. Out of the corner of her eye she saw that Erica was naked.

'And how grateful are you going to be, tonight? Mmm?'

Mandy remained silent, her mouth dry, her hands prickling with a sudden sweat.

'I worked out your escape route. I know you hid in the storeroom. I found the glove.'

Mandy burned with shame, bitterly resenting Erica's discovery.

'That storeroom is full of interesting items, isn't it? I don't blame you for succumbing. I have selected –' her voice dropped to a thick whisper '– a few of the pieces stored there. I think you might find them interesting.'

Canes? Whips? Paddles? Mandy's bare bottom tightened.

'I don't – ' Mandy stammered.

'I find them very interesting,' Erica said softly. 'I am sure you are going to agree. After all, the mistress need never know about your naughtiness, need she?'

It was not a question. It was a veiled threat. Mandy knew that she was now completely at the mercy of the cropped blonde. Though they were both naked under the neon lights of the gym, Mandy felt vulnerable and afraid. She hung her head. She was Erica's now, utterly and entirely – and they both knew it.

'Put this on,' Erica murmured, approaching Mandy and whipping her bottom playfully with a black rubber brassiere.

The soft rubber weighed heavily on Mandy's open palm. Her nipples thickened as she gazed down at the moulded cups. Slowly, she eased her bosom into it and fingered the stretchy straps. The cups had been talcumed, allowing Mandy to fit and fill the soft rubber with her swollen bosom. To her surprise, her nipples peered out and then emerged through the peek-a-boo holes: forced out through the rubber slits by the weight of her breasts settling into the brassiere. The rubber gripped, feeling strangely tight and undeniably sensual. Mandy's nipples stiffened into firm peaks, becoming pink stubs against the black of the rubber cups.

Erica lowered her face to Mandy's left breast. Closing her lips around the exposed nipple, she sucked hard. Mandy squeezed her buttocks tightly together in an attempt to deny her delight. Gazing down, she saw the cropped blonde, naked and bending, sucking fiercely at her nipple. Erica buried her face in the warmth of the rubbered breast, then applied her rasping tongue, and finally her nipping teeth, to the nipple. Mandy felt the wetness of her slit oozing forth. She closed her eyes and shuddered.

Erica withdrew her mouth and murmured, 'Now try this.'

It was a rubber mask. Mandy felt her belly tightening. She hesitated.

'I want you to put it on.'

Mandy held it in her right hand, her fingers sinking into the black softness.

'You know of course how severely the mistress deals with failed runaways. Most severely,' Erica remarked in a conversational tone. 'They're often whipped three times a day for at least a week.'

Mandy donned the mask. It fitted tightly, pinching her face and flattening her cheeks. Tiny holes allowed her to breathe at the nose and mouth – but speech, like sight and hearing, was denied to her. Surrendering to the overwhelming sensation of the rubber, she tasted its harsh tang and, with that tang, the bittersweet taste of submission. Deprived of her essential faculties, she felt mute, blind and utterly helpless.

Erica led her captive across the polished floor of the gym to a vaulting horse. Mandy came to an abrupt halt as her belly collided with the solid flank. She felt a dominant hand at her bare bottom, urging her to mount. She climbed up, and then lay face down across the horse. Mandy's rubber brassiere kissed the scuffed hide: her nipples tightened exquisitely. Mandy felt Erica pulling her arms behind her back, then drawing her passive wrists together and positioning them at the point where her spine tapered into the swelling curve of her bottom. Handcuffs snapped silently into place, pinioning her into helpless submission. Mandy sensed that Erica had donned a single rubber gauntlet; she felt the softness of it as a palm caressed her bottom firmly, then the severity of it as the spanking began.

The sensation was as eerie as it was deliciously dire. The soundless spanks from the rubber-gloved hand exploded as if out of thin air across her upturned cheeks, flattening their curved crowns and burning them with a slow, spreading fire which licked at her cleft and labia, flickering down to ignite her pulsing slit.

The splayed fingers of the dominant hand pressed her rubber-encased head down into the horse. Mandy's tongue and lips tasted the tight rubber of the mask, finding it just as disturbingly delicious as her bare buttocks found the rubber-gloved spanking. Soon she was coming, her wrists in their handcuffs intensifying her sense of utter helplessness and total submission.

Unable to see or hear – or even touch herself – the unique experience of orgasming in restraining bondage was shattering. Her belly imploded as hot waves rippled down to her spasming flesh below. Did Erica know? Was she scrutinising and savouring Mandy's helplessness? These thoughts and half-formed fears fuelled another – and then another – climax. Dizzy with the dark delights of discipline and total domination, Mandy squirmed and writhed across the leather of the vaulting horse.

A rubber-sheathed finger probing at her wet slit presented Mandy with an unpleasant truth: Erica was not only aware of her orgasm, she was clearly examining – indeed coaxing and controlling – the sequence of climax upon climax. The spanking had ceased after the second of the orgasmic paroxysms, but the rubbered fingers returned to caress her cleft and tease her oozing slit.

The rubber fingertip tapped her anal whorl enquiringly, as if testing the rosebud for the heat of its stickiness. Mandy squeezed her buttocks together as another climax gripped her in its implacable violence – but the probing finger would not be denied its desire. Mandy stiffened, gasping into the moist heat of her rubber mask. The finger worried her tight sphincter determinedly, forcing it to open up like a rosebud. It accepted the intrusion unwillingly, the spasming muscle making entry difficult rather than a smooth glide. Threshing in her bondage, Mandy inched her breasts and belly along the back of the leather horse in a desperate bid to evade the firm finger at her secret flesh. Three severe spanks exploded silently across her hot cheeks, stilling her and staying her tortuous progress. She sank down on the leather, crushed under the cropped blonde's supreme authority and absolute domination.

Then nothing. What was happening? Where was Erica? What was the cruel dominatrix planning, doing? Gone to collect a wooden spanking paddle or a length of bamboo cane? Was Mandy's bare bottom to suffer, suffer until Erica herself came? Was the lustful tormentress seeking to achieve her own hot orgasm with a crop in her rubber-gloved hand?

Mandy wriggled, feeling the wetness of her own climax on the leather horse beneath her. The silence, the helplessness, the darkness at her eyes – suddenly these tortures became unbearable. She screamed a silent scream, giving mute tongue to her delicious dread, hearing only a mournful echo of her anguish in her spinning brain. Where was the cropped blonde? What was she doing? Gazing down upon and relishing Mandy's utter helplessness? Would Mandy shortly be doomed to feel Erica's tongue, lips and teeth at her spanked cheeks?

Suddenly, before she fully understood what was happening, the handcuffs were removed. Mandy was so startled that she kept her hands and palms together in unholy prayer, at the swell of her punished buttocks. She felt Erica taking her arms and arranging them so that they now stretched out before her. She felt, but could not see or hear, the handcuffs being snapped back at her wrists. Erica withdrew, leaving Mandy helpess and immobile again. In her renewed bondage, Mandy lay still, her mind feverish with dark anticipation and dread imaginings.

Then she remembered the picture. When she was just seventeen, Mandy had stayed at a friend's flat after catching a Bruce Springsteen gig. Fingering between the paperbacks on a shelf while ice cream, cake and coffee was being rustled up by her old school chum, Mandy had discovered the folio of lascivious French prints. One had made a lasting impression on her curious, pubescent mind.

It was one of a set of naughty-nineties prints from Lille, which the Bishop of Paris had ordered to be publicly destroyed, and Freud had consulted in his essay on female sexuality: it depicted three Belgian firemen surrounding a naked Frenchwoman in her bedroom. The legend at the bottom of the print briefly explained that, while visiting her sister in Ghent, she had overturned her night table, causing her lamp to spill and set fire to the carpet. In the print, the young naked beauty shrank back, cowering in shame from the three uniformed officers, who were each trailing nozzling hoses up between their parted legs. Two of the shining nozzles were dribbling against the woman's belly and thighs; the third was still squirting a jet from its stiff hose upon her naked bosom.

It was a picture that haunted Mandy's imagination: a powerful study of shame, humiliation and erotic power. Mandy had often summoned up the image when playing with herself at bathtime or in bed: it was her favourite fantasy. Sometimes she was in the room, as voyeur; sometimes she was the naked beauty penned in by the uniformed firemen; always, when enjoying the potent image, she came.

It had been her first glimpse of female masochism, and it had fuelled many a pussy-rubbing climax. But now, masked and handcuffed across the leather horse, she was experiencing the velvet violence of total domination and discipline. The burning image in her brain of Erica, naked and predatory at the side of the vaulting horse, was infinitely more disturbing than firemen with their splashing hoses.

She felt a hand at her left shoulder, then one gripping her right forearm. Erica was mounting the horse – and then mounting Mandy, easing her pubic curls down on to the hot cheeks of the spanked bottom. Pinning Mandy's shoulder down as her thighs straddled the buttocks between them, the cropped blonde rode the cheeks she had just chastised. Mandy felt the rasp of the pubic curls against the swell of her buttocks, and jerked and bucked violently to topple the unbidden rider. Erica's hands slid between the rubber brassiere's cups and the scuffed hide of the horse. Squeezing dominantly, she instantly asserted her supremacy over her victim. Frozen in her fearfulness, Mandy lay prone and still, unwillingly accepting and all the time hating the outrage visiting her naked bottom. She shuddered as the cropped blonde's labia splayed apart, smearing her hot ooze on Mandy's cheeks.

The hands at Mandy's rubbered bosom taloned the flesh mounds savagely. Mandy squealed a mute protest. Erica's open flesh-lips grew hotter and wetter against the passive buttocks – soon she was hammering herself into Mandy's soft bottom. The rhythm broke: the rider stiffened, her thighs taut. Mandy could not smell the feral juices, could not hear the primal scream of ecstasy – but despite being deaf, dumb and blind to Erica's orgasm, Mandy knew that the cropped blonde had come.

She had been brought, blindfold and naked, to the room an hour after sunrise. Erica had made no mention of Mandy's escape attempt – or the sequel of punishment and domination – as she led her stumbling captive down the carpeted stretch of the Long Gallery. They had turned abruptly to their left; Mandy knew at once that she was being shepherded into the lair of a dominant resident. Inside, having forced Mandy to kneel, Erica withdrew.

The sounds of sucking filled the air: of lips devouring juicy flesh. Grapefruit, Mandy decided, decoding the noise. She would have to remain kneeling patiently while the dominant devoured her late breakfast. Mandy strained to catch the sounds of the breakfast table, the chink of a coffee cup, the scrape of a buttered knife across golden toast. Only the sound of the fierce sucking greeted her efforts. Mandy felt uneasy, hating the blindfold at her eyes.

She decided to risk a quick peep. If detected, it would only earn her a stripe or two across her bare buttocks. Clenching her cheeks expectantly against the sudden lash, she pretended to draw her hand back through her hair, surreptitiously lifting the blindfold a fraction as she did so.

Two naked beauties, locked into a *soixante-neuf*, lay curled up on the carpet before her. The sucking intensified as both mouths worked hungrily: not at the moist pulp of breakfast grapefruit as Mandy had supposed, but at the more succulent flesh of wet labia. The blindfold had only been inched up for a split second, but Mandy had captured the scene before her in its entirety. It remained etched vividly on her retina: the curled, naked women; the embracing, sinous limbs; the hot eyes drowning in lust; the delicious blonde curls tossed in abandon and, above all, the fact that the two naked women were identical twins.

The sucking became more frenzied. Gasps and smothered moans filled the air. Mandy felt her own slit prickle with interest as the carnal feasting came to a climax. From the sounds that followed, she sensed that the couple were now stretched out on the carpet, momentarily spent and sated.

'Take off your blindfold.'

The voice was Nordic. Finnish, Mandy thought. It had a peculiar sing-song lilt, the tone sinewed with a metallic crispness. Whatever its origin, Mandy knew that it was the voice of an accomplished disciplinarian and dominatrix.

'Quickly.'

Mandy obeyed, her bosom rising as she raised her hands to untie the blindfold, then bouncing softly as her fingers fumbled at the knot. The scene that greeted her gaze was unsettling. Two naked thirty-year-olds, severe and unsmiling, were standing hip to hip, thigh to soft thigh. They stared down at Mandy, devouring her kneeling body with hungry eyes. Mandy gazed up shyly, secretly astounded at how similar they were. Never before had she seen twins so utterly identical: and their nakedness emphasised the likeness. She marvelled at the untamed, tumbling blonde curls, the ice-blue eyes, the slender shoulders, the heavy breasts and tapered hips. It was exactly as if there were one deliciously dominant nude standing next to a long mirror – but then Mandy spotted the difference: one nude was shaven at the pubis, the other sported a bush of golden fuzz.

Mandy raised her left hand up to her ear lobe and tugged at it nervously. The twins advanced, their thighs brushing gently, their heavy bosoms bobbing. They trod the carpet with naked feet, their silent footfalls loud with exquisite menace. Mandy, kneeling, suddenly found her lips three inches from the shaven pubis. Her mouth went dry. The pulse at her throat gathered momentum, becoming deep and rapid.

'Lick me. I want you to lick me,' came the lilting command.

Mandy pressed her warm lips against the delta, parted them and flickered her tongue out. The flesh was soft and sweet, like probing a ripe damson. Working her tongue cautiously, she teased the pink clitoris.

'Harder. You can do better than that. Or be made to do better.'

Redoubling her efforts, Mandy lapped feverishly, knowing that, if she failed to please, the cane or crop would surely fall down across her bare bottom.

'Faster,' came the stern injunction.

Mandy closed her eyes and tongued the sweet flesh furiously. To her alarm, the other twin stalked around behind her and straddled Mandy's shoulders with warm, wide buttocks. Mandy flinched from the graze of pubic fuzz at the nape of her bowed neck, but the delta kissed her skin firmly as, above, the twins embraced and kissed.

71

Opening her eyes and looking up, she saw the delicious swell of the breasts, nipples peaked, of the shaven twin. The naked blondes kissed passionately, and the rounded bosoms bounced, as Mandy's wet, muscled tongue probed deeper and deeper.

The dominant being tongued gave Mandy crisp commands. When doing so, the shaven nude spoke distinctly in almost perfect English. Between themselves, they chattered rapidly, their clicking consonants and terse vowels alien to Mandy's ear. Icelandic, she decided eventually.

They spanked her next. It was, at the beginning, a playful bout of erotic dominance in which they imprinted their authority with smooth palms across Mandy's quivering cheeks. She was arranged across the thighs of the shaven twin and trapped into the punishment position: one slender hand at her neck, one slender leg trapping and controlling her thighs. Before the slaps rained down, a flattened palm had circled her naked cheeks firmly, exploring every inch of the helpless, supple flesh. Mandy tightened her buttocks as the palm curved, expertly moulding itself to the swell of her cheeks. A dominant finger – whose, she did not know – traced the outline of each peach-cheek before settling halfway down the crease of her cleft at her anal whorl.

Mandy inched her bottom up, unashamedly relishing the imperious fingertip. Deep in her cleft, her rosebud grew warm and sticky. Aroused, she was now impatient for the stinging caress of the spanking hand across her upturned cheeks. The dominant twins were in no hurry. They inspected Mandy's vulnerable nakedness intimately, dimpling the crowns of her creamy flesh-mounds with squeezed fingertips while working their thumbs at her sphincter.

The suspense made Mandy's belly coil up like a tightened spring. She wriggled across the naked thighs, wobbling her cheeks invitingly, but they did not succumb, choosing instead to maintain their absolute dominance and total control. Mandy writhed under their reign of supremacy, and struggled to provoke the punishment she had dreaded, but now desired.

The shaven blonde swept her hand across the soft curve of both cheeks. Palm upward, she dragged her knuckles across each heavy buttock, then knuckled the cleft, spreading the cheeks apart. The second twin lowered her face down. Mandy could feel the warm breath at her sphincter, and the controlling hand at her neck tightening. Mandy clenched her buttocks in self-protection, but the tongue dipped down to taste the flesh splayed apart by the knuckled hand.

Mandy threshed, squealing and protesting, as the unshaven twin knelt firmly against her, burying her entire face into the softness of her bottom. Soon the lapping, then the probing, became unbearable. Mandy felt her inner muscles spasm as the thick tongue explored the length of her velvety cleft.

The spanking followed immediately. Across the thighs of the more dominant twin, Mandy sweetly suffered three and a half minutes of severe, intimate punishment. The sharp staccato of spanks echoed around the room as the chastised cheeks bounced and slowly turned pink, then crimson, then scarlet.

Mandy ground her wet slit across the supporting thighs over which she was spread and pinioned. Delighting in the discipline, she surrendered her bare bottom to the blonde. The spanking ceased, for the moment. With maddening politeness, the dominatrix relinquished her ownership of the hot cheeks and offered Mandy's buttocks to her twin to chastise. The kneeling blonde, who had tongued Mandy so expertly, accepted the offer and spanked Mandy harshly. Mandy bucked and squirmed, the climax welling up within her now imminent – only a few sharp spanks away.

The spanks did not come. Suddenly, Mandy felt the heavy bosom of the shaven nude, over whose lap she was stretched, crush down and pin the other twin's hand to the cheeks she had just punished with her palm. The trapped hand slowly slid out from beneath the breasts, leaving the deliciously warm weight nestling dominantly on the spanked cheeks. Mandy cried out with raw pleasure as the fiercely peaked nipples burned into the satin skin of her buttocks – then whimpered as her orgasm spilled out in spasms of gentle violence.

With the bare breasts dominating her spanked bottom, Mandy came. As she paroxysmed, the kneeling twin fingered two slits: Mandy's and her own wet crease, probing each tightened flesh in rhythmic unison. Rocketing into a fresh orgasm, Mandy moaned long and loud. The nude twins remained cool, silent and seemingly aloof, their very indifference fuelling Mandy's renewed climax.

Iceland: the home of volcanic steam, boiling lava and frosted ice. They came from the land of glacial fire embodying the eternally frozen inferno. This knowledge, and the knowledge of their self-control, burned with a sweet heat in Mandy's brain, torching a third, then a fourth orgasm. Control and domination, she had discovered, were sweet, but to be so hot, punished and naked, to be so stickily aroused and so urgently kindled by the lips, tongues and hands of these identical ice-maidens was sweeter still – the sweetest surrender and submission she had ever known or imagined.

Leaving her curled up on the carpet, they withdrew, pausing to sip vodka and champagne cocktails from a single, fluted glass. The shaven twin took the ice cube from the cocktail and plied her labia with it, rubbing the smiling, flesh-lips with firm, downward strokes. Taking the red cherry out of the glass, she sucked on it hard then thumbed it into her flesh just below the clitoris. Kneeling, her twin plucked out the glistening cherry between her teeth. Mandy shuddered as she watched the teeth slice the cherry in half, and shuddered again as the two pieces of cherry disappeared into the naked blonde's mouth.

Mandy, now kneeling on the carpet, was studiously ignored. She ached with resentment, eager for their acknowledgement and chafing at their indifference. Momentarily exiled from their erotic realm, she desired to be readmitted – on almost any terms imaginable.

Abandoning the cocktail, the twins returned to where Mandy knelt, encircling her with soundless footsteps. The dominant twin stood, legs astride, in front of Mandy, while her twin knelt down behind: Mandy shivered at the rasp of the pubic curls against her recently spanked – and still sore – bottom. Cupping Mandy's breasts, the kneeling twin held them in a squeezing, vice-like grip. Mandy thrilled to the sensation of her nipples thickening into the controlling palms. Pulling her captive backwards, the twin pulled Mandy down on to the carpet. Swiftly mounting, the unshaven twin lowered her fleshy buttocks down on to Mandy's upturned face. The soft warmth of the descending bottom squashed and smothered Mandy for a brief moment, a brief moment in which sight and breathing were denied, a brief moment of exquisite torment and delight. Shuffling slightly, the twin eased her buttocks slightly, allowing her victim to breathe.

Mandy gulped for air, her hands pawing at the carpet as the scissoring thighs tightened their grip, trapping and controlling her torso and rendering her immobile. The heavy cheeks pressing into her face rose a fraction as her tormentress leant forward and threaded her arms beneath Mandy's knees. Then the plump rump settled firmly down again as the arms gathered Mandy's legs and dragged them up from the carpet. Once her legs were raised up, strong hands parted them at the thighs, exposing her wet fig. Mandy could not see, but could both sense and then feel, the presence of the other twin, the shaven vixen, kneeling down at her exposed delta. The unseen mouth closed on her, lips and tongue busy at her slit. Mandy struggled, but to no avail. These devilish twins were determined in their enjoyment of her: one pinning her down contemptuously with her bare bottom, the other mounting her splayed labia with absolute impunity.

The tongue at her slit lapped slowly, luxuriously, at first. Then the rasping became more urgent; soon the thick muscle was probing. Mandy felt its firmness inside her, the angle of approach affording deep penetration. Her squeals were muffled by the soft flesh of the buttocks on her face. As the tongue explored her inner, most secret flesh, the buttocks above commenced a rhythmic joggling. Cruel hands grasped and squeezed her breasts once more, punishing and pleasuring the helpless flesh-mounds and tormenting her nipples up into peaks of fire. Above her face, the swollen cheeks were riding her ruthlessly, the heavy flesh raking her mouth so that Mandy could taste the bitterness of the hot cleft. With a cunning dexterity, the rider managed to drag her slit across Mandy's mouth with each thrusting sweep, and backward jerk of the hips.

'Tongue her.'

The command came from the twin mouthing Mandy's labial flesh, not the naked twin who was to be tongued.

Mandy's tongue protruded, thrusting up into the acrid cleft, the tip just touching the rosebud sphincter.

'No, not there,' the twin cried, wriggling her bottom. 'There,' she hissed, lowering her gaping flesh-folds down on to Mandy's mouth. 'There.'

Perched above her victim, the unshaven nude planted her hot slit over Mandy's tongue just as the other twin's tongue at Mandy's own slit started to trigger a climax.

The three naked women were briefly frozen in their frenzied lust. Fusing hot flesh to hotter flesh, they quivered as violent orgasms raked their nakedness. Mandy screamed into the buttocks above, biting them in her passionate paroxysms, as the tongue at her opened furnace stoked fresh flames. Driven into the fury of her climax, Mandy tongued the sweet flesh above with renewed vigour and violence. The naked rider gripped her mount and ground her slit down, coming furiously on to Mandy's shining, slippery face. Mandy sensed the weight of the buttocks above shifting as her tormentress knelt up, and felt the tongue at her slit withdraw as the shaven dominatrix also knelt. In mute understanding, the blonde twins were now locked in a deep French kiss above her pinioned, helpless nakedness.

The dildo, they informed her, both fingering its length in harmony, was carved from an Icelandic walrus tusk. It was over two hundred years old, the cherished relic of initiation rites performed in the long, dark nights before spring came to melt the ice that bound the iron land. Mandy saw that the gleaming curve of ivory was etched with runic inscriptions: an unholy pagan prayer dedicated to the goddess of ice-fire. Mandy quailed at its sinuous, wicked length, clamping her thighs and clenching her buttocks at the very thought of its penetration. The twins perceived her token resistance and exchanged slow, knowing smiles.

Tied to the bed, her arms and legs splayed and secured at the wrists and ankles to the wooden posts, Mandy gazed up fearfully. Kneeling in silence at either side of her bed of bondage, the nudes played with their ivory shaft, probing one another's mouth with its blunt tip. Mandy had been gagged tightly with a cruel band of crimson serge. Above it, her eyes were wide with fearful apprehension. She shook her head from side to side vigorously, signalling her unwillingness. To her relief, both twins gazed down at her, nodding their understanding.

'Not until you plead with us,' the shaven dominatrix murmured. 'Not until you beg us,' she added in a curdling whisper.

Mandy heaved a sigh of relief, certain in the knowledge that she would never want – or whimper for – the dildo.

'But you will,' the whispering voice continued, as if the naked blonde had been reading Mandy's troubled mind.

They removed the tight gag and, hands entwined tenderly around the ivory shaft, fingers interlocking in the carnal unison, the twins guided the phallus to Mandy's mouth, using it on her lips like a lipstick. Denying what seemed to be self-betrayal, Mandy found herself opening her lips wide as if eager for the blunt tip inside her mouth. It slid in, probing her wet warmth. She tightened her lips around its cool length, sucking gently at first, then with a fierce desire to possess. Inside her, it teased the roof of her mouth, then dominantly flattened and tamed her tongue. It was intimately erotic, and Mandy juiced down at her hot slit. The twins, eyes darting down to note her involuntary response and reaction, played with the dildo for several more minutes, plying it into her mouth until the patches of sheet beneath Mandy's parted thighs were stained dark with her wet ooze. Then, hands still wrapped around the dildo, they guided it slowly, teasingly, down over her chin, against the arch of her straining neck to her breasts below.

The hard tip of the ivory shaft traced the soft contours of her naked bosom with exquisite delicacy, delighting her silken flesh as it faithfully fingered its passive swell. The tip addressed each nipple in turn, tapping each tiny pink bud up into pale-purple peaks of fierce pleasure. Mandy writhed, the bondage at her wrists and ankles burning into her bound flesh. At her pouting labia, the sparkling ooze of her arousal widened the spreading stain. The gag was firmly replaced, the crimson serge biting into her mute mouth, renewing her sense of utter helplessness – a help-lessness as absolute as her capitulation and desire for the dildo.

Mandy struggled to resist her innermost yearnings, stunned at the possibility of her submitting eagerly to the shaft. Taking her breasts, one in a left hand, the other in the kneeling twin's right hand, they nosed the dildo down along the swell of her hip, across her flattened, tense belly and across to her upper, outer thigh. Mandy jerked as the blunt tip dimpled her soft flesh. Riding her dominantly, it descended into, then against, her ultra-sensitive inner thigh. Mandy squealed as the solid weight of the phallus scored her satin flesh just above her right knee. Slowly, with maddeningly tantalising circular sweeps, it inched back up towards the hot pulse of her open slit. She jerked her hips and pounded her buttocks as her splayed thighs were ruthlessly teased, her mind no longer certain that it would be able to deny what her aching body desired: the thrust of the dildo inside her tight warmth.

It inched up a fraction closer, and then a fraction more, the clasped hands nudging the tip up to kiss-tease her tiny, erect clitoris.

With a supreme effort, Mandy shook her head. No. No. She mouthed her protest into the wet gag, still denying her desire for the dildo. Ignoring her totally, the guiding hands at the ivory shaft directed it to finger her wet labia with firm, downward strokes. At each stroke, the cunning hands swiftly speared the shaft up along the crease of her cleft, briefly forcing the firm length between her tightly clenched cheeks.

The delicious torture lasted for a full eight minutes. Mandy's aching body burned with the effort of her denial but burned more fiercely with the seething flame of desire. Suddenly, the spasms inside her told her – and told the predatory eyes of the watching twins – that she was rapidly approaching the point of no return. Her orgasm would be soon; her climax was imminent.

Gasping audibly, she nodded, signalling her readiness for the cruel shaft. Further denial and resistance was useless: they had smashed her resolve completely and broken her spirit. They had crushed her rebellion, and bent her mind and body to their lustful will using the dark skills of erotic prowess and the spells of sexual witchcraft. Shuddering, she submitted and surrendered, closing her eyes and expecting the blunt thrust.

It did not occur. Opening her eyes, she stared up in bewildered frustration to see the bottom of the unshaven twin hovering over the bed, the plump cheeks held apart to receive the probing dildo. Pumping the phallus deep into her twin's anus, the shaven nude guided the shaft into the tight sphincter. Mandy threshed in her fury and confusion, and threshed with renewed violence as she felt the drip, drip of the hot juices splashing down on to her breasts from the weeping slit of the speared twin.

She heard their harsh laughter and then the taunting words of the dominatrix.

'We made you want it, no? But you cannot have it. Not even if you beg. It is sweet, is it not, to light the flames of desire and then douse them with denial? Yes,' the alien voice from the land of fire and ice reflected aloud, 'it is sweet.'

For Mandy, her capitulation tasted as sour as her subsequent humiliation: sour and bitter.

AMANDA IN THE PRIVATE HOUSE

Esme Ombreux

Esme Ombreux has a remarkable reputation when one considers that she has written only two books for Nexus. These aren't just any two books, though: the first, *One Week in the Private House*, sold out within weeks of first publication and has been reprinted twice, and the long-awaited sequel, *Amanda in the Private House*, more than lived up to expectations when it was published last year. She also edited the first two *New Erotica* books, and used to write *Letters from Esme* in the back of a number of Nexus novels – all in all, a true devotee of erotica. When we asked Esme if she had any plans to return to the Private House, she left us with the tantalising hope that we could indeed expect a third visit to that ever-popular house of hedonistic perverts. We can only wait.

The following extract is taken from *Amanda in the Private House*. In this novel the naïve Amanda has travelled to France to find her missing housekeeper, Tess. During the search Amanda has met Michael, an artist with bizarre sexual tastes who has awakened in her a love of the shameful delights of discipline. Amanda has taken enthusiastically to her new-found sexual freedom, voluntarily submitting to extreme indignities of punishment and humiliation as she is targeted by the Private House. They have been keeping a close eye on her until now, but in the following extract she finally undergoes a personal inspection of one of their members.

'This is the place.' Michael said. 'An unlikely premises for the making of dirty videos, but this is definitely the address I was given when I phoned the number that was hidden inside your vibrator.'

Amanda looked up at the house: it was a tall, stone-built structure with thin windows and narrow gables; the large garden that surrounded it was well-tended and tastefully landscaped. Most of the windows were shuttered.

'It looks deserted,' she said.

'Only one way to find out,' Michael replied, and pushed the button set into the wall next to the wrought-iron gates. After a moment the gates swung open.

'Someone's in,' Michael said.

'Perhaps I should do this on my own,' Amanda said. 'I've bested some redoubtable captains of industry and some formidable corporate lawyers in my time. I doubt if I'll have any trouble with an actress from a porn video. And the instruction was that I should come alone.'

Michael pretended to look offended. 'I suspect you're looking forward to this rendezvous and you don't want me sharing the fun,' he said. 'More to the point, you don't speak French. And although this woman obviously can speak English when she wants to, it might be useful to have me there as an interpreter. And anyway, I want to look after you. Do you want me to come with you?'

Amanda looked into his eyes. She felt herself blushing. 'Yes,' she said. 'Of course.'

They walked hand in hand along the curved gravel path

that led to the portico of the house. When Amanda reached for the doorbell button, Michael pulled away her hand and gathered her close to him. Their lips met, and Amanda thought briefly, in the midst of the warmth and passion that always coursed through her when Michael kissed her, that each time he kissed her it felt as fresh as the first time and as natural as if they had been kissing for ever.

She felt his hands untying the belt of her coat and then opening it. His arms snaked round the back of her dress, pulling her towards him. Through the thin cotton of the dress her body was pressed against his. He was warm and hard. Her nipples felt like living stones, hard against his chest and yet achingly sensitive. His hands, busy behind her back, had pulled up her skirt and now grasped her naked buttocks. She gasped, her breath entering his mouth. Her sex felt like liquid, tingling heat, and she was sure that at any moment his fingers would discover the shameful wetness of her desire for him or, even worse, he would merely have to touch a fingertip to her anus, and she wouldn't be able to restrain the exclamation of pleasure that would reveal how much she liked that particularly intimate caress.

Abruptly, Michael broke away from their embrace.

Amanda looked up, saw the direction of Michael's gaze, and turned to find that the door behind her had opened. A slim woman with dark hair cut in a severe style was standing in the doorway and had obviously seen everything that Michael had been doing with his hands.

Amanda couldn't help blushing, but she made sure she displayed no other signs of her mortification as she brushed down her skirt, re-tied her belt, and returned the woman's insolent stare.

'I'm Amanda,' she said. 'I believe you have information about the whereabouts of my friend Tess.'

'I'm sure you recognise me,' the woman said, without smiling. 'You have seen me on video, *n'est-ce pas?*'

'Nicole,' Michael said, in a voice that sounded to Amanda rather too flirtatious. He was right, however:

Amanda had also recognised the pretty, sharp-featured woman as Nicole. She suddenly remembered, in vivid detail, Nicole sitting astride Tess's face, Nicole holding Terss's legs in the air while Tess's bottom was being whipped and, of course, Michael bringing Amanda to a climax just as Nicole, on video, was brought to a climax by Tess's tongue.

Nicole glanced disdainfully at Michael and made a point of speaking only to Amanda. 'I asked you to come alone,' she said.

Amanda was in no mood to stand for any nonsense. 'Well, I'm not alone,' she said. 'You can speak to both of us. I don't want to keep anything secret from Michael.'

Nichole raised an arched eyebrow. 'No? But perhaps there are things which I wish to remain secret from him.' She gave a sigh of impatience. 'I won't let him come into the house.'

'We can probably sort this out here on the doorstep,' Amanda said. 'Do you know where Tess is? And how much do you want for the information?'

'How much?' Nicole seemed infuriatingly naïve.

'Money,' Amanda snapped. 'Sterling. Francs. Whatever.'

Nicole laughed, and Amanda began to experience yet again the feeling that she was slipping into a weird parallel world which was controlled by rules that were subtly alien to her. The feeling had something to do with becoming sexually aroused, and she found herself very conscious of her knickerless state and of the pulses of excitement that were still thrilling in her pudenda.

'I don't want money,' Nicole said, and leant forward until her face was close to Amanda's. Her voice became a whisper. 'But I am interested in entertainment. And for that you must come into the house. Alone.'

Amanda heard Michael start to protest, but she silenced him with an abrupt signal. 'And you'll tell me where Tess is?' Amanda asked, her steady gaze and low voice matching the French woman's.

'But of course,' Nicole said, finishing the phrase by

shaping her lips slowly and unmistakably into a kiss. 'If you entertain me, why should I not?'

Amanda assumed that Nicole wanted her to perform oral sex, perhaps in the way that Tess had in the video. Amanda had never done such a thing with a woman, and she had no doubt that Nicole would take pleasure in making the experience particularly difficult and degrading for her. But that, she knew to her shame, was a large part of why she would agree to whatever the French woman demanded. She recalled again the image of tall, athletic Tess held captive between Nicole's thighs, and felt her treacherous nipples tingle with excitement.

She turned to Michael. 'I'll have to do this on my own,' she said. 'It's the only way. I'm sorry, but I know what I'm doing.'

Michael was quite obviously dumbfounded. The silly boy looked as hurt as if she'd slapped him. 'Amanda, sweetheart. You can't. I mean, how can you trust this whole set-up? There's something strange going on here. At the airport I'm sure I saw – '

'It's all right,' Amanda said firmly. 'Leave me here. I'll call you at your hotel. I can look after myself. Don't make a fuss.'

Amanda knew she was being curt, but she didn't like to see Michael being indecisive and wimpish. She didn't want Nicole to see him like that, either. And she was keen to find out what Nicole had planned for her.

Michael managed a wry smile. 'All right, angel,' he said. 'We'll do it your way. I'll be looking out for you.' He turned and made his way briskly along the path and into the boulevard.

The two women watched him until he was out of sight, and then turned to face each other again.

'Come in, Amanda,' Nicole said, opening wide the door and stepping back. 'Come into a world of pleasure.'

Michael's already taken me there, Amanda thought as she hesitated on the threshold.

Nicole extended a hand. Amanda took it, and stepped through the doorway. She hardly noticed the dark opulence of the hall because Nicole gave her hand a gentle squeeze, which Amanda returned, and she had just enough time to register a thrill of excitement before Nicole pulled her close.

The two women were almost exactly the same height, and similar in appearance. Amanda's features were less sharp then Nicole's, but both had large eyes, stylishly short dark hair, and heart-shaped faces with broad, full lips.

Curiouser and curiouser, Amanda thought. It's rather like looking into a mirror. Perhaps this is what you see when you look into mirrors in this weird parallel world. This world of pleasure.

'I'm going to kiss you,' Nicole said.

'Yes,' Amanda said, and urgently pressed her lips against those of her perverted reflection. Nicole's lips were soft and warm; her scent was as sharp and pretty as her face. Her arms were around Amanda's waist, and Amanda found it natural to reciprocate the embrace. Amanda was aware of the softness of Nicole's breasts, and wished that she wasn't wearing a coat.

'I'll tell you where you can find Tess,' Nicole whispered. 'But you must promise to do exactly as I tell you.'

Amanda knew what she had to ask, but she held on tightly to Nicole and kissed her willing lips for several moments while she summoned the courage to say the all-important words.

'Are you going to tell me to do things that are very indecent?'

Nicole kissed her, and stroked her face. 'Yes, of course.'

'All right, then,' Amanda said, as if clinching a deal. 'I accept.'

'Very good,' Nicole said, and gently separated herself from Amanda's embrace. 'In that case, welcome to my house. Let me take your coat.'

It was precisely the sort of offer that anyone would make when inviting a person into a house, Amanda thought as she shrugged off her coat, but Nicole's words seemed to contain undercurrents of meaning. They

89

implied that Nicole was starting to undress her; that Nicole wanted to see Amanda's body. As Amanda gave her coat to Nicole she felt as if it was an act of surrender, a removal of a layer of protection.

Amanda remained standing in the hall as Nicole walked round her to hang the coat in a cloakroom. She was conscious of Nicole's gaze on her body and of the fact that her dress was of thin, clinging cotton with a skirt that barely covered her stocking-tops. She wondered whether the French woman had been able to tell that she was wearing no knickers.

'We will go upstairs now,' Nicole said, and indicated that Amanda should precede her. 'Everything is ready.'

Amanda knew that Nicole's ominous words should fill her with trepidation, but she felt nothing but impatience to find out what was in store for her. She stepped on to the curving staircase and realised that the French woman, behind her, couldn't fail to notice that she was naked under her skirt, and aroused.

'Lift up your skirt,' Nicole said. 'I want to watch your arse as you go up the stairs.'

Amanda put her hands behind her and pulled her skirt up to waist. Her bottom, sensitised by the spanking Michael had given it, felt as if it was flowing with embarrassment as much as her face. She had obeyed the French woman's instructions without question, and she hated feeling so stupid and helpless. But she also had to admit to herself, guiltily, that although Nicole hadn't even touched her sex she could feel that it was already almost dripping with her juices.

'Very pretty,' Nicole said. 'Now go up the stairs quickly, Amanda. I want to see your pretty arse move.'

Nicole seemed to have a knack of making comments that could have been designed to cause maximum embarrassment, Amanda thought. As she trotted up the stairs she was acutely conscious of the swaying of her hips, the jiggling of her buttocks, and the fact that in lifting one leg and then the other she was repeatedly giving Nicole glimpses of her sopping vulva.

She stopped on the landing, catching her breath and looking over the wrought-iron balustrade into the hall below. She didn't lower her dress; she knew that it was immodest to stand there showing off her bottom, but guessed – she hoped – that Nicole might want to touch her. She remembered reading Tess's notebook, and realised that her situation was similar to that of Becky, one of Tess's many conquests. Becky had been made to bend over at the top of a staircase; Tess had given her bottom a spanking. Was it possible that Nicole knew about Tess's exploits? Could Nicole know that Amanda had read Tess's secret stories?

Nicole came to stand close behind Amanda. Amanda's hands, clutching the material of her skirt, made contact with Nicole's. Amanda felt Nicole's breast touch her back, and moved to press against them slightly.

'Keep still,' Nicole warned, and stepped back.

Nicole's hands were cool as they gently explored the curves of Amanda's bottom. Without thinking, Amanda moved her legs further apart and leant forward on to the balustrade. Nicole laughed, and Amanda realised with a rush of shame just how brazenly she had displayed herself.

'You're beautiful, Amanda,' Nicole said dreamily. Her fingers were tracing circles at the very tops of Amanda's thighs, frustratingly close to the tingling lips of her vulva. 'And very sexy. Your bottom is a delightful colour. Quite bright. Have you been punished today?'

Amanda took a deep breath. The French woman could tell. Well, there was no point in denying it. 'Yes,' she breathed. 'Michael spanked me.' Saying the words gave her a thrill. She pushed her bottom out further. Please touch me, she thought; please touch my arsehole and my clitoris. She didn't dare to plead aloud.

'Men!' Nicole said, and touched the tip of a finger to the seeping line between Amanda's outer labia. 'They are useful, but sometimes they are not sensitive enough. I think that only a woman knows how to punish another woman.'

Amanda realised that Nicole wasn't going to spank her.

The French woman had something else in mind, and said, 'Come with me, Amanda. Come into the bathroom.'

Amanda followed Nicole into a room that was even grander than the largest bathroom in any of Amanda's properties. The floor and walls were entirely tiled in white ceramic; the effect would have been antiseptic, like a hospital, but for the colourful rugs on the floor and the great swags of dyed muslin that hung from the ceiling and were gathered around a scintillating chandelier. In addition to the usual bathroom fittings there were a jacuzzi and an open shower area; a corner was furnished with black leather-upholstered sofas and glass-topped tables. Vast mirrors hung on all four walls. The most incongruous item, however, was a large, reclining chair, shining with chrome and polished black leather, that had been placed in the shower area. It looked to Amanda like a sinister cross between an old-fashioned dentist's chair and an operating table, and she was sure that it was going to feature in Nicole's plans.

'Take off all your clothes,' Nicole said. 'They must not become wet.'

The room was warm, but Amanda shivered with anticipation as she removed her shoes, her dress, her stockings, her suspender belt and her bra. Each time she glaced up she found that Nicole's eyes were hungrily admiring her body. She knew she was blushing furiously, and had to stifle a sob when her breasts fell from the cups of her bra and she heard Nicole's appreciative exclamation.

'Come here,' Nicole said, and Amanda's trepidation increased as she was led towards the complicated, metallic throne.

'You like to show your body, don't you?' Nicole said.

Amanda, in all honesty, had to nod in agreement.

'Then sit here,' Nicole said, 'and make an exhibition for me. Show me your private places.'

Amanda bit her lip and approached the chair. The seat and the armrests were covered in shining black leather. Every part of the complex structure appeared to be jointed, so that the whole thing resembled a futuristic machine more than a piece of furniture. She turned, looked at Nicole, whose smile was encouraging but also predatory, and placed her bottom on the smooth, cool leather.

'Sit at the front end of the seat,' Nicole said. 'Look, I will move the back of the chair to support you.' Nicole turned a steel handle, and the entire back of the chair raked inwards, inclining towards the small of Amanda's back as she sat perched on the front edge of the seat. Amanda relaxed into the slightly concave, leather-covered surface. Nicole moved a soft headrest so that Amanda was supported from her hips to her cranium.

Amanda was feeling very comfortable now, and was prepared for almost any indignity which Nicole might inflict on her. She became aware of a rustling noise, and turned her head to find that Nicole was undressing. She had already removed her crisp blouse and her short silk skirt, and was wearing only a lacy bra and hold-up stockings. She noticed Amanda watching her, and moved close to the chair.

'I am as pretty as you, don't you think?' she said, and covered Amanda's mouth with her own in a passionate kiss. Amanda felt Nicole's hand caressing her right breast; the nipple hardened immediately, and Amanda felt Nicole's smile. 'But I have not such big tits,' Nicole went on, breaking off the kiss. 'Perhaps we should give your tits some support while you are in the chair. Would you like that?'

Amanda didn't know what she was being asked to agree to, but if it involved Nicole touching her breasts she couldn't refuse. 'Yes, please,' she said.

Nicole reached behind the back of the chair and produced, from either side, an array of straps and elasticated ribbon, all in black. 'I will make a bra for you,' she said. 'But first, I must make your tits as big as possible.' And, to Amanda's writhing delight, she proceeded to stroke, fondle, pinch and massage Amanda's breasts, paying particular attention to the nipples.

Amanda closed her eyes and surrendered to the

sensations. She remembered, suddenly, that at school her precociously large breasts had caused her abject embarrassment. She realised now that it had been envy that had prompted her classmates to give her the nickname Busty; at the time she had cried herself to sleep in the dormitory. She still found it hard to believe that anyone could find her big tits attractive. Michael did, of course, but then she expected an artist to have strange notions. Nicole's enthusiasm was also unfeigned.

After only a few minutes her breasts felt swollen and acutely sensitive, and she arched her back to offer them to Nicole's increasingly rough treatment and to watch her engorged, pink globes being manhandled. The pinching and slapping stopped. Amanda's breasts were reddened and heavy. Nichole was stretching the straps and ribbons across Amanda's chest, enclosing her breasts within a web that ran above, below and between the swollen orbs, constricting them, supporting them, and pushing them into shining, prominent, distended spheres which appeared separated from Amanda's body by the tight bonds but which were in fact, as Amanda found, throbbing with desire.

Nicole stood back to admire her handiwork, and then swept forward and placed her lips over Amanda's right nipple. Amanda discovered immediately that bound breasts are particularly sensitive; she gasped at the intensity of the thrill that ran through her as Nicole's tongue described a circle, and when Nicole's teeth nipped her taut skin she would have leapt from the chair had she not been tied to it by her peculiar bra.

Nicole laughed and flounced away. 'Do you like your new bra?' she said.

Amanda recovered her breath. She had never had her breasts tied up before. She had had no idea that the sensations could be so powerful. Her breasts looked strange, surrounded by stretched black straps and pulled into firm balls of smooth flesh. She moved in the chair, and found that even a slight movement caused a shock of feeling in her nipples. 'Yes, thank you,' she said.

Nicole pressed a button with her foot and Amanda felt the chair begin to rise. She could no longer touch the tiled floor with her extended toes, and she feared that only the straps round her breasts would prevent her slipping from her precarious perch on the edge of the seat.

'Hold the armrests,' Nicole said, a little testily.

Amanda did so, and felt more secure.

'Well?' Nicole said, coming to stand in front of the chair. 'Are you going to show me what you have between your legs? That's what you want, isn't it?'

Amanda knew, with a sinking heart, that Nicole was going to make Amanda very aware of each stage of her step-by-step humiliation – and that she, Amanda, wouldn't be able to stop herself enjoying every minute of it.

'Yes,' she said defiantly, 'of course.' And she parted her legs so that she was sure Nicole could see her pubic hair and probably the topmost part of her labia.

Nicole laughed unpleasantly. 'You stupid girl,' she said. 'I want to see everything. I want your legs much wider apart than that. Put your feet in the stirrups. You see them? Like on a horse.'

Amanda hadn't noticed that the chair was equipped with footrests; now, with her breasts tied to the chair, they were at the edge of her field of vision. Like the rest of the chair they were made of metal and lined with soft leather, and they were connected to the mechanisms at the base of the chair by long, jointed, steel rods. They were also very far apart.

Amanda stared at Nicole, who returned the look with a frown. The French woman really did expect her to stretch her legs that wide. Amanda knew that she would look obscene with her legs splayed out. She also knew she would have to do it.

It was difficult for Amanda to keep any part of her bottom in contact with the seat, and she had to take much of her weight on her arms as she stretched her legs and manoeuvred her feet into the rests. She was disappointed that Nicole didn't even comment on her success, but crouched at each of the footrests in turn to secure Amanda's feet in them with leather straps. 'For safety,' she said, but Amanda suspected that Nicole wanted to be sure that Amanda couldn't close her legs.

'Now,' Nicole said, 'we will adjust the position.' She started to turn another handle, and Amanda realised that the chair was gradually moving: the seat, the back, the headrest and the footrests were tipping backwards together. Her legs and hips were being lifted into the air as the top half of her body reclined. Nicole continued to turn the handle until the back of the chair was almost horizontal, and Amanda found herself looking up at chrome-plated struts and leather belts that formed part of the framework round the chair.

Instead of resting against her ribcage, Amanda's breasts in their tight black bondage were erect and thrusting upwards. Nicole flicked the nipples with a fingertip and made Amanda cry out.

It had occurred to Amanda that Nicole, wanting to prevent any show of modesty from Amanda, would probably tie Amanda's hands to the armrests of the chair. Amanda had guessed correctly; securing Amanda's arms was Nicole's next task, and was quickly accomplished. Amanda's forearms were strapped to the leather armrests with the black bands, and Nicole then turned another handle to move the armrests up and apart so that Amanda's hands were held in a position alongside her reclining head. Nicole removed her bra and stockings and now, completely naked, taunted Amanda by letting her breasts brush against Amanda's imprisoned hands.

Nicole came to stand in front of the chair, and Amanda suddenly remembered that her thighs were held wide apart. 'Now I can see almost everything,' Nicole said, after staring at Amanda for a long time. 'I can see your big lips, all hairy and wide open.' Amanda moaned on hearing the demeaning description of her sex. 'And between them,' Nicole went on remorselessly. 'I can see your little pink lips. They are very, very wet. There are drips of wet coming out! I can see them, coming out of the hole of your cunt. Can you feel how wet you are?'

Amanda struggled against her bonds. Her breasts jolted with electric thrills with every movement. She didn't understand how she had allowed herself to be treated in such a squalid way, but she couldn't deny the physical evidence of her arousal.

'Yes,' she said. 'I know I'm wet.'

'There is a problem,' Nicole announced. 'I cannot see your arsehole very well. You want me to see your arsehole, don't you? We will have to move your legs.'

Nicole made more adjustments to the chair, and Amanda watched helplessly as the footrests began to rise towards the celing, taking with them her feet. She could feel her bottom being lifted off its perch on the seat; then the footrests, on their long steel rods and still as far apart as ever, began to move into a position above her head. Before she knew it her splayed legs were above her reclining torso, and her knees, had they been closer together, would have been touching her breasts. She was bent double, and a glance into the mirror on the opposite wall confirmed that she was secured in the most shameful position imaginable, with her arsehole now very visible indeed and her open vulva pointing upwards.

'That's better,' Nicole said. Now that she was naked the French woman seemed unable to resist the temptation to caress Amanda's helpless body. She touched the crinkled skin around Amanda's anus tentatively at first, but when she discovered that Amanda couldn't conceal her pleasure when touched there, she concentrated her attentions on the prominently displayed hole.

Commenting all the while on Amanda's perverse and disgraceful enjoyment of such intimate caresses, Nicole first spent several minutes lubricating Amanda's anus with both Amanda's copious juices and her own. Nicole inserted and quickly extracted one finger, and Amanda tossed her head with mortification when she couldn't conceal the tremor of a small orgasm. Nicole merely laughed, which added to Amanda's discomfiture. Amanda felt the fingers of Nicole's other hand circling her clitoris, and she knew that she would come again if the French woman did anything at all to her anus.

'Two fingers?' Nicole said. Amanda felt the familiar pressure against her sphincter, felt the muscle relax, and felt a sudden stretching fullness that sent her into another climax.

'Very, very good,' Nicole said. 'But there is still a problem. I cannot see everything. There is too much hair. You are too hairy. And you want me to be able to see everything, don't you?'

Amanda opened her eyes. Nicole was no longer standing at Amanda's upraised buttocks, framed with Amanda's lifted legs. Amanda turned her head. Nicole was standing beside her. In one hand she had the rose of one of the showers and a safety razer. In the other she held a small pair of scissors.

'Now we will play at being at the barber's, no?' Nicole said.

'What are you going to do?' Amanda gasped, although she had already guessed the next humiliation that Nicole had in store for her.

'I am going to make you completely naked, Amanda. You must not move.'

Amanda immediately tried to move her hips and found that she couldn't. She found her enforced stillness strangely reassuring.

Nicole pulled one of the rugs in front of the base of the chair and knelt on it. She placed her left hand on the back of Amanda's right thigh, and leant forward. She blew softly into the cleft of Amanda's vulva, and Amanda shivered.

'First,' Nicole said, 'I will cut away all the long hairs.' She started at the top of Amanda's pubic mound, where the dark curls were thickest and still relatively dry. Amanda could hear nothing but the snip of the scissors. She began to relax. She had had hair down there since puberty; she knew that it was quite respectable for a woman to keep her pubic hair trimmed, but she was still sure that only vulgar women shaved everything. She guessed that Michael would like it: he liked anything perverse like that.

Amanda's reverie was interrupted by the tugging of Nicole's fingers at the hairs on her labia. The hairs, sparser here but long and curly, were blackly wet with Amanda's juices and slicked down, but even so Nicole seemed to be pulling harder and more frequently than could possibly be necessary. Amanda couldn't squirm in protest; she could only lift her head and say 'Oh'. Nicole took no notice, and in any case Amanda found that no matter how she craned her neck she couldn't see what Nicole was doing because her view was blocked by her bound and swollen breasts. She suspected that Nicole was pulling and pinching at her private parts long after the long hairs had been snipped away; she was sure that from time to time she felt Nicole's lips brushing close to her clitoris, and every now and then one of Nicole's fingers would stray into the gaping well of Amanda's anus.

If Nicole was trying to remind Amanda that she was tied up, helpless, obscenely exposed, and thoroughly aroused, then Amanda had to admit that Nicole was succeeding.

Nicole stood up, stretched, and came to stand beside the headrest of the chair. Amanda turned her head, and found herself gazing at Nicole's naked body. Nicole slowly slid her feet apart until her thighs were parted almost as widely as Amanda's. Amanda licked her lips; would Nicole want Amanda to use her mouth now? Amanda watched in reluctant fascination as Nicole pushed her hips forward, put a hand behind her back and between her legs, and used her fingers to part her sex-lips. She was wet and pink inside. Amanda breathed in the sharp scent of Nicola's arousal.

Amanda realised she could hear the sound of running water. The shower head, held in Nicole's other hand, came into view. A fine spray of water struck Nicole's belly and cascaded through her black pubic hair. Warm drops splashed on Amanda's face; she saw rivulets of water

99

stream between Nicole's parted lips and drip from them to the floor.

She looked up at Nicole's face. The French woman was striving to retain her haughty mask but couldn't help gasping with pleasure as the water flowed across her sensitive membranes.

'You must not come when I wash you and shave you,' Nicole said. 'If you come before I tell you, I will not give you the information you want.' She flicked the shower head towards Amanda and sprayed Amanda's face.

When Amanda had blinked the water from her eyes, Nicole had resumed her position kneeling at Amanda's upthrust private parts. Suddenly the spray was splashing all over Amanda's vulva and trickling into her vagina and her anus. She immediately felt the tremors of an orgasm beginning, and squeezed shut her eyes as she fought against the sensations.

There was to be no respite, however, and Amanda had to bite her lip and toss her head from side to side to counteract the waves of pleasure. Nicole was doing something else now, something almost unbearably exciting; a soft, cool, moist, circular movement all around Amanda's sex lips. Amanda realised what was happening: Nicole was brushing shaving soap everywhere between Amanda's widely spread thighs.

Just when Amanda thought that she could no longer prevent herself cresting the wave of a spectacular climax, the brushing stopped.

'Keep still,' Nicole said, and something small and cold and hard touched Amanda's pubic mound, slid across it delicately, and then was gone, leaving behind a sense of exposure as if to a cool draught of air. Nicole was shaving her.

The razor touched her again, a little lower this time, a little closer to the hood of her clitoris, and Amanda shivered. Again and again the razor touched her briefly, tantalisingly, and each time Amanda felt more exposed, and the shivers began to run together into a trembling that was taking Amanda once again to the brink of ecstasy.

When Nicole used her fingers to press Amanda's sex lips first to one side and then to the other as she shaved the valleys at the very tops of Amanda's thighs; when Nicole pressed Amanda's outer labia flat and shaved them, one after the other, with the gentlest of tiny strokes, Amanda was sure she would come.

But Nicole suddenly said, 'Finished. For the moment, at least. Now I must wash you again. No coming, you understand?'

This time the jet of water was stronger; very warm at first, and then cold. Through the swarm of sensations Amanda realised that she could tell that she was now hairless; the water ran quickly off her newly exposed and tingling skin.

If the water had remained warm she would have come, but the change to a cold shower, while exciting because it revealed to her just how naked she was, restored her partially to her senses. She opened her eyes and saw Nicole watching her expectantly and brandishing a pair of tweezers.

'For the little hairs near your arsehole,' Nicole announced. 'You want to be completely naked, no?'

Amanda moaned. Was there no indignity she was to be spared? She was tied up in the most degrading position imaginable; her breasts were strapped up and bulging like balloons; her denuded, yawning pudenda were more exposed than they had ever been; and her doubled-up, pulled-apart legs were beginning to ache.

'Well?' Nicole said.

'Oh, I suppose so,' Amanda replied, and settled back to enjoy guiltily the nipping sensations as Nicole extracted the tiny hairs growing close to the rim of Amanda's anus.

'The little mouth is opening,' Nicole said. 'Would you like a finger inside it?'

Amanda, completely subjugated, could only sob in reply. Nicole's finger slid easily into her anus, and Amanda once again couldn't understand how such a despicable thing could make her feel so contented in the depths of her abject shame.

At last Nicole leant back. She cast a critical eye over the shaved area; Amanda could almost feel Nicole's gaze inspecting every fold and surface of her private parts.

Nicole sprayed Amanda again with cold water, and ran her hand from Amanda's belly to her anus. Amanda could feel that Nicole's fingers met no resistance; her sex was completely smooth.

Nicole's hand continued to stroke Amanda while she ducked under Amanda's raised leg and came to watch the expressions of pleasure that Amanda couldn't help showing on her face as Nicole's fingers caressed the denuded flesh.

'Would you like me to kiss you?' Amanda said. 'I mean, lick you. Down there.'

Nicole smiled. 'Not today. Today is for you to learn more things about your body. Now it is time for the final thing.'

Nicole busied herself for a few minutes with tidying away the shaving implements. She left the bathroom but returned almost immediately. The first thing that Amanda noticed was that Nicole was now wearing a black collar and black gloves. Then she noticed that Nicole was carrying a short, thin, leather strap.

'You look very smooth now,' Nicole said, tickling the backs of Amanda's thighs with the end of the strap. 'Very smooth and naked and shining. I'm going to smack you until you come. You will see that a woman knows best how to punish you. And then I will tell you how to get to where Tess is.'

Amanda wasn't surprised to be told that she was going to receive another spanking. She knew that she deserved to be punished: she couldn't deny that all the things that Nicole had done to her had aroused her, and her wetness betrayed her wicked perversity. The residual tingling from Michael's spanking had gone now; the strap, she imagined, would sting more sharply than Michael's hand, but

102

she welcomed the thought of sharp strokes landing across her taut, rounded buttocks.

It was strange, Amanda thought, that Nicole was standing between her raised legs, looking down on Amanda's shaved sex, rather than to one side. Then Nicole lifted her arm, and Amanda heard a soft hiss as the leather cut through the air.

Amanda heard the slap of leather against her skin, felt the stinging pain, and enjoyed the sexual thrill that clenched in her vulva and her stomach, before she realised that Nicole had struck not her bottom but the inside of her right thigh.

The next stroke was on the inside of her left thigh; a little higher this time, almost where her thigh met her crotch.

Nicole wasn't giving her time to think. The next lash followed almost immediately and smacked on to her pubic mound, quite close to the hood of her clitoris. It was pain and pleasure simultaneously. Nicole was hardly raising her arm between strokes; by merely flicking her wrist she was able to bring the strap down in rapid, stinging beats that gave Amanda scarcely time to draw breath, let alone to cry out.

There was no respite: Nicole plied the strap relentlessly on Amanda's denuded pubic mound, the tops of her thighs, and the innermost slopes of her bottom. Within a few minutes the whole area around Amanda's vulva and anus felt blazing hot and sore. Whenever the strap landed near the covering of her clitoris Amanda attempted to lift her body to catch more strokes; she sensed that her vagina was gaping open, she could feel her juices flowing, she wanted Nicole's fingers in her cunt and her arsehole.

The smacking stopped. Amanda, panting, felt perspiration cooling on her body. Between her open thighs and buttocks she felt pulsing heat, everywhere except where she wanted most to feel it: her vulva and her anus, which felt cold and ignored. She opened her eyes.

Nicole was standing beside her, and smiled. She leant

103

forward and kissed Amanda's mouth, and then lifted the strap and stroked its tip across Amanda's breasts.

Amanda felt her nipples hardening. Her breasts felt exquisitely sensitive.

'No one has whipped your tits, ever?' Nicole asked.

Amanda shook her head. 'If you want to,' she said.

Nicole laughed. 'Not today. There will be plenty of time in the future.' She spent a few moments pinching Amanda's nipples. 'But now I am going to smack your cunt and you will come.' She returned to her position standing at Amanda's upturned bottom. 'Try not to come quickly,' Nicole added. 'I want to make your cunt very sore and shining, like a fire.'

It wasn't painful. Nicole's smacks were quite gentle, but in any case Amanda was so aroused that each stroke of the strap was merely a nudge towards the brink of orgasm. She tried hard to obey Nicole's instruction to delay her climax, but she couldn't resist the tremors that began to grow and merge from the first stroke that landed on her shaved labia.

When Nicole started to concentrate her smacks around the top of Amanda's cleft Amanda knew that the dam was breached. Her orgasm blossomed throughout her body. She heard herself crying out, again and again. She felt Nicole's finger pressing against her anus. The aftershocks seemed to go on for ever.

'A little rest now,' she heard Nicole say. She felt her legs being lowered; her arms were freed. She felt too weak to move. 'And then I will tell you what you want to know.'

CITADEL OF
SERVITUDE

Aran Ashe

Aran Ashe is a writer of unique talents, and has deservedly collected something of a cult following in his years of writing for Nexus. The most extreme violations are described in a loving and lyrical detail which can only add to the power of the prose. He is best known for writing erotic novels in a fantasy setting, but has also written a dark tale of Edwardian intrigue, *Choosing Lovers for Justine*. His first series of erotic fantasy novels, *The Chronicles of Lidir*, have been bestsellers for Nexus. The mythical principality of Lidir is a place where taskmistresses and overlords slake their lust on the flesh of the young initiates of the Castle. The novels comprising the Lidir series are *The Slave of Lidir*, *Dungeons of Lidir*, *The Forest of Bondage*, and *Pleasure Island*. The second of Aran's series is *The Chronicles of Tormunil*. The first book in the series, *The Handmaidens*, sold out extremely quickly and is still in high demand; the second book in the series, *Citadel of Servitude*, served only to strengthen Aran's position as one of the finest writers of erotic fiction working today.

The following extract is from Aran's most recent Nexus novel, *Citadel of Servitude*. Here the hero, Josef, finds himself in a curiously arousing situation with a number of strange and highly sexed creatures, the Kelthlings.

Before Josef was an open door which seemed to beckon. Without thinking he stepped through. He was in a garden. It looked almost like the garden of Ladyseer but there were differences: the plantings appeared less contrived and more luxuriant, and the air was warmer and more humid than expected, engendering a feeling of enclosure, as though everything were inside a vast glasshouse. But he could see no frame or panes, only the blue of the sky. And though it was early afternoon the lighting was peculiar and golden; all the flower colours seemed intensified and surreal. Even the grass felt warm against his bare feet. But there were no insects. And when he turned round the door had disappeared.

His mind jarred. He closed his eyes and tried to think: had he taken any steps after passing through the door? Was it hidden in the foliage? He opened his eyes; the nearest bushes were too far. There was no door. In desperation he even began testing the air with his fingers. The disorientation he was experiencing was far more distressing than any anxiety he might have felt at simply being lost. He panicked – he did not run, but still, his heart was palpitating. He was not thinking straight and it was panic. He must have covered several hundred yards at a rapid walk, circling – he hoped – the area. There was no door, nor artefact of any kind, and soon he was back at his starting point. So this was not a dream: for the scene had retained its integrity, nothing had shifted. And there was no feeling that his consciousness was elsewhere.

It must therefore be that, somehow, the way that he had arrived here could not provide an exit. But there had to be one somewhere.

The ground sloped away from him; he reached a clearing. A warm breeze was blowing upslope. He decided to walk towards its source, hoping it might yield an exit. For many minutes he continued, through several open thickets between the clearings, all the while telling himself that, however beautiful and fragrant his surroundings, as long as the way out remained undiscovered they were, nevertheless, a prison.

Then he felt very thirsty. No sooner had the thought crystallised than he heard the sound of running water. Ahead and to the right was a sunlit dell. There he found a stream fed by a spring of sweet refreshing aerated water. Sitting on a smooth rock in the warmth of the sun, he drank copiously. Gradually the refreshment calmed him. The still warmth of the dell in sunshine left him almost pleasantly lethargic. Stretching back he closed his eyes for a few seconds and inhaled the powerful fragrance like the frangipani and oleander he had known in the hothouse as a child. He could hear birdsong in the distance, but a more intricately melodious birdsong than any he had encountered. And for the first time he felt almost at ease with being naked.

Suddenly his eyes snapped open. There were sounds much closer by: someone was running through the bushes. He sat up quickly, automatically covering himself. The sounds came nearer. By the time he knew he had to hide it was too late.

Crashing down above the opposite bank came a young man as naked as himself. The newcomer was totally unsurprised at meeting him.

'Have you seen them?' the young man cried agitatedly, scanning the woodland and the valley, mopping his brow. He was wild-eyed, urgent, but pale and so thin as to be on the verge of emaciation. Yet he was very visibly well endowed and his penis bore a thick vein which testified to intense and vigorous usage. Seeing the bubbling water, he scrambled down and began drinking thirstily before repeating his question.

Josef shook his head: 'Seen whom? What is this place?'

'Then you've only just arrived?'

Josef nodded.

The other stared at him then gave a low whistle. 'Then welcome to heaven. My name is Brandreth.'

'Josef.' They shook hands. 'Why are we – '

'Shh!' Brandreth cocked his head. 'Listen – can you hear?'

Josef frowned. There was only the birdsong from the valley. It chimed again.

'Kelthlings. Come on . . .' And the young man hurried off down the valley and was soon out of sight. Josef followed cagily at a discreet distance, sweeping a wide arc. Soon he could hear the rush of a small waterfall. Then the distinctive birdsong came again, growing louder. Crouching, he picked his way through the dense aromatic foliage above the stream. Then he saw them.

It was like a magical painting. Again he wondered if he could be dreaming. They were strange, beautiful and fragile – sylph-like creatures – pure-white of skin, with hair in golden wavy cloaks down to their hips, breasts small and full, nipples perched like bright-red cherries. And through their pouted lips emerged the birdsong he had previously heard. One creature sat on the bank; two stood in the stream, their naked bellies bulging, water bubbling through their open thighs, drawing the tips of their golden cloaks downstream like trains behind them.

There was a noise beside Josef. It was the young man Brandreth, now peering with avid eyes through the leafage. 'If we can only find their nest now, while they are occupied, we can cuckold them. If they return and find us they will not think it strange.'

None of this made any sense to Josef. But he could not take his eyes from the beautiful creatures. 'And then?' he whispered.

'They crave it – this.' Brandreth pointed to his thick-veined penis. 'Once you have been with them, no human girl can ever compete.'

'No human?' said Josef. The strange pleasure of the Succubus haunted his mind.

A few minutes later, the two men were standing at the foot of the largest of three ancient spreading oaks. Its lower branches were draped with tangled chains of ivy which provided easy footholds.

'Can you smell it?' whispered Brandreth, throwing back his head.

'Oleander,' Josef answered. 'But there are no bushes of it here.'

'Exactly. Wait here.' Josef watched his accomplice's naked thin form disappear rapidly into the canopy. When nothing more happened, Josef stepped back and began circling the tree. Its girth was enormous; the trunk was cracked and gnarled. As he continued to move round it, he glimpsed amongst the foliage of the highest branches, close to the trunk, a large pale-coloured structure. It looked like a cankerous growth or a giant beehive. When he stepped further back it was hidden in the canopy of green. Taking hold of a thick mat of ivy against the trunk, he tried to pull himself up to gain a clearer view. The ivy broke away revealing a hollow like a doorway into the trunk.

Once inside he was standing in a lofty chamber and staring up an irregular chimney lit by shafts of light from on high. A flimsy spiral narrow ropewalk of vines ascended the inner circumference. As he began cautiously to climb, it sagged and groaned under his weight. Several times he bumped his head on protruding knots of ivy wood and clumps of aerial root. At intervals there were narrow landings leading out on to the major branches. There was no sign of Brandreth. Josef kept climbing. At the top he emerged but not into daylight.

The space in which he stood was cocoon-like, with no clear division between floor and walls, which tapered upwards to an opalescent silken dome, uneven and glowing with a creamy light. Curvilinear and undulations radiated across the floor; he realised they were the buried branches over which the cocoon had been woven. The interior was wholly covered in a substance resembling fine fleece; the surface on which he stood was soft, as if underlain by layer upon layer of it. It shimmered like spun silk. But this place was nonetheless a home and not a nest: the walls were garlanded with flowers; there were fragrant pomanders made of woven reeds and there were other artefacts, even some brightly coloured scarves and blankets. In a hollow he found a cache of gold and silver chains, bright beads and jewels, men's rings but also veined stream-pebbles and worn fragments of coloured glass. In another place he found a small store of food – nuts and fresh fruit and bunches of leaves, but also pots of honey and silver flasks of cordial. There was a multiplicity of silk ropes of various gauges. But there was no true furniture, only fleece-covered cushions and raised shaped places with hollows for the limbs. It was a sea of fragrant softness with waves and troughs.

The structure, although built around the trunk of the tree, was irregularly shaped; it was also very extensive, with tunnels leading off at waist height in several places, following the branches then expanding upwards into miniature versions of the main cocoon. These he assumed to be the bedchambers. Cast about were objects of cork and rope silk and smooth wood but also gold. And there were instruments which seemed unnaturally out of place here.

He heard a rustling sound behind him.

'Where were you? They're coming back,' Brandreth whispered hoarsely. 'Lie down!'

'Where?'

'Anywhere. Just keep quiet. Don't do anything until they accept you. Have you anything you can offer as a gift? Never mind. Keep quiet.' Brandreth sat perfectly still against the curve of the wall.

Josef lay on his side and watched the entrance. There was no sound. Then suddenly they were in the cocoon – Kelthlings, two of them, pale and nubile, cherry-nippled, doe-eyed, staring inquisitively at him. Never had he seen creatures so perfectly formed. They were naked but for thin silvery-grey silken panties. Their reaction had been of surprise but not fear. They began to speak to each other in their musical tones, discussing the two intruders. Then Josef realised what their pointing and giggling meant: they were choosing. At that thought a soft sinking feeling moved inside him.

The Kelthlings appeared to be twins, not quite identical, but equally perfect, each one a distillation of fragility and primal beauty. Yet they were distant, other-worldly, as if they had been cast from a human mould but were not of human substance, not of human soul. Their eyes spoke this. But the mould was delightful. They were exquisite soft blonde doll-like creatures, open-lipped, small-breasted yet full-nippled; and he could see the shape of each naked sex through the clinging thin silver-grey panties. They communicated in this strange beguiling musical speech he could not understand. But they had no problem in communicating their desires to the two men whom they would take as lovers.

Brandreth held his hand out to the one who had shown an interest in him. In it was a gift of a pebble bisected by a shiny vein. She took it with obvious delight and studied it. Then she showed it to her friend, who admired it then stared expectantly at Josef. He had nothing to give and she was looking at him with such trustful anticipation. His eyes sank away, downcast. And suddenly this beautiful perfect creature was upon him, whispering musical words of selfless comfort, staring into his eyes and leaning over him to take the first kiss, a kiss so perfectly soft and beautiful that he could not have contained his arousal even should he have wished to.

She wanted to play. She pointed to Josef's naked penis and said something, tilting her head to one side. She had asked him a question. Mystified, he shook his head. Brandreth could not help. He was sitting with the other Kelthling, who appeared more shy. The first one took Josef by the hand and led him to one of the larger side chambers. Again she pointed to his penis then she swept her arm across the surface of the fleece and nodded eagerly. Josef moved closer. Nestled in the fleece were various toys. They seemed so out of place here. She indicated one of several dildos, so realistic that it might have been cast from a penis. It had balls that moved independently. It had a hole down the tube and a piercing point in the same place as Josef's. And inserted through it was a ring. This was what she had wanted to show him. His being pierced had aroused her fascination. She kept touching the piercing and the ring through the dildo and crooning to herself. Then she touched Josef's chest; her fingers were soft, her skin oily smooth. Scattered across the silk fleece he saw other toys, straps and braided silk ropes, gold balls, clamps and small chains. A little further away he glimpsed clysters and broad glass flasks of cream – instruments of the Abbey. He stared down: the fleece was marked. He touched it. Amongst its soft curls were others that were firm and shiny, glued by the juices that these sweet beautiful creatures, in their love play, had exuded.

The girl closed her soft lips about his nipple and sucked it. Her fingertips kneaded his breast just as if it might give milk. His erection came on hard. Brandreth with his girl now joined them in the chamber.

Josef's girl proudly displayed the dildo, rubbing and squeezing it where the ring was pushed through near the tip. It seemed uncannily like his own piercing. The balls rested on her naked thigh. When she sat back he could see her sex lips pouting through the tight silk of her panties.

She pointed at the other girl and said something in that sweet shrill voice. It sounded like 'Lhirrahje'.

'Lhirrajhe,' Josef repeated: it must have been her name. Brandreth had her on his knee.

'Herazhaan,' the first girl pointed solemnly at herself.

Josef opened his mouth to tell his name. Herazhaan cut in quickly: 'Zhozef.'

Dumbstruck he turned to Brandreth but Brandreth was too immersed in the delights of Lhirrajhe. Her panties were down; she was on his lap trembling everywhere that Brandreth was touching – jellied breasts, smooth soft thighs, slim bare sex, small dimpled pot belly.

Herazhaan was at first concerned by what Brandreth was doing to her friend. But very quickly she became interested and was soon wanting to help him. For Lhirrajhe, despite her shyness, was experiencing pleasure at his hands; her legs stayed freely open. She looked so sweetly alluring in that pose. Watching the two Kelthlings – their innocent expressions, their unleashed lubricity as the games progressed – swept Josef's inhibitions aside.

Lhirrajhe's silk panties were round one quivering ankle. Herazhaan, sitting very erect and still, watched absorbedly with the dildo still in her fingers. Every so often she glanced excitedly at Josef. Each glance of those wide doe eyes made him want to melt inside. Her hair hung like a curtain not quite touching her back. Like her friend she was long limbed, very slim – with prominent shoulder-blades, the small immature-looking cuspate breasts, plump red areolae, a deeply recessed spine, and tight buttocks all balanced on the upturned soles of her delicate feet. Her fingertips moved continuously, nervously playing with the dildo above her small pot belly. Even as she crouched there he would have loved to draw her panties down and slide his fingers down from back and front – just one finger from each side – to tease apart the creases.

His erection had firmed to constancy. He did not move to hide it. She gazed at it. Then Brandreth called her over. She seemed to know to kiss him – her reassurance to him, but with no concept of any jealousy Josef might feel. Her full lips lingered on Brandreth's. She touched his long stiff penis, pressed her small fingertips knowledgeably against the thick vein as if testing its pulse. Then again she glanced happily at Josef. Her wide eyes flashed at him, transmitting the pleasure she was experiencing at this touching of the living penis. Her friend Lhirrajhe murmured. Brandreth was completing the detachment of her panties. Against the emaciation of his body his engorged cock looked very thick. He put her ankle down in such a way that her legs stayed open. For this last part of the operation, she had been turned face down on his lap, covering his large erection, which pressed against her belly.

Josef moved across. His penis too felt large between his legs. It swung, brushing against the cool fleece as he squatted. Herazhaan had expected him to come to her. Now her head turned slightly to one side as if questioning him. Then she glanced down at her friend lying prone across Brandreth. Josef could see the girl's bottom properly. Brandreth was lifting her to make his cock more comfortable against her. When he put her down, her legs were more open.

There is something very deeply arousing about the perfection of a female anus. Its beauty is intrinsic, its skin is velvet to the fingers, its embraces are illicit, sensual, wanton, profane. It is not simply the vision of its distension as the prober goes inside it. It is more the witnessing of the responses in the victim to the pleasures that distension brings. And Lhirrajhe's pleasure-seeking anus was responding. Her friend was doing her by hand – two upturned fingers rimming, reaming deeper. Josef felt the sexual pulse-beat in his erection.

Brandreth made a swishing motion with his fingers. 'Smack,' he ordered. 'I want to smack her here.' Herazhaan seemed to understand. She slid her fingers out then scampered away across the silken fleece. Lhirrajhe understood too. She became restless. Her legs which had been so open to the fingering now began to close from sexual fear. Recollections of the discipline of the Abbey came to Josef. It was always so before a spanking, however much a human girl might want it and even if she subsequently came to climax while the spanking ran its course. As it was with the novices, so it seemed to be with Lhirrajhe. Everything about her behaviour was entirely human.

Brandreth turned her head so she was lying on her cheek and looking at Josef. When a girl is made to look upon her watcher, her pleasure runs deeper. He drew aside her long wavy tresses of golden hair and rested his

117

open hand against her neck. With this gesture he was holding her anxiety in check and her body in place for the spanking. This pose looked so erotic. Her buttocks made a smooth white whaleback breaking through the waves of golden hair. Then he split this smooth whaleback gently open, making it clear to her what she would get and exactly where she would get it. He gently prised the deeper cheeks apart. Josef's erection began to throb and pulse again when he saw her lovely rosebud. Soon this tight young rosebud would be made to swell.

Herazhaan had returned with a crop made entirely of silk. It appeared specifically designed for anal whipping – the stem being wound stiff and very flexible, and carrying a thick shiny knot of silk loosely fastened to the end. She handed it to Brandreth then took on the responsibility of keeping Lhirrajhe's rosebud intimately exposed.

The whippings by this knot of silk quickly brought on a kind of erection specific to that place. She squirmed; he whipped it; after every few strokes, he gently teased the swelling rosebud with the round tip of the stock as if using a finger or the apex of a penis. And all that sweet while, cheek to the silk, Lhirrajhe kept her eyes open, looking at Josef. Her lips were parted, and Brandreth's free hand lay gently but firmly at her neck, keeping her down. But her open bottom was rising gradually into the air – reaching for the smacks – and her legs were getting wider and wider open to allow the snapping knot of silk to focus ever more precisely to the sexual mouth of the spreading rosebud in the crack. But oh, it must have hurt so sensitive a place, more used to being licked or tickled or gently stretched by a well-oiled clyster.

Her friend now sat back on her heels, her fingers again playing with the dildo agitatedly, her breathing in concert with Lhirrahje's, each breath locked up inside her beautiful breast then expelled by the next snap of the silk.

Brandreth then displayed his handiwork: there was a raised hot ring where once there had been a cool inviting crater. Brandreth pushed the silk knot inside it. Lhirrahje squirmed. The crop hung between her legs. Herazhaan

shivered. It was like the shiver that comes when a girl is
trying to conceal or delay a climax. Josef reached across,
taking hold of Herazhaan's foot. 'Come here,' he whispered. The ankle in his hand seemed so cool and frail. He
wanted to kiss it and kiss her there between the legs where
she had shivered, and let his tongue slip down to linger in
the tight place where her friend, gently trembling, was
very slowly yielding up the knotted silk to Brandreth's
tugging fingers.

Herazhaan made directly for Josef's erect penis, placing
her cheek against his belly. She stared up at the clear fluid
welling down his shaft. Soon it would come thicker. She
nuzzled closer. Her fingertips made contact with the sticky
fluid. They stroked it back up the underside of his penis
and touched the piercing. The flow lazily increased. But
inside he was aching. She put her fingers to her lips,
painting them with his fluid. Then she ran her tongue-tip
round her lips and put her fingers back to where the fluid
issued from the mouth of his penis. This time she sucked
the issue coating her fingers. She closed her other hand
round his hot shaft. The flow strengthened. She kept
gathering it on the tips of her fingers and transferring it to
her mouth as if she were collecting honey from a leaking
comb. Then, turning on her back, she stared up at him so
innocently. Her arm was back, her hand still gripping his
penis, her armpit nakedly smooth. But her little finger was
through the ring of the dildo. She tugged it, milked the
tip. She put her head back. Her lovely face was pillowed
in the fullness of her wavy golden hair. She shaped her
lips to an inviting 'o'.

'You want me to suckle you?' said Josef. Her lips
widened. 'You want me to feed you?' Her tongue made a
sucking movement against her upper lip. She still had
hold of his penis. A drop of his fluid was sliding down her
little finger. She raised the dildo to her lips and took the
ring between her teeth and tugged until the ball of the
torc pulled through the piercing. Then she drew herself
upright and sat back on her heels, the gold ring glinting

between her teeth, her belly pushed out, the lips of her sex pouting suggestively through her panties.

She murmured when he pulled the waistband open, took the ring and dropped it down the front of her panties. As he eased her back, her thighs stayed open so that the shape of the ring was very visible through the tautness of her panties. Her flesh inside was nude. Josef had seen it when first he drew the panties open, nude perfect pubic lips sitting pressed against the silken gusset.

Progressing only through the gentle pressure of the tips of Josef's fingers, the protruding ring moved down under the taut silk skin. It now balanced on the ridge of stimulated flesh. Josef gently rubbed it, squeezed it against her, turned it, worked her slippy flesh around it, pressed it gently in. Herazhaan gasped. It disappeared inside her. He kept his hand there, squeezing her sex gently through the silk.

Lhirrajhe was being turned face up. Brandreth's cock bounced up from under her then brushed between her legs. But it was not destined to be used as he had not finished with the crop. He asked Josef to help. And he showed him a little clitoral shield that he had found and now intended to use. 'I want to whip her sex – just inside it, on the lips,' Brandreth explained, then, 'Oh, my – she understands. Look at her.' Josef left Herazhaan spread and sitting on her heels and he moved closer to Lhirrahje.

All her tremblings had returned. 'Down here, my dove, is where I shall whip you,' whispered Brandreth. He took her by her ankles and pushed her knees back. Her sex opened. 'Never whip too hard, Josef, not in here. If you whip too hard, they go too tight. But when you get it right – oh, God – and go inside them then, hard after the whipping . . . So hot, they are, so puffy . . .' And now he touched her anus, already so visibly subjected to the rigours of the knotted crop. 'Feel it. There, you see?' Her hot bulging crater tightened round the tips of Josef's gently stroking fingers.

Behind Josef, Herazhaan's breath snagged; she was jealously aroused. But Josef persisted, examining her friend's anus intimately and not attempting to hide the ferocity of his erection. Brandreth continued: 'Lift her up. We must put this on you, darling, so you do not come from the kiss of the crop.' Its cord, interthreaded with gold, encircled her waist and dropped down between her legs. It carried a tiny silk cup to shield just the clitoris. Below it, at the end of the cord, hung a polished gilt stopper. She shivered sexually when Brandreth fitted the cup. He tightened it by twisting the cord around the stopper which he then inserted into her sex. The fat, near-buried stopper pushed her labia partly open. He clamped dangly gold weights to them to keep them so. The gold strings radiated like tiny sunbeams out across her belly. Her sex was out-turned, openhearted, moist, soft pink. 'Angel wings . . .' Brandreth whispered, detaching the silk knot from the end of the crop, leaving it bare-stemmed. 'Fine kisses are what they need.' He whipped them – quickly, with her knees tucked up beside her breasts, whose areolae bulged and shook. Then he opened her bottom with the stock of the crop. 'Let the stings bite awhile,' he whispered, one hand stroking her brow, the other drawing the weights radially out again across her belly, stretching her naked angel wings, now adorned with fine raised intersecting lines.

Josef returned to Herazhaan, who was still kneeling. He slid behind her. His penis was against the hollow of her back. He put both hands down the front of her panties and toyed there while she shuddered. His fingers teased her labia open. His fingernails gently scratched the moist inner surface. He felt the knob of the thick torc that was still inside her. He pressed it. She moaned. Her head fell back against his shoulder. Her little jellied breasts stood out as she watched the stock being withdrawn from her friend. Josef felt that Herazhaan would climax in his fingers if she saw another whipping.

'Come on, now, drink from me.' Sitting, he drew her down and made of his thigh a pillow for her cheek. She kept one knee bent, still inviting him to touch her while he suckled her with his cock. His arousal, with his hand down her panties, holding those nude wet lips, made his fluid run heavily. She was milking him with her mouth. And he could suckle a girl continuously now because of what the Succubus had done to him: the flow never really stemmed while he remained erect. Moist greedy murmurs issued from Herazhaan's lips. She became demanding of him when she heard the crop, and she slid her fingers up inside him to stimulate the gland.

The crop began snapping down inside Lhirrajhe's pubic lips. Herazhaan suddenly moaned, stopped sucking and her belly turned rigid. Her fingers slid limply out of Josef.

He gently eased her up, with his fingers still inside her. She sat against him, her knees up, splayed: she was near to climax. He slid his free hand underneath, drew her panties down and nipped her anus as his other fingers searched about inside her for the ring. He kept pausing to suck those small red fat-nippled teats. The ring had worked in deeply. Eventually he drew it out. Her anus tightened. He nipped a little whorl of skin and gently pulled it. The perfect symmetry of her anus was now blemished by this small skin flap. Then he sent her for the dildo. As she began to crawl away, he stopped her, pressing his hand into the small of her back until her breasts were in the silky fleece. He wanted to look at her again, her panties round her knees, her naked bulging sex slung under her little anus with its small temporary skin protrusion, so sexually teased out of her, and now in need of wetting. He did this with his penis, which was still leaking seminal fluid. The mouth of her bottom turned slippery. Its little bulb of skin slid back inside. The cap of Josef's penis followed. He drew apart the cheeks. She moaned. Her bottom opened properly. Her back hollowed deeply. The cap disappeared inside; the mouth of her anus clutched it lovingly. As Josef stroked the edges of Herazhaan's labia with the tips of his fingers, her hips rose sensually up and down, her bottom sucked the end of his penis as neatly as had her mouth.

He drew out. She collapsed sideways, reaching for him open-mouthed, panting gently, her lips now secure round the fluid-soaked head of his penis. The little bulb-crowned mounds of her breasts poked out to each side. 'Oh – you little beauty,' Josef murmured. Her open sex was lifted like an animal in heat as she sucked the scent of her anus from the end of his penis. 'Oh, you sweet little fucker,' Josef groaned in pleasure.

'Tl-*fugher!*' she blurted round the mouthful of his flesh.

Brandreth was beside him. He had left Lhirrahje spread-legged and swollen. He was fastening a thick cord around his waist. A second cord went through it, then round the base of his penis, above his scrotum, then up between his buttocks. He drew it tight. His cock immediately expanded larger than ever and the balls were drawn back, making the shaft longer. 'Let me,' he said. Josef baulked, but Herazhaan, knowing, wanting, stretched out on her back, her mouth yawning open. 'Look – she wants to swallow it whole.'

'Oh, God,' Josef murmured as he watched it sliding, inch by thick-veined inch, down her willing throat. Her legs writhed gently with the pleasure of swallowing. She was like a snake gorging on its prey. Brandreth crouched to get the angle, pivoted to get the depth of thrust.

Josef spread her lovely sex and held it open. She moaned with sexual pleasure at the stretching. And her lips were still seeking, her head pushing up between Brandreth's legs. It seemed she wanted every inch of shaft. She tried to get her fingers inside his anus. Josef shuddered to see her; he felt her sex tighten, wanting to close; then he saw her throat rippling, contracting like a soft squeezing sheath round the glans of the pumping penis.

Brandreth drew out stiff and dripping. The Kelthling licked the last thick drops, then groaned. Her head had twisted to one side and Josef still held her sex lips open. Her clitoris was in hard erection, her labia very soft and yielding to the touch. He resolved to keep her that way.

He made her fit the heavy gold ring on to his own penis. Then he lifted her on to it, open-sexed, legs astride. It went all the way up inside her. He felt it press against her womb. And she was gasping, holding herself open,

123

wanting to get it deeper yet. She moaned, rubbing the torc against her. Her bare wet open sex lips suckered to his pubes. Her knob was standing out from its swollen thin-skinned hood. Josef took a silk cord to it. The cord quickly turned wet and slippy as he rubbed it back and forth. She pressed her little breasts against him, kissed him, sucked his tongue. He kept the taut cord moving, masturbating her gently with it. She started gasping, chirping words he did not understand. Suddenly she sat bolt upright against him, very still and put her head back, groaning. Her labia stood open, her knob bright-red. He made to rub the cord against it, but she stayed his hand, then leant against him and clasped her hands around her buttocks. 'Udtha-cock. Fugh-it.' And she pressed her breasts tightly to Josef's chest, pressed her lips against his neck, because it would hurt, it must surely be too full a penetration. There seemed so little space from front to back to take even one fully extended penis. Her anus was already compressed and pushed up by the thickness of Josef's shaft, which was by the second gaining girth.

He felt the other penis push, the anus stretch and tighten. Then the push came again. She gasped sweet sexual tongue-filled shudders into Josef's mouth. He felt the other penis sliding up against him – tight, so tight and small, her anus felt. He tried again to get the cord across her knob. He pulled it down; she bucked; he pulled it up; her knees jerked outwards. She started riding, writhing on two shafts. Brandreth drew her back, squeezed her little breasts to bursting, kissed her. The Kelthling tongued his open mouth. Between her legs, her sex was bulging out. She put her hand down, pressing as if to stop Josef's ringed penis bursting out. Josef tried to close her labia. He rolled the wet cord into a ball and rubbed it against her. She arched away from him and came. And because the two knobs were enveloped in the compass of her sucking muscle, with the ring trapped between them, stimulating each bunch of nerves, the semen flooded. It just kept coming. Her muscle just kept sucking.

After this they watched her do her friend with the

squirting dildo. She pushed it up her bottom. The girl was on her back. The oil-filled balls were between her legs on the fleece. Herazhaan teased her knob and when the pleasure was about to come, she stamped on the balls of the dildo. The squirting of the oil up inside Lhirrajhe brought on the climax. Because her knob was no longer being touched, the climax was prolonged, driven only by the squirtings up inside her.

Herazhaan was kneeling over her friend. Josef made her stand, then spread her slim legs and bend from the waist. As he fingered her and opened her, the fluid stored hot inside her sex and bottom started escaping down her thighs. Lhirrajhe drank of it greedily. It seemed to fuel their desire; Herazhaan was thirsty again.

Josef languorously watched the two of them making love to Brandreth to the point of his exhaustion; still they wanted to continue. It was as if the later issues of fluid were more intoxicating to these creatures. Lhirrahje was sitting astride his face and letting him suck her clitoris which now stood out like a nipple. It seemed to be secreting some form of liquid. Brandreth was becoming wild eyed, groaning with pleasure. Herazhaan was sucking his penis so strongly that the thick vein stood out purple. He passed out but she kept sucking; he climaxed while asleep, the fluid overflowing her lips. And once Brandreth was left drained and comatose they turned to Josef.

The balance was changing; these beautiful creatures were now stirred by desire. They came to Josef. Herazhaan crouched over his face and Lhirrajhe removed his penile ring and sucked him. His glans slipped beneath her tongue, which seemed to mould around it, holding it, milking it, inducing a peculiar pleasure at the mouth of the penis as if something fine and narrow were being pushed very slowly down it. He imagined the fine beak of a humming bird drinking, or the proboscis of a butterfly, delicate and long – that was the feeling. The pleasure was unique. He gasped; it felt as if it were extending down the full length inside his erect penis, licking keenly, searching out the entrance to the inner gland. If the inside of the penis could taste then the taste that she was somehow putting there was as tantalisingly sweet as aniseed. And at the other end, the secretion Herazhaan was delivering from her clitoris into his mouth was like sweet almond oil, softly dripping. All the time it was coming he could feel the other one's proboscis slipping down him and now sucking inside. He tried to resist the urge to climax; the pleasure was exquisite; it made him shiver; his shivering stimulated the steady flow. Lhirrajhe put her fingers into him and massaged the gland. The dull ache came: it felt as if the proboscis was going down the very tubes into his balls. His climax came and he passed out into a delicious sleep.

He awoke with the feeling that he was about to climax. They were using a clyster on him. Herazhaan, open-mouthed, was awaiting his ejaculate. She held his penis clasped tightly at the base. When the plunger of the clyster pushed the contents up inside him, Josef spouted. And Herazhaan drank his liquor as if he were a fountain. Again she fed him almond oil from her clitoris. Again they used the clyster. Again he passed out with the intensity of the sexual feeling. Each time he slept he awoke more tired.

When he awoke again it felt as if a thick silk tube was emergent from his penis. It filled the girth and felt attached. The slightest movement brought peculiar pleasure. He could not see what had been done because one of the Kelthlings was crouched aside his belly and was gently slapping his balls to stimulate the flow of fluid. He could feel one of them taking suck from the tube. He felt as if he was in sexual bondage deep inside. She sucked deeply and the feeling was of belly-piercing pleasure.

He had not the strength to move. But still they some-how kept inducing pleasure. Eventually he did not know whether he was asleep or awake. Darkness followed day-light repeatedly. It was like a slow delicious creeping fever which never would abate.

AGONY AUNT

G. C. Scott

G. C. Scott has written a series of extremely successful and popular bondage and domination novels. *The Passive Voice, His Mistress's Voice* and *Agony Aunt*, make up a masterful trilogy exploring the joys of erotic confinement and feature the dominatrix Harriet and her submissive slave Tom. *His Mistress's Voice* remains the only Nexus novel to be concerned exclusively with female domination, and has been one of our most popular titles. Another title, *A Matter of Possession*, is also a bondage and domination novel, but features the submissive Barbara, one of the author's most convincingly lewd creatures, involved in some very special kinds of loving.

The following extract is taken from *Agony Aunt*, the author's most recent novel for Nexus. Here Harriet's slave Tom returns to the flat to find her all tied up, and decides to turn the tables on her.

Don't waste any opportunity – that's my motto, Harriet told herself. The trick is to recognise an opportunity. On the face of it this wasn't one, but she had plenty of time to examine it. Not two hours ago she had been in her cellar workshop entertaining herself and two women friends with a little creative B&D. They were the victims (if that is the right word for the subjects of a highly diverting and pleasurable exercise) and she had been administering the discipline and generally controlling things. Now she lay bound and gagged in her own bed, as helpless as her erstwhile 'victims' had been.

Like everyone else who has ever been tied up, she had tried to get free as soon as her captors had left her alone. It hadn't worked, and in her mind's eyes she now saw herself as she would be seen by anyone who found her: an attractive woman dressed in nothing but stockings and suspenders struggling in her disordered bed to get free of the ropes that held her prisoner. Her hands were tied in front of her but she couldn't get at the knots. The men who had tied her were too clever for that. They had taken a piece of rope from her wrists down between her legs and up again behind her back, tying it around her waist so that her bound hands were held down against her mons veneris. She was unable to bring them to her mouth in order to use her teeth on the knots. And in any case she was gagged, a wad of cloth held inside her mouth by a scarf tied around her lower face and knotted behind her head. Her legs were tied at her knees and ankles. Finally giving up, Harriet rolled over on to her back and lay staring up at the ceiling as she considered her limited options . . .

She had already tried twisting and jerking at her bonds, but that hadn't worked. She had discovered earlier that the rope between her legs touched her in a very sensitive spot. Her tugs and jerks had brought on several rather enjoyable orgasms as the rope rubbed against her clitoral area.

Harriet was not unduly worried by her predicament. For one thing, as a practising B&D person herself, she enjoyed all the erotic aspects of bondage even when, as now, she was the one who was tied up. Usually she had the job (if *that* was the right word) of tying others for their sexual pleasure. There was a surprising number of people who got their kicks that way, and she was much sought after for her enthusisam and expertise in ministering to them. For another, she knew that Tom, whom she had trained as her servant/assistant, was due to come in that morning. When she didn't answer the door he would let himself in and find her. That was something else her captors had doubtless thought of – they weren't passing robbers who didn't care what happened to their victims.

Harriet relaxed as she remembered the previous evening activities. She had arranged for the three 'intruders' to burst in on her while she was putting her two guests through their paces. The idea was to make the others think that strangers had found them while they were most vulnerable. Harriet thought that the 'intruders' would contribute to the ambience, playing the part of passing thugs so that the other two women could pretend that they had been taken by strangers. Harriet had even arranged for the three men to tie her as well, so as to lend an air of verisimilitude to the proceedings. They had done just that – but she hadn't planned on becoming part of the entertainment herself. Once she had been made helpless, and before the three men turned their attention to the two guests for whom all this had been arranged, they had given Harriet a bit of the same bizarre sex she had planned for the other women.

They had stripped her down to her stockings and suspenders and then strung her up by the wrists to one of the many overhead hooks in her cellar. They had gagged her as well, so that when things took an unexpected turn she couldn't give the game away. And things had taken such a turn almost immediately. Two of them had turned their attention on her, alternately lashing her with one of her own straps and then arousing her sexually until she couldn't tell the difference between pain and the pleasure. Then one of the men had entered her from behind while his companion had continued to lash her breasts and belly and the fronts of her thighs. At that point there *was* no difference between the pain and the pleasure.

And at that point Harriet had tried to shout 'Oh God!' but the gag had prevented her. She had only been able to squeal and snort as they made her come again and again. It had been a long time since she had been on the receiving end, and as they pleasured her a part of her wondered why she had let herself forget how good it felt to be sexually aroused while bound and helpless. It was possible to become too wrapped up in one's work, she now told herself. But at the time she had been mainly occupied in coming. When the man inside her had reached around and begun to fondle her heaving breasts, she had come very near to fainting with pleasure. But the man with the strap had kept her awake as he lashed her belly and her straining thighs.

After that they had left her hanging by her bound wrists for a short time while she recovered. She remembered hearing the cries of her two guests as the 'intruders' turned their attentions to them as she had originally planned. Harriet hadn't had the strength left to envy them – nor much time either. When the men came back for her she was almost dismayed. Surely they didn't expect her to do all that again so soon?

But apparently they did. One of the three – she guessed it was Jean, but couldn't be sure because they were all

wearing dark ski masks – spread her legs and tied her
ankles to either end of a broom handle. Then he lay on
the floor between her legs while another of his companions
slackened the rope that held her stretched tautly upright.
The two of them guided her down on to the erection that
was waiting for her. She didn't do anything to make the
task difficult for them.

Lying bound now in her own bed, where they had left
her, Harriet smiled as she remembered how she had felt
stretched as she took him inside her. She wished there was
some way to repeat the experience there and then. The
original sex fiend, that's me, she told herself without
reproach.

When she was fully impaled and squatting atop the man
whose cock seemed to reach to her back teeth, the rope
was tied off so that her upper body was erect and her full
breasts jutted out invitingly to whoever was in the vicinity.
They were just out of the comfortable reach for the man
between her thighs, but his companion knelt behind her
and took one in each hand. He had begun by stroking her
nipples until they stood stiffly erect and Harriet was
panting with excitement. During all this time Jean kept
still. He held her down on his cock with a hand on either
hip. His thumbs massaged the taut muscles of her lower
belly, moving her clitoris softly against his cock. Harriet
felt a trickle of sweat run down her ribs and into her
crotch. She glanced down and saw that her stockings were
stained darkly in places by sweat from her earlier
exertions.

That was some indication of how she had enjoyed the
first session, but she was only marginally interested in that
now. There was more urgent internal business, and it
looked like she would be adding more dark patches to her
stockings soon. The hands on her breasts were maddening. She felt as if she would burst from that alone, but at
the same time she wished that Jean – or whoever it was –
would do something. There was such a thing as too much
restraint, and he was practising it.

Harriet's solution was to raise herself by straightening

her bent knees. At the same time she pulled herself up on the rope that held her arms over her head. 'Ahhhhh,' she sighed as she slid up the pole. With a deeper 'ahhhhh', she came back down. The fingers that rubbed and stretched her lower stomach muscles added their own excitement to her motion. This was going to be a long process, but Harriet knew that it would be better than the first. Second attempts so often were. And sometimes third and fourth, if she could last that long.

The three men she had invited for her guests' benefit seemed to be more interested in her – perhaps because there were comparatively few occasions when she could be manoeuvred into the vulnerable position she was now in. Or maybe they found her more attractive – a pleasant thought but hard for her to believe. I'll have to do this more often, Harriet told herself, before she lost interest in keeping mental notes.

As the arousal went on, Harriet's cries changed pitch, the soft 'ahhhs' changing to sharper 'ohhhs' and the intervals between the cries becoming shorter as her climax approached. She cried out steadily in sharp exclamations of pleasure as she was shaken by her orgasms. The cock inside her and the fingers manipulating her breasts pushed her over the brink time and again. In one of her short lucid intervals she looked down at Jean. She could see from the expression on his face that he was trying to hold back so that she could enjoy herself. Harriet wanted to tell him not to bother, to come now, but her gag prevented any verbal encouragement. She caught his eye and nodded vigorously to tell him that she was ready, that he too could let go, that she was ready for – Oh God, here it came. Harriet lost herself in the waves of pleasure that swept her away.

She was having trouble catching her breath in the excitement, and she was tugging madly at the ropes that held her prisoner as she cried out. Dimly she was aware of Jean moving with her as his own climax took him. Harriet felt him pushing inside her and she lost control for perhaps the tenth time. She mewed like a kitten as she

135

came. Even afterwards she was shaken by small shudders, the aftershocks of her climax. Jean was patient, allowing her to enjoy them at her leisure, while his companion continued to tease her breasts and nipples until gradually she subsided and hung once more by her bound wrists. Tired as she now was, Harriet felt a small glow of triumph as she considered that she had been able to bring Jean to climax before her own resistance ended.

They had helped her dismount quickly, Jean holding her upright on her shaky legs while his companion untied the rope that had strung her up to the ceiling. But they weren't done with her yet. The man lowered her aching arms and quickly brought the rope up between her legs, pulling her hands down against her mons veneris. The rope was pulled taut in her crotch and tied around her waist. As her bound hands lay against her pubic hair, Harriet could feel how damp it was. The rope sawed at her clitoris each time she tugged on it.

They untied her ankles from the wooden pole that spread them apart and led her to one side of the cellar where there were gym mats covering the floor. Then she was laid down on her back and one of the men tied her legs at knees and ankles. While she was left to recover, the men turned their attention on the two other women again.

Harriet twisted herself over on to her side, the rope between her legs providing some interesting sensations as she heaved herself about, so that she could see what the three men would do to her two friends. Even if she couldn't participate in the action, she could still play the voyeur. She knew she would enjoy watching the other two being done, and she hoped they had enjoyed the show she had provided as much.

Both of her guests were lying on gym mats like her, and both were nude. The three men handcuffed Liz's wrists around the base of one of the pillars that supported the ceiling, then spread her legs apart and tied her ankles to ring bolts in the floor of Harriet's basement workshop. Janet was spread out starfish-fashion with her wrists and ankles tied to the same kind of ring bolts. Neither of them were gagged. The cellar was soundproof, so there was no danger of them being heard in the adjacent houses. Nor did it matter what they might say to anyone present.

After what they had done to Harriet, the treatment the other two got was almost anti-climactic, although Liz and Janet certainly seemed to enjoy it as the men took turns in arousing them and mounting them. But they weren't lashed as she had been, and except for being tied helplessly, their experience wasn't much different from normal sex. She listened to their cries of pleasure as they came, and marvelled at the stamina displayed by the men. Was it her imagination that the one who had done her last – the one she guessed was Jean – seemed to be a bit tired himself after the ride they had had? She liked to believe she had given him as much pleasure as she had received. Things seemed so much more balanced that way.

As she watched her guests and listened to their cries, Harriet found herself becoming excited all over again. She twisted on the floor, tugging at her bonds, and the rope between her legs rubbed against her clitoris as she heaved and jerked. While Liz and Janet were being made to come by their partners, Harriet brought herself to the brink – and over – by her own efforts. As with the other two women, part of her own excitement came from being bound and helpless. Her soft cries were muffled by her gag and went unnoticed by the others.

When it was over, the three 'intruders' had untied Liz and Janet and let them go to the toilet. Then, still nude, they were bound hand and foot, gagged and blindfolded, and carried out to the van Harriet used for collecting those of her clients who didn't come of their own accord. She had arranged for them to be dropped off at their respective homes, though the two women hadn't known where they were being taken when collected earlier. When the others were ready for transport, the men had come back for her. One lifted her shoulders while another supported her under the knees. The third one had gone ahead and opened doors for them. They had carried Harriet like a sack of potatoes up the stairs to her bedroom two flights above and deposited her, still bound, on her bed. Before leaving her alone Jean bent to kiss her nipples and eyes. She liked to think that he would have kissed her between her legs as well if they hadn't been tied so tightly together. Then they had gone. Harriet heard the doors close as they left, and she was alone in her bed. That was just as well, because by now she was worn out. She heaved herself into a comfortable position and fell into an uneasy sleep.

Not surprisingly, she dreamt that she was bound and gagged. She woke several times in the night, turning herself over laboriously before falling asleep again.

When she finally woke, the room was bright with the morning sun, and she had company. Tom was standing beside the bed. She wasn't sure, but she had the impression that he had been standing there for some time. He was staring at her, and Harriet was suddenly aware that this was the first time in their relationship that Tom had seen her helpless. From the beginning she had been in control, giving him the orders. She had never allowed Tom to see her completely naked or have sex with her. She supposed that he could have overpowered her at any time but had chosen instead to obey her. But now she was not in control. Harriet wondered now if Tom had ever thought of turning the tables on her when she was putting him in bondage. He was now in the dominant position, and the look on his face told her he was considering what to do with her.

The choices were really quite simple. He could either untie her immediately, thereby restoring the familiar mistress/slave relationship they had developed over the past seven or eight months, or he could take advantage of her helplessness to assert some sort of control – even if only temporary – over her. As Harriet knew very well, there is something appealing in the sight of an attractive woman who is naked and bound. But Harriet had enough confidence in her training regime to believe that he would revert to his former position, although she felt she had to make an effort to reassert her control, especially in this situation.

'Uhh eye eee owe!' she grunted through her gag, jerking vigorously at the ropes that bound her. Her meaning was unmistakable even if her words were not. But Tom continued to stare down at her.

Harriet saw the moment when he decided to have her, and was both excited, gratified and annoyed at the same time. She didn't like the idea that he could break training at this stage, but she was also turned on at the idea of being had while unable to deny her partner. And she was gratified that Tom thought her attractive enough to risk her wrath by taking advantage of her in this way. His decision revealed that the training had not wholly broken his spirit of mischief and fun. Now that she knew what he was going to do, she lay waiting for him to work out how he was going to go about it. Bound as she was, Harriet was safe from the normal methods of penetration and sexual intercourse, and Tom wouldn't want to untie her because he knew she would immediately try to reassert her own dominance.

Tom must have come to a similar conclusion. He left the room and Harriet could hear him descending to the cellar – doubtless to collect what he thought he would need. The student was about to use what he had learnt against the mistress, and Harriet would soon discover if her training in the art of human bondage had been thorough. The notion of having her skills turned against her was embarrassing, but at the same time every good teacher values a good student.

On his return, Tom carried some more of the rope the three 'intruders' had used to tie her. Harriet approved of his choice while at the same time trying to signal with a withering glance that she expected him to untie her forthwith. But Tom planned no such thing. He sat on the bed and turned Harriet over until she was lying on her back. Then he carefully straightened her legs out, taking the time to caress her through the sheer nylon stockings. Harriet had learnt very early on that Tom, like most men, had a weakness for women in stockings and suspenders, and she liked to have her legs stroked and admired. She had allowed Tom to caress her legs on several occasions, usually when she was wearing tights, and she knew he was excited by them. At the time she had been gratified to be the unattainable object of his admiration, but now she found herself excited by his attentions while she was unable to control him.

Tom spent a good deal of time merely rubbing his hand over her legs, pausing when he reached the ropes to touch them and assure himself that she was securely tied. It was as if he couldn't believe that she had allowed herself to be manoeuvred into this position. Harriet shivered as he fingered the ropes at her ankles and knees, reminding her that she was bound. He moved to her feet, stroking the hollows of her ankles, touching her ankle bones with a feather's touch of fingers, then running his hands into the hollows behind her knees. Harriet sighed as he touched her in those places which so few men ever thought about. She was excited by the way he paid attention to her details, exploring all the places and smells of her body now that he had the opportunity. It was rare for a woman to be so cherished.

Tom's hands travelled up her legs once more, tracing the swell of calf and the fullness of thigh. He ran his fingers back and forth over the place where her stockings ended and bare flesh began. Like crossing a border into another place, she thought. She felt his fingers forcing their way between her thighs, and she tried to make room for his explorations. Tom touched her labia, even though it was a tight fit, finding the rope that ran between them and pushing against it where it passed over her clitoris. She was already sensitive there from the long contact between rope and flesh, and she jerked in pleasure when he touched her again. She let out a long 'aaahhhhh' of satisfaction.

Even with Harriet's help and encouragement, there wasn't enough room to explore that area very well, but that was one of the problems Tom would have to solve on his own – Harriet could only let him know when he was on the right track. He apparently came to the same conclusion, withdrawing after a few more strokes. Her hands were the next thing he touched. They were held palm to palm, pulled down against the mat of her pubic hair by the rope between her thighs. Tom caressed her fingers one by one, then clasped both hands, tugging gently on them to make the rope move against her clitoris. This was even more exciting than his fingers had been, and she drew in a sharp breath at the touch. Tom took her wrists in both his hands, holding them together as if to show her that she was *his* prisoner. Hers were the hands that had wielded the whip over him whenever she thought fit.

Still holding her by the wrists, Tom bent to kiss each of Harriet's nipples, drawing a gasp from her as his lips brushed the sensitive flesh. She wanted him to keep on, to take them between his teeth, teasing them until she could stand no more. She knew that would make her come, and she twisted her shoulders and arched her back, trying to thrust her breasts closer to his mouth, but he was already gone. It came to her then that he was toying with her, bringing her to fever pitch and then leaving her hanging as she had done with him time and again. She was being repaid in her own coin, and she could see the rueful justice in that. She would have done the same thing had their roles been reversed.

Abruptly Tom stood up and began to take his clothes off. When he got his trousers down Harriet could see that he was erect. She took that as a tribute to herself – both to her looks and to her helplessness. However, she still had no idea what he was going to do with the evidence of his arousal. Somehow he would have to part her legs and free her hands before he could get that inside her, and she wondered what it would feel like. It occurred to her that she was about to lose her virginity as far as Tom was concerned. This would be the first time he had penetrated her. She waited expectantly but Tom made no move to untie her.

He returned to stand beside the bed, then bent down and picked her up, grunting with the effort as he lifted the weight of her compact, sturdy body. One arm supported her shoulders and the other held her under the knees.

Ah, Harriet thought. Having made her his captive, the caveman was about to take his prize back to his lair. She smiled at the idea while enjoying the experience of being carried by him.

But Tom only went as far as the armchair across the room before setting Harriet down on her feet and steadying her when she seemed about to fall. He turned her until the chair was behind her, then sat down in it and spread his legs. In the mirror Harriet could see his cock standing up in his lap. Then he grasped the rope tied around her waist and tugged sharply on it.

Harriet lost her precarious balance and fell backward into the chair. She was taken by surprise and let out a dismayed grunt, thinking she was going to fall to the floor, but she landed between his knees and he pulled her tightly against him. She could feel his erect cock between them. It seemed to reach halfway up her back, and she experienced brief regret that she wasn't able to take it inside her at the moment. It seemed too good to waste, but she had 'wasted' similar erections in the past when she was teasing him. Now she wondered why – with the reversal of their roles, Harriet had undergone a change of viewpoint. But the etiquette of the B&D game (not to mention her gag) prevented her from communicating this to Tom, and the stubborn part of her kept insisting that she would suffer a great loss of face if she admitted to him that she wanted to be had so thoroughly. Mistresses didn't say that to their slaves, even when the slaves had them – temporarily, she told herself – in their power.

Tom settled her comfortably in his lap and bent to kiss the nape of her neck. Harriet could feel the warmth of his breath against her skin and the touch of his lips felt fiery on her. She moaned softly. Tom had once told her that he liked this position best of all. Both his hands were free to touch and stroke and arouse the woman, and all her most sensitive areas lay open to him from behind. Of course, Harriet had never allowed herself to be put into this position. But she had to admit that everything she owned was within his reach – or would have been if she hadn't been tied. But Tom doubtless had something in mind, and she could do nothing except wait for him to begin what had to be his show.

Still kissing her back, Tom reached around and took her full breasts in his hands. In the mirror Harriet watched as his fingers closed over her. The woman in the mirror flushed as he cupped her breasts, weighing them in his hands. The areolae were darkening and becoming larger, the tiny points that surrounded them becoming prominent. This always happened when she was aroused. She leant forward, pressing herself against the living bra that supported and stroked her. The woman in the mirror struggled to get free, to open her legs, to speak to the man whose hands sent shivers through her.

She closed her eyes to concentrate on the sensations flooding through her. Her breasts felt heavy and hot, as if filled with molten lead, while her stiff nipples ached deliciously at the touch. Tom stroked them from base to tip, elongating and stretching them. Harriet felt herself grow warm between the legs, and knew she was becoming wet inside as she was fondled and kissed. She felt a small shudder at the base of her belly, a tingling in the insides of her thighs that preceded her orgasm. Her breath caught on a gasp and Harriet gathered herself for the climax.

Tom guessed what was happening and abruptly stopped. It took Harriet a moment to realise what he was doing; then she twisted violently in his lap, trying to make him continue what he had started. She moaned in frustration. Damn you, she thought, recognising at the same time that this was exactly what she had done to him. She had required him to hold back for as long as possible – part of the training, she insisted. And she had often simply denied him the pleasure of orgasm by refusing to finish what she had started. But she had forgotten the efficacy of her own methods when she was on the receiving end. Mortified, Harriet resolved to be less obvious.

She forced himself to relax and wait for the next move.

Tom seemed in no hurry. He too sat relaxed, his hands merely cupping Harriet's breasts as if weighing them. She glanced at herself in the mirror and was gratified to see he was admiring her. He had told her often enough that he found her attractive, but like most women, Harriet had difficulty in believing that she was the right size or shape, no matter how often others told her she was.

She was glad she had allowed her brown hair to grow longer. The shoulder-length cut softened her face and made her look much more youthful. She tended to be thick in the waist and heavy of hip and thigh without being fat – not an easy feat for anyone. Her calves swelled nicely, and she had often been complimented on her legs. Indeed, Tom had seemed more than pleased to caress them whenever she had allowed him to do so. And the way he cupped and stroked her full breasts should have reassured even the most sceptical of women that he was taken with her. As she looked at herself, Harriet realised that Tom's actions indicated an appreciation of her body. And the erection that still lay between them said the same thing. She lay back against it, wishing he would get on with things.

Presently he did. His hands resumed stroking her breasts, pinching the nipples and stretching them until once more they were stiff and sensitive. Harriet sighed as she felt herself becoming warm all over again, especially between the legs. This time Tom varied his approach. When it became obvious from her accelerated breathing and involuntary squirmings that she was once more becoming excited, he used one hand to clasp her bound wrists, tugging them and causing the rope in her crotch to saw against her clitoris. Harriet hissed through her gag. She could feel herself gathering to a point somewhere beneath the mons veneris, a tingling and a warmth that she hoped would grow.

It did. She felt a small shudder of pleasure as she came, but this first orgasm was a ladylike thing. She didn't even moan, but she was glad none the less. This time Tom didn't stop – apparently he had decided on a change of tactics. She was on the verge of another climax and was no longer worried about holding back for the sake of policy. This man knew her well, even though this was the first time she had ever been driven this far by him. He knew which buttons to push.

There was no hiding the next orgasm. Harriet felt it building at the base of her spine, warm waves flooding through her belly and down her thighs. She tightened herself around the lovely sensation, and the sudden hunching of her body must have told Tom that she was going to come again. He didn't stop, proving himself more merciful than she had been when their roles were reversed. Her breath caught on a gasp, and this time she couldn't stifle the moan of pleasure as she was shaken by her climax. And, yes, here came another one hard on its heels. Harriet was on the verge of losing all control, and she was past caring as the waves of her orgasms lifted and dropped her, one after another. She writhed on Tom's lap, feeling his erection against her back. The ropes were tight around her legs, holding them together around that grand eruption at the centre of things. Now she added her own tugs to the rope in her crotch while Tom still held her bound wrists and stroked her breasts in turn. She wanted to shout her pleasure out, but the gag limited her to a series of high-pitched moans.

Tom, bless him, seemed intent on driving her wild, and she was content to be driven, if content wasn't too mild a word to describe what she was feeling. A long 'unnnhhhhhh' signalled the next climax. Harriet bent herself at the waist and jerked her hips as it rippled through her body. She was in danger of slipping off on to the floor, but Tom paused long enough to steady her before resuming the cycle of arousal and climax. When he finally stopped, Harriet lay back against his chest and gasped for breath. She felt his arms around her waist, holding her steady as the earth gradually regained its equilibrium for her. It was nice being held like this.

Tom let her rest while her breathing and pulse steadied and slowed. Then Harriet felt herself being lifted and turned so that she lay across his lap, her back supported by his left arm and her legs hanging over the opposite arm of the chair. He smiled crookedly at her and leant forward to kiss her earlobe before fumbling one-handedly at the ropes that bound her knees and ankles. When the ropes finally fell away, Harriet let her legs fall apart and flexed them. She was stiff after being tied for so long, and she was tired out after last night's and now this morning's, frolics – but not too tired to watch carefully for Tom's reaction as she moved her legs. She was glad to see his look of approval.

'Bathroom,' he told her. 'I'll be along in a minute to dry you off. Try not to make too big a mess.' Once again he stroked her legs fondly through the sheer nylon of her stockings before he helped her to stand up.

As Harriet left the room he was gathering up the pieces of rope and tidying the bed. He was still half-erect, and she imagined it wouldn't take too much effort to bring him back to attention. In the bathroom she suddenly realised how badly she needed to use the toilet after being tied up for nearly ten hours. As luck would have it, the lid was closed, and with her hands bound tightly against her belly she couldn't lift it. Being this near the goal made her afraid she would wet herself. She clamped down hard and at the same time tried to call for help. 'Ummmmm!' There was no response, and she felt herself leak a few drops. She tried once again, louder and longer; 'Ummmmmmmmnnngg!'

Tom came a few moments later. She nodded her head desperately at the closed toilet lid and jerked her hands to show him she couldn't open it, nearly causing the floodgates to open as the rope sawed at her crotch. His smile infuriated her, and she grunted in annoyance once more. He seemed to be taking his time.

'I should let you wet yourself,' Tom told her. 'You made me do that often enough. But I don't feel up to changing you right now.' He lifted the lid and stood aside.

Harriet squatted hurriedly and relieved herself. It felt almost as good as a small orgasm. She suffered the indignity of being wiped dry in silence, remembering how she had put Tom through the same ritual. Having to be helped with one's most intimate acts was a good way to learn humility and obedience, she had told him. And so it was. The rope between her legs was damp. Placed as it was, that had been unavoidable. He could have spared her that if he had loosened it.

Nor did he loosen it now. He took her elbow and led her downstairs. 'Breakfast time,' he said tersely. He seated her on the couch and went through to the kitchen. Presently he came back with toast and coffee. 'Boiled eggs in a minute or so,' he said as he removed her gag.

Harriet worked her tongue around to moisten the inside of her dry mouth. He held the coffee cup for her and she drank thirstily.

'Another, please,' she said when it was empty. There were many other things she wanted to say, but first things first. What she had to say to Tom would keep until they had eaten. Now that the sharp edge was off her sexual desire, Harriet was thinking it was more than time for her to reassert her authority. But she was at a double disadvantage – her hands were still tied and she was considering the possibility of further sexual gymnastics in the near future. Maybe she should wait until that was over before resuming control of the relationship. Though she couldn't admit it to him, she was rather looking forward to finding out what sort of a lover he was. But it didn't do to let the servants get above themselves, so she kept quiet.

Harriet saw that the time was approaching 9.30 a.m., rather later than she normally had breakfast. That explained why she felt so hungry. As she waited for Tom to return she decided that she had to try to reassert control over the situation, even if that meant she would have to forego the anticipated pleasure of allowing him to go on. It was more important that she regained her authority as soon as possible. One had to make some sacrifices to be true to oneself, didn't one?

Tom returned with a tray, which he set down on the coffee table. Toast and boiled eggs, marmalade and coffee

– it all looked tempting on an empty stomach. His cock looked tempting on an empty –

She stifled the thought and summoned her most severe look. 'Tom, this has gone on long enough. I insist that you untie me this minute and resume your duties. What you did this morning was a serious violation of our agreement and will be dealt with in due time.' She felt slightly foolish as she remembered how much she had enjoyed his 'serious violation of our agreement', but she had to say the words. She knew she sounded pompous as well.

Tom looked directly at her. He appeared to consider her words for a moment before he said 'no'.

Harriet was taken aback. She had expected him to obey the command and resume his role as her servant/slave. She tried again. 'Tom, I warn you that your behaviour is making me very angry. You are only making things worse for yourself by continuing this disobedience.'

'You didn't look very angry in the bedroom a few minutes ago,' he replied.

Harriet felt herself flush as his remark hit home. He had unerringly put his finger on the weak spot of her argument. Nevertheless she persisted. 'Don't argue with me. You took advantage of me when I couldn't resist. That's done. Untie me now.' She looked down at her bound wrists to emphasise her determination.

Still he made no move to obey. By way of reply he buttered a slice of toast and spread marmalade on it before offering it to her. Harriet knew that to eat from his hand would be a further sign of submission. After all, she had taught him the same trick during his first week at her house. But he was turning her own training against her now. He had spirit, she had to admit. He continued to hold the slice of toast close to her mouth. Harriet could smell the butter and marmalade, and her stomach rumbled: she felt betrayed by her own body. Tom's grin didn't improve her temper.

'Not hungry?' he taunted her. 'Or would you prefer this – ' he indicated his cock ' – with butter and jam?'

Harriet knew then that the argument was lost. She opened her mouth and took a bite of the toast. It was delicious, and she made no further demur as he fed her the rest of the breakfast. She ate everything. When she was done he sat down and ate his own. He didn't ask her permission to sit or eat in her presence. Full of himself, Harriet fumed, even as she felt the familiar churning in the stomach that preceded sex. She hoped it wouldn't be too long before he did her again. With difficulty, she restrained herself from letting her anticipation show. At the same time she was planning how she would make him pay for his disobedience. I'm such a hypocrite, she chided herself.

Tom finished eating and rose to clear away the remains of their breakfast. Harriet had to admire his deliberation. He knew he'd have to pay for this day's liberties, but he never wavered. He must want me very badly, she told herself, if he's willing to go this far to have me.

When he came back, Harriet felt her stomach go hollow with anticipation. His erection was back and she knew that was due to thinking about her. She was happy to accept the tribute. Without speaking, Tom helped her to stand and guided her upstairs with a hand on each of her elbows. She too remained silent during the trip, but her thoughts were full of what was happening. It's now. He's going to do me now, Harriet thought as he led her to the bedroom. He's going to put that up me and I know I won't be able to keep quiet. She resolved to try not to be too obvious, but was afraid he would know anyway.

Harriet reflected that the relationship between the sexes was often spoilt by an unwillingness to show one's true feelings and responses for fear of betraying a weakness in oneself. She herself had been an offender in this respect. Joni Mitchell's couplet came back to her about not letting them know, not giving your thoughts away. She wondered if this might not be the time to change her own policy; to abandon her reservations wholly.

The pressure of Tom's hand on her elbow suddenly brought her to a stop alongside her bed. She felt him working on the knotted rope behind her back, and abruptly the pressure on her labia and clitoris eased as it came free. Harriet brought her arms up and over her head, stretching the stiffness from them and easing her cramped shoulder muscles.

'Lie down on the bed, Harriet,' Tom commanded her.

It was the first time he had addressed her by her name since she had taught him to call her 'Mistress'. It was another sign of the change in their relationship, at least for the time being. She wondered if it would ever be the same again. Before today everything had been predictable. She gave the orders and he obeyed. It might not be so easy to go back to that state now, and she felt slight loss and regret. She lay down on the bed, her bound wrists resting on her stomach.

Tom pulled her arms up over her head and tied them to the headboard of the bed with the rope that had run between her legs all night. She could smell the faint odour of herself on it. Her heart was beginning to pound in her chest, and her breath came short. All the muscles in her stomach knotted as she imagined what was coming. When she looked at Tom he was still erect. She looked away quickly. Don't be the nervous virgin, she chided herself. You've seen him often enough. And he's certainly not the first. But still she knew that once his cock was inside her, things would probably never be the same between them.

'Do I have to tie your ankles to the bedposts?' Tom asked.

With a start Harriet realised her legs were pressed tightly together. It was purely reflexive. And pointless. If she resisted, he could simply subdue her with more rope. Harriet thought fleetingly that it would be nice to feel herself spread helplessly for him, but she allowed her legs to part slightly.

Tom spread them wider, then she felt the bed sag as he positioned himself between her. He lowered himself until the tip of his erect cock touched her labia. No foreplay this time. He eased inside her and she felt the warmth of him slowly penetrate her, filling her full, and then she was wet, welcoming him inside her. Harriet bit back a moan as he slid home. There was no hiding her other reactions.

Once inside her Tom made no further move. She looked at him and realised that he was going to force her to react. All right, she thought, clamping down on him as she tightened her vaginal muscles. He smiled down at her and held still. He was going to make her do the work, but luckily, it was not in Harriet's nature to play dead during the sex act. She moved her hips ever so slightly, enjoying the first slow slidings the motion gave to their joined bodies. She felt him tighten himself in response. Then this was going to be a slow fuck, she realised.

Tom bent his face close to her, kissing her eyes and cheeks and ears. Then he found her parted lips and kissed her mouth, pushing his tongue inside there as well. Her breath grew ragged with rising excitement as she felt him move for the first time. Short in-and-out motions, sliding deliciously as she held him tightly. If her hands had been free she would have pulled him down against her fiercely. She wanted him to do some of the work, not force her to give herself to him utterly. A girl's got to have some dignity, she told herself, even though she knew she was going to have a hard time holding on to any of it.

She felt herself shudder with the first signs of her arousal. Tom must have felt it too. It began in her belly and spread slowly to her legs. She felt herself opening widely to him, her legs parting further to allow him full access. He was taking his weight on his forearms to spare her, but he managed to get his hands to her nipples. Harriet gasped as he touched her there, knowing she was going to lose control at any moment. Then she did, coming in spasms that drove the breath from her, which was just as well because it prevented her from shouting his name. Mistrsses, even when in the throes of orgasm, are not supposed to go that far. It might give the other an exaggerated sense of their worth or prowess.

Tom paused while she recovered, then resumed the slow in-and-out motion while continuing to tease her nipples. She could sense him trying to hold back, and she

151

decided that she would work on him as he was working on her. She tightened and relaxed around him as he probed her, feeling the contractions in his cock as he pulled himself back from the verge several times.

She was satisfied that she could give him as good a ride as she was getting, and that was very good indeed. She wondered why she had held back so long from trying this man out, realising that she had missed a great deal by holding on to her position of dominance. She felt him tense inside her and knew he was about to come. Her own orgasm had crept up on her as well, and they finished almost together, Tom's breath hot against her face as he hunched himself, driving deeply into her. Her own cries were forced from her as she came, jerking wildly at the ropes that bound her wrists to the headboard.

Afterwards he lay beside her, holding her in his arms with his face buried in her hair, letting her come down gradually. Harriet was glad he didn't speak. There weren't that many things one could say, and speech, she felt, would somehow diminish the event. Also, she might blurt out something she'd rather not have him know. It was going to be hard to go back to the game of slave and mistress after this, but she had nothing else to offer at the moment. Time, that's what they needed. Time to get used to being lovers. Maybe she would relax a bit . . .

ANNIE AND THE COUNTESS

Evelyn Culber

Evelyn Culber certainly knows how to put her pretty young heroines through their paces. In her classic series 0of Edwardian erotica, *Annie*, *Annie and the Society*, *Annie's Further Education* and *Annie and the Countess*, Annie swiftly learns her duties as a new maid, performing indelicate entertainments for a variety of observers and enduring some harsh lessons before her education is complete. Evelyn has also graced us with two contemporary novels, both featuring the delightfully enthusiastic Sherrie, keen both to administer and receive punishments on her bare bottom. The first is *Sherrie*, and its sequel, *Sherrie and the Initiation of Penny*, featured Sherrie's friend Penny being initiated into the depraved games she has never before dared to play.

The following extract is taken from *Annie and the Countess*, Evelyn's most recent novel for us. Here Annie is taken for a special kind of cleaning, and is introduced to the delights that can be derived from the gentle insertion of a clyster.

On Wednesday morning I remembered my assignation with Mme Dupont. I freely confess that I anticipated our imminent appointment with some trepidation. Further reflection on the prospect of having my bowels thoroughly purged lessened the potential attractions with every minute. Still, as I told myself as I climbed into my carriage, I had committed myself and so had no honourable alternative but to submit with as much grace as I could muster.

I had changed into black for this more-or-less public engagement but kept my underclothes to a minimum in order to facilitate access to the area under threat. My nervous tremors were alleviated somewhat when the good lady opened the door to me. Her relatively humble address had suggested that for her to have a servant in residence was unlikely, but far from feeling superior about this, I was most relieved that my forthcoming embarrassment would not be witnessed, however indirectly.

Welcoming me volubly, my new acquaintance ushered me into her small drawing room. The quality of the furnishings came as a very pleasant surprise. My first impression that she was a woman of taste had been correct and I assumed that her reduced circumstances were probably of a temporary nature.

She produced a bottle of good red wine and, while we conversed in slightly unnatural tones, I sipped away, rather wishing that she had offered me tea instead. Not for long, however. Her ebullient nature and the wine soon

157

began to put me at my ease. Then she cleared away the bottle and glasses and returned, clearly in the mood for business. She had tied her hair back and was wearing a voluminous white apron. My heart began to pound and my initial blush warmed my cheeks. My bottom-hole began to tingle nervously. She smiled at me with such sympathetic warmth that I began to feel better; then she asked me for details of my personal habits, which even I found almost intrusive. Sensing that I was troubled, she came across to me, perched on the arm of my chair and smiled. The close proximity to her in general and her hip in particular reminded me forcefully that I had been attracted to her from the outset. Suddenly the thought of presenting my bottom seemed less embarrassing! Presumably my expression gave away my change of mood because her smile broadened noticeably and she squeezed my hand. Then she dropped her bombshell!

'I do appreciate that you are a little nervous, Mrs Milford,' she said, and something in her tone made me stiffen. 'But I assure you again that the process will not be at all painful. And you will certainly feel a great deal better afterwards. And to reassure you further, I have taken the liberty of inviting a friend of mine to join us. Her name is Mrs Arbuthnott, she is a widow like yourself and, if not as beautiful as you are, still a most attractive lady. She is also a devotee of my treatment and I felt that it would help to put your mind at rest if you were to watch her undergoing it beforehand.'

I looked up at her anxious face, my thoughts in something of a whirl. Presumably the unexpected visitor would expect to be able to watch me being dealt with and this did not please me greatly. I could not, however, summon up the courage to protest, so I agreed to stay.

In the event, my fears were not realised. Mrs Arbuthnott proved to be an enchanting woman in her middle thirties and, as Mme Dupont had described, very attractive. As she had been delayed somewhat, there was not time to finish the wine and we moved into the treatment room as soon as the introductions had been made. Mme

Dupont left us alone, saying that she had to make her preparations.

I stared around me, intrigued, despite my growing apprehension. The only item of furniture was a well-padded couch against one wall. It was covered with a clean white cloth and so looked encouragingly clinical. A wash basin stood in one corner and, next to it, a table with some strangely shaped items just discernible under another cloth. Just as I was trying to assimilate my surroundings, my fellow sufferer broke the silence.

'Mrs Milford, I usually take the treatment in a state of complete nudity – it is so much more convenient. I hope that you will not be offended?'

My interest quickened. The prospect of seeing this handsome woman all bare put a completely different complexion on the proceedings. Doing my utmost to keep any trace of excitement from my voice, I hastened to assure her that I would not.

'Would you like me to assist?' I asked innocently.

'Oh that would be kind!' she exclaimed. I moved forward and helped her undress until she was reduced to a light chemise and drawers.

She seemed quite unperturbed as I stared openly at her near-naked form and this encouraged me to voice the admiring thoughts which had already crowded through my mind.

'What a beautiful complexion you have, Mrs Arbuthnott,' I said with genuine feeling. 'And a splendid bosom. But that mine were as round and generous.'

'Thank you, Mrs Milford,' she replied, blushing in a most becoming manner. She slipped her chemise down off her shoulders, stepped out of it and folded it tidily with her other clothes and then, with apparent modesty, turned to face the couch before removing her drawers.

I held my breath as I studied her naked bottom. It was a little larger than I had expected but delightfully broad and smooth, with especially wide folds. I was just debating to myself whether a spoken compliment would be seemly in the circumstances – and if so, which feature to select – when she peered over her shoulder, smiling shyly.

'Do you find the sight of my bare bottom unappealing, Mrs Milford?' she whispered.

I looked her straight in the eye. 'Far from it, Mrs Arbuthnott,' I replied warmly. Then I took a deep breath as I ostentatiously returned my gaze to those splendid buttocks. 'It is without question a splendid bottom and I feel honoured that you feel you can expose it to me without embarrassment.'

Her smile broadened. 'I am pleased that you like it. And I do hope that you understand my desire to see yours in the same state.'

This reminder of my mysterious ordeal reawakened my fears but I considered that to show any sign of them would be craven. I bobbed a little curtsey. 'You compliment me, Mrs Arbuthnott. I trust that I shall not disappoint you.'

'I have no doubts on that score, Mrs Milford. Rest assured.'

At that point, our hostess bustled back into the room, carefully carrying a large jug on a tray. Steam rose wispily from the top and both my curiosity and nervousness increased.

Mme Dupont placed the jug on the table and turned towards her waiting victim, studying her bottom with undisguised admiration. Rubbing her hands together, she turned to me.

'Did I not tell you that Mrs Arbuthnott is admirably formed, Mrs Milford?'

'You did indeed, Madame,' I agreed fervently, 'and I could not agree more.'

'Assume the usual position, if you please, Mrs Arbuthnott,' Mme Dupont asked politely and once again I held my breath as she moved to obey. At this stage, the displeasing aspects of what was about to happen faded from my mind and I was able to derive full enjoyment from watching this handsome and comely woman arrange her bottom. My eyes glued to the alterations in its aspects, from the moment she raised her left knee on to the couch to her final shift, when she arched her back and stuck it high into the air. As I have indicated, I was most taken with her figure and her bottom was of the highest quality. Nor was I disappointed when I leaned forward to make a close examination of that tight little orifice so obviously a central part of the proceedings.

I do find pleasure in looking at a pretty feminine bottom-hole. Partly because it is normally well concealed and therefore exposing it – either by prising apart the buttocks or by placing the owner in the sort of revealing pose which Mrs Arbuthnott was now adopting – produces in me a sensation of utmost intimacy with the other. If I am punishing in earnest, I usually make a point of such an examination at least once during the proceedings. The idea is, of course, to remind the culprit of her vulnerability. On those occasions where sensual pleasure is the sole purpose, the intention is to increase the delight.

It is also a deliciously sensitive part. If any of my readers have not plucked up the courage to try caresses here on their lover (or, of course, lovers) then I urge them to experiment; although it is always important to remember that cleanliness is next to godliness.

So, I drew closer without the slightest hesitation and could sense Madame's approval as I bent my head to peer right into the open division. Her little orifice may have lacked the pink and hairless perfection which Bertha and Arabella enjoyed but was pretty enough for all that. The wrinkled surround was a nice shade of pale brown and the opening itself was protruding sufficiently to give a hint of pinkness in the centre. A few fine hairs grew haphazardly around it and a quick lowering of my eyes showed that the plump, parted lips of her cunny were quite profusely covered.

Sensing that both the others were quite content to let me satisfy my curiosity, I decided that it would be wrong for me to conceal my interest and experience, so extended the forefinger of my right hand and gently tickled her. She gasped and immediately jerked her hips inwards, trapping my finger in the softness of the closed divide. I assumed

161

that her reaction was surprise rather than outrage and was proved correct in an instant, for she wriggled her bottom slightly and then pushed it back out, pressing her anus against my soft touch.

'Oooh!' she whispered. 'That *is* nice!'

Thus emboldened, I let my fingertip roam freely around the inside of her bottom while my left palm happily stroked the taut satin of her prominent buttocks. As I did so, I saw a small drop of moisture emerge from her major opening and cling to the hairs, glistening like a tiny pearl. As the scent of her excitement reached my nostrils, the last of my inhibitions dissipated and my own cunny and bottom-hole began to tingle insistently. Suddenly impatient, I stepped back. Up to that point, it had all been reasonably familiar to me. It was not the first time I had watched a woman disrobe and present her bare bottom in such a blatant manner and Mrs Arbuthnott's anus was not the first I had seen and caressed. But from that moment, I was a witness to the unknown.

Madame was most solicitous, both to me and her patient. She explained all her actions to me and treated Mrs Arbuthnott with consideration. The first thing to do, she told me, was to prepare the anus properly.

'I always use as much oil as is necessary, Mrs Milford,' she said as she coated her forefinger liberally with the contents of a large phial. Our heads were almost touching as we bent to the application. She carefully covered the anus, dipped her finger in the phial again and pressed it against the actual opening. I sensed that Mrs Arbuthnott actually tried to thrust her bottom into even greater prominence in anticipation of the rude intrusion, but it was so tightly bent that I could not swear to it. In any case, Madame's finger paused for a moment and then moved forward. The pink sphincter closed tightly round the slender digit in apparent welcome, an impression confirmed by the blissful sigh from the other end. I watched with bated breath as Madame pressed in until she could go no further and then wriggled around, ensuring that every possible inch of the clinging tunnel was oiled.

The finger slid out with a tiny plopping sound. Madame moved across to the table and beckoned me over. As she whipped off the covering cloth, my hand flew to my mouth and I gasped. The purging instrument looked more like an instrument of unrefined torture than an aid to good health. It was essentially a large syringe with a red tube emerging from the narrow end and a round handle at the other.

Madame picked up and caressed it lovingly while I looked on with awe. 'It is quite simple, Mrs Milford,' she said, her voice low and steady but unable to quite to contain her excitement. 'I fill the main part with water, like so – ' as she spoke, she grasped the handle and pulled it smoothly out ' – and then press the plunger back in and the water is expelled into the bottom.' Once again, she demonstrated; there was an audible hiss from the nozzle as she did so and the tube writhed threateningly.

With her smiling acquiescence, I picked up the tube and stroked it. The thought of its sinous length sliding up first Mrs Arbuthnott's bottom and then mine thrilled me. I looked across to the couch and was again struck by the lasciviousness of the sight which greeted me. Those splendid white, rounded buttocks framing the pale and gleaming anus, in a pose which was superficially utterly submissive and yet with a touch of eagerness in the naked woman's attitude.

When I turned back, Madame had placed the end of the nozzle into the jug and she then slowly pulled the plunger out to its fullest extent. I could hear a gentle gurgle from the device's innards and found this quite thrilling. As she withdrew, I stuck a finger into the water and was a little surprised at its heat.

'The water has to feel hot to the touch,' Madame informed me. 'The interior of the *derrière* is considerably warmer than the outside skin.' I had slipped my finger up enough bottoms to know that and was not surprised. I nodded wisely and we walked the few paces back to Mrs Arbuthnott.

Without further ado, more oil was spread over the end of the nozzle; the clyster – as I now knew to call it – was laid on the couch between Mrs Arbuthnott's parted feet, and the penetration commenced. Madame took a firm grip of the nozzle in her forefinger and thumb and raised it until it was brushing against the very centre of Mrs Arbuthnott's anus.

I held my breath. Mrs Arbuthnott sighed softly as she felt the touch and then Madame's hand moved forward and the tiny ring of muscle seemed to open out in welcome. I peered as closely as I could, entranced by the sight of the tube disappearing up her fundament. The guiding hand progressed until its fingers were nuzzling against the inner surfaces of the surrounding buttocks, then moved about three inches back, resumed its grip, and moved remorselessly inward again.

Mrs Arbuthnott moaned quietly, whether from pleasure or discomfort I could not be certain. By this stage, she had six inches of tube inside her and, while the thickness could not have pained her in the slightest, I wondered whether the length was irritating parts of her bowel beyond the reach of more usual intrusions. I comforted myself that I would shortly discover this for myself; my breathing returned to normal as Madame picked up the clyster, raised it so that the tube was slanting downwards and pressed the plunger inwards.

The water gurgled happily from the tube into the passage, which provided me with the only sign that the process had begun. There was no rection from the owner of the passage – apart from an audible exhalation. Needless to say, I found the absence of moaning and groaning quite reassuring!

Once the plunger had been pressed to the end of its travel, Madame carefully extracted the tube. Once again, I peered closely as the glistening length emerged, noting that Mrs Arbuthnott's anus pouted to facilitate the invader's exit. I then waited nervously for the next stage, conscious that the distasteful part of the operation was imminent. I was wrong.

With a friendly pat on the nearer buttock, Madame went back to the table and refilled the clyster. Having witnessed that operation once, I felt that I would not learn anything new by watching it again, so spent the few moments of inactivity happily gazing at Mrs Arbuthnott's delightful posterior.

'How do you feel?' I asked.

'Oh perfectly at ease,' she replied gaily. 'The first dose presents no discomfort whatsoever. The second fills me up and I shall feel a trifle cramped before it is all inside me, but then it would not be nearly so beneficial otherwise.'

'Oh,' I replied, in some confusion. There was a pause while I tried to think of another question to ask but failed to. I devoted my full attention to her bottom, feeling brave enough to stroke the tautly curved cheeks without asking permission. She clearly found my caress much to her taste, for her bottom swayed under my palm. Just as I was about to tickle her anus again, Madame reappeared with the recharged clyster; I stood to the side and avidly watched the tube make its second voyage.

As Mrs Arbuthnott had suggested, the second injection was more testing. I could sense the tension in her muscles as the plunger forced more water into her and I heard her initial sighs changed to groans.

The tube slid out again. 'Wait for a few moments more, Mrs Arbuthnott,' Madame ordered, not unsympathetically. After perhaps two minutes, during which the groans and wrigglings grew in intensity, Madame administered a ringing slap. 'Relief is at hand,' she cried gaily.

'Oh thank heavens!' Mrs Arbuthnott exclaimed and clambered gingerly down. She straightened up slowly and then hobbled with undignified haste out of the room, her ample bottom quivering quite deliciously.

Madame turned to me and the hollowness once again invaded my vitals. She smiled reassuringly. 'I do hope that what you have seen has not made you change your mind, Mrs Milford?' she asked.

'Certainly not,' I replied, more positively than I felt.

'Excellent. I shall now attach a new tube to the clyster and we can proceed with your treatment. Perhaps you would like to begin to disrobe?'

'Yes, of course.' My fingers moved to the buttons of the simple dress I had purposely chosen with this eventuality in mind and, as I undid them, I asked where Mrs Arbuthnott had gone.

'Oh, Mrs Milford, do forgive me!' Madame cried. 'I should have explained properly before we commenced. There is a water closet just along the corridor. When I have finished, you make use of it and have a wash. She will have finished quite soon, I imagine. I believe that she is as anxious to see you naked as I am.'

Blushing at this compliment and relieved that the inevitable conclusion of the purging was to be carried out in complete privacy, I set about undressing with a lighter heart. I had just placed my chemise on the spare chair when Mrs Arbuthnott returned, catching me in just my drawers and stockings. Had I been the modest young girl of three years past, I am sure that I would have found such exposure embarrassing. As it was, I found that I had instinctively pulled back my shoulders in order to add even greater prominence to my bosom. I noticed the sparkle in Mrs Arbuthnott's eye just before I lowered my gaze to her equally bare protuberances, and we stared contentedly at each other's breasts for several minutes.

I then came out of my reverie and turned my back to remove my last garment. I am not ashamed to admit that I did my best to bare my bottom as sensually as I could manage, swaying my hips as I worked the waist over my buttocks and bending down to ease the rumpled silk off my feet, hoping that they were both enjoying the view. I then walked sinuously to the couch and arranged myself according to the example set by my predecessor.

I freely confess that my cunny began to tingle in concert with my bottom-hole as I knelt. The knowledge that these two singularly attractive ladies, one of whom was unashamedly still naked, were staring at my elevated and naked bottom was most exciting. I was aware of two faces peering closely into my gaping cleft – I could actually feel warm breath on the sensitive skin in that region – but I cared less and less about their actions and reactions. An oily finger moved slickly around my bottom-hole and I cried out softly as the thrilling waves surged into my vitals. After a brief interlude, it pressed against the opening of my bottom and I instinctively did what I had painfully learnt to do when I was being buggered and pushed against the intrusion, so that my little orifice provided an unresisting welcome.

I gasped in pleasure at the slight stretching and there-fore only just heard Madame's whispered '*bien fait*', as she expressed her appreciation of my compliance. There were other murmurings in the background but I ignored them. The delicious feelings suffusing the whole of my bottom were all-enveloping.

Then, when the finger finally withdrew, I tensed again. I was now entering the realms of the unknown and these demanded my full attention. I felt the end of the nozzle touching the opening of my anus and bore down again. It slipped in easily and provided a sensation very different to the penetration of either a male member or my wooden dildo. These stretch my anus in a way that is deliciously painful and this feeling, initially at least, overwhelms the fulfilling plugging of my rectum. The tube was thin enough to titillate my opening but did not numb the parts inside it, so that I could easily feel it as it wriggled its way into me.

It stopped and I held my breath expectantly. Madame kept me waiting in the same way I had made dear Cook wait for the first spank only a few days previously. I crouched there, my eyes closed and breathing heavily through gritted teeth as I waited. Just as I was on the point of calling out, I felt the flow and exhaled in a gust of relief and surprise.

Relief because the waiting was over and surprise

because the liquid rush was far more pleasant than I had dared to envisage. It surged remorselessly, filling me far more dramatically than I would have believed possible. And it went on and on and on. My bowels seemed to swell beyond comprehension and suddenly a cramping sensation made me cry out and tuck my bottom inwards in a vain attempt to stem the flow.

I heard soothing voices and gentle hands stroked my buttocks. Another reached beneath and gently rubbed away at my swollen belly. The cramps faded and, with a sigh of relief, I thrust my posterior back into its original blatant pose. The flow resumed and then stopped. My breathing was loud in my ears and I cried out again – this time with pleasure, not distress, as I felt the tube slide back out. Its passage made my anus tingle anew and, when it eventually plopped out, the lining of my back passage clung on to the memory of its presence.

The need for relief of the pressure grew strong as I knelt silently awaiting the second dose and my ears strained the catch the faint sounds of Madame refilling it. The pressure began to overwhelm me and I was on the verge of pleading for release when I felt a sharp little slap on the tautest part of my left buttock. Knowing what it meant, I groaned in relief and only just heard Madame speak.

'I think that for the first occasion, one infusion will suffice, Mrs Milford.'

'Oh thank you, Madame,' I cried weakly as I clambered down on to trembling limbs. I made for the door with utmost despatch, aware as I fled that my bare buttocks were wobbling away behind me with even more vigour than Mrs Arbuthnott's had done.

The water closet was as welcome a sight as an oasis must be to a lost traveller in the desert. I hurled myself backwards on the seat and let the water stream out, groaning in sheer bliss. I sat there, panting heavily for some moments, and then everything that Madame had said about the process being beneficial came true. I completed my ablutions with the blood racing through my veins and, when I returned to the room, my broad smile and skipping walk were more eloquent than any words.

Laughing, I flung my arms around Madame and hugged her to my naked bosom, babbling out my thanks and appreciation. To my delight, she laughed as happily as I and then reached down and placed her hands on my bare bottom. Her touch was quite delicious and the flow of sensuous well-being that flooded through me waxed even more strongly.

It was then that I had an inspiration which provided a splendid climax to what had already been a richly educational afternoon.

'Madame Dupont,' I began. 'You told me when we first met that you yourself find a good purging of immense benefit. May I be so bold as to ask who performs the task for you?'

She blushed and looked down. 'Nowadays I apply the clyster myself,' she whispered.

I smiled happily at her. 'That is most unsatisfactory, Madame,' I announced firmly. 'We have both had to expose every last secret of our innocent little *derrières* to you, and I am of the firm opinion that it is high time Mrs Arbuthnott and I had the opportunity to feast our eyes on yours.'

I suppose that I had expected her to fall in with my scheme with some gratitude, so her immediate protestation that the idea was quite out of the question took me aback. Then I looked at her rather more closely and saw a flash in the depths of her eyes which I interpreted as a longing for something more than I had originally offered. I frowned at her in mock irritation, tapping a stockinged toe rhythmically on the floor while I furiously tried to identify her secret wish. I was still at a loss when she spoke again.

'No, Mrs Milford,' she stammered. 'I am quite content to operate on myself and you cannot force me to submit.' Her face showed an inner yearning quite at odds with her words and then I understood.

'I cannot force you, Madame?' I asked sweetly, advancing on her with clear intent. 'I am sure that I can. Especially with the help of Mrs Arbuthnott.' I turned to my hoped-for ally. 'I am sure you agree with me, Madame, that our friend here would benefit from a good purging. I feel enormously improved by mine and the thought of her doing it herself and thus depriving us of the opportunity to help her is amazingly selfish.'

'I am in complete agreement with you, Mrs Milford,' she enthused, rubbing her hands vigorously – an action which made her bosoms quiver most enticingly – and, in complete accord, two naked women advanced purposefully towards the clad one, who shrank against the wall, mewing piteously in her apparent distress.

Firmly, but with no undue violence, we stripped the good woman. My suspicion that the worthy Mrs Arbuthnott was as sensual a creature as I was confirmed as soon as we had bared Madame's breasts.

'A charming bosom,' she judged, staring at the trembling orbs with clear satisfaction. 'May I suggest, Mrs Milford, that you go behind her and hold her arms back? This will thrust her breasts into even greater prominence and allow me to fondle them without interference.'

'I would be delighted to oblige,' I replied, and did so.

Madame wriggled ineffectually in my grip as her bosom was subjected to a lengthy manual examination, after which Mrs Arbuthnott and I changed places. I was relieved to find that French breasts showed no sign of special qualities lacking in English ones and I enjoyed manipulating them no less than I had all the other bosoms I had toyed with in my short but eventful life.

I soon had her large dark nipples straining against my touch, their owner groaning in assumed shame and real pleasure; then I grew impatient to move to even more fertile pastures. Looking up, I caught my ally's eye. 'I think we should now bare her fat little bottom,' I said with gloating relish.

Madame groaned theatrically, Mrs Arbuthnott agreed wholeheartedly, and in a trice we had the writhing woman face down on the floor. I sat on her shoulders and my friend held her knees down in the same manner. The smoothness of Madame's naked back beneath my bare bottom was quite delightful, but the sight of her posterior emerging as we manoeuvred her clothes down to her ankles was sufficient to distract me from even that pleasure.

I had referred to her as having a fat little bottom and when it loomed into full view I saw that my judgement had been surprisingly accurate. She was certainly narrower in the hip than Mrs Arbuthnott – and, probably, than me – and her cleft was appreciably shorter. On the other hand, her cheeks were deliciously round and the temptation to fondle them rigorously was unbearably tempting. My hands roved freely, while Mrs Arbuthnott wrenched clothes and stockings off a pair of feebly kicking feet, and then I graciously sat back and beckoned to my new friend to help herself to as much buttock as she wished.

As I watched, I thanked my good fortune for introducing me so unexpectedly to two new bottoms of such quality, for Madame's was, for all its different form and consistency, no less desirable than my partner's.

By this time, I was very impatient to proceed and we soon had Madame's beautiful white bottom properly positioned. We anointed her in turn and then I generously allowed Mrs Arbuthnott to operate the clyster. Apart from a muted squeal of protest that the water was cold, Madame took the first load in silence. I then assumed command, refilled the cylinder, joyously thrust the glistening tube up her fundament and pressed the plunger home in one smooth push, making her gasp and squirm. I extracted the device slowly and placed it on the floor; Mrs Arbuthnott and I spent a happy minute or two, standing close together stroking the other's bare bottom while we peered at Madame's twitching anus.

At last we let her fly to relieve herself. I sighed deeply and turned to Mrs Arbuthnott with genuine respect. 'I enjoyed that very much indeed,' I said contentedly.

171

'So did I,' she whispered, 'especially the forcible stripping. And I have long felt a desire to see her bottom. And to administer the clyster myself. It was all most satisfying.'

'We must try and persuade Madame to invite us both to return,' I suggested.

She smiled at me. 'I do not think that it will be hard to persuade her. The expression on her face while she was looking at your bottom made her admiration quite clear.'

'How nice,' I responded, quite embarrassed.

'And if you will forgive me for being so forward, my admiration of your figure matches hers.'

Laughing aloud, I flung my arms around her and kissed her with genuine affection. Then Madame returned, looking exceedingly content, and we took it in turns to embrace her in the same way.

I reluctantly said that I should be getting back to the Academy but was persuaded to stay for tea, which we took fully dressed and with a decorum which made the events of the previous hour seem quite unreal. I made my farewells with genuine reluctance which was considerably mollified when Madame reminded me that she was due to visit me to discuss 'matters relating to physical punishment of young women'. A little disconcerted at the way she had let slip our plans to another, I frowned in annoyance.

'Oh how exciting!' cried Mrs Arbuthnott. 'Madame, please tell me exactly what transpires.'

My heartbeat fluttered in excitement. 'Will you honour us with your presence, Mrs Arbuthnott?' I asked softly.

'With the greatest pleasure,' she assured me.

Very content, I climbed into my carriage and Tom drove home with his customary expertise.

THE TRAINING OF
FALLEN ANGELS

Kendal Grahame

Kendal Grahame specialises in writing quality, arousing erotica with highly unusual settings and plots, which are always a delight to read. Kendal's books for us have included *Fallen Angels*, in which Janet and Lisa must perform every lascivious act known to mankind in order to discover the identity of their mysterious mentor; *The Cloak of Aphrodite*, a highly erotic interpretation of the tale of Jason and the bewitchingly gorgeous Medea; *Demonia*, in which luscious female vampires live off the essence of sexual arousal; *Pyramid of Delights*, a tale of secret erotic rituals set in Ancient Egypt; and *The Training of Fallen Angels*, which continues the adventures of the libidinous Janet and Lisa. A story set in Roman Britain, *The Warrior Queen*, is due to be published in December 1998.

The following extract is taken from *The Training of Fallen Angels*, Kendal's most recent book for us. Here Janet, Lisa and other willing pupils are undergoing strict instruction in the art of arousal by the fearful Madam Stone – but this lesson looks like it's going to be a little more fun than most.

Madam Stone stood haughtily before Lisa and Janet, her hands planted firmly on her broad hips. The two girls had been summoned to see her in the library and had been quick to obey. It was a large, airy room towards the rear of the sprawling manor. Rows of desks and chairs had been arranged in the form of an old-fashioned classroom. Lisa and Janet were seated at two of these desks, facing their mentor.

'Today will be your final lesson,' said Madam Stone, her voice booming with confident authority. She was dressed in a severe outfit consisting of tailored trousers and a smart jacket which, for once, concealed her voluptuous figure. Following instructions, the two friends had dressed themselves in similar garments. 'I will take this class,' continued their instructress. 'It will be a general lesson, to outline the rest of the week's goals and to discover the knowledge that our students may already possess. Afterwards, they will split into four groups. You will each take one of these groups, the others will be instructed by your colleagues, Paul and Mike.'

'Instructed?' queried Lisa. 'What are we going to teach?'

Madam Stone smiled and moved over to her. She rested a hand gently on her shoulder. 'You have both shown the areas where you have the most expertise,' she said, 'and you have learnt the art of teasing and torment. You will combine these talents and instruct the students accordingly. You, Lisa, will teach the girls the techniques of giving good oral sex, both to men and to women. You will

177

be ably assisted by two male members of staff, as will you, Janet.'

'And what will I be teaching?' said Janet excitedly.

Madam Stone smiled broadly. Lisa had a very good idea what she was going to say. 'You, my dear, will explain and demonstrate the delights of anal love, a subject which, I am told, is near to your heart.'

Janet looked across at Lisa, who quickly glanced at the floor, blushing noticeably. 'Bitch!' hissed Janet as she realised her friend's indiscretion, although in truth she was quite pleased.

They heard noises from outside the room. It was the sound of many footsteps echoing in the hallway.

'Right,' said Madam Stone as she moved two high-backed chairs to the centre of the room and turned them to face the desks. 'Sit here. Do not speak unless asked to.'

The door opened and the students began to troop in silently. They were dressed uniformly, which gave even more credence to the classroom effect. The outfits had obviously been provided by Mr Gee for just this purpose. They consisted of short, black mini-kilts, crisp, white shirts and striped ties. The uniforms were completed by light blue blazers which sported a badge proclaiming the legend 'Grantham Manor' on the breast pocket.

Once they had all entered the library the door was closed behind them and they stood in a group at the back of the room. Madam Stone clapped her hands loudly. 'Right, ladies,' she barked. 'Sit at the desks.' The students obeyed, filling the room with the sounds of sliding chairs as they took their places.

Madam Stone stood in silence as they made themselves comfortable. Lisa surveyed the sea of faces with admiration. Although they were all at least seventeen or eighteen years of age, the uniforms made them appear much younger. They were all lovely, and some were positively beautiful.

The oriental girl who had so captivated Lisa when the group had arrived that morning had sat at the front of the rows of desks. From her vantage point, Lisa could glance under the desk. She had to bite her lip as she noticed that the gorgeous student's legs were slightly parted to offer a tantalising glimpse of the tops of her black stockings and the tiny 'V' of her white panties. Lisa enjoyed sex with other women, of course, but she had never felt such a powerful desire for one of her own sex before. She looked back at the girl, and their eyes met. This time, the student didn't look away but held her gaze and smiled coyly. Her legs opened a little further then she closed them quickly, as if realising her indiscretion. Lisa felt a familiar dampness between her own thighs and took a deep breath.

At last, Madam Stone broke the uncomfortable silence. 'Ladies, you know why you are here. Your host, Mr Gee, has explained everything. Today we wish to learn about you. You must speak openly, always tell the complete truth and, above all, speak frankly. Grantham Manor is no place for shyness. Is that understood?'

A few of the girls nodded.

'I said, is that understood?' repeated their tutor. Her face was stern and her eyes glared angrily.

'Yes,' chorused a number of voices.

'Yes, madam,' demanded the tall woman as she paced the floor. 'My name is Heidi Stone, but you will always address me as madam, especially when I am having sex with you.'

Lisa noticed that a couple of the girls looked at each other apprehensively at these last words. Others seemed not in the least surprised, and a few looked positively excited at the prospect. She looked at the small, oriental student. Her legs were open again and her eyes were firmly fixed on Madam Stone's dark features. The young girl allowed the tip of her tongue to play across her upper lip. Lisa's immediate thought was how lovely it would be to have that same tongue fluttering over the hard bud of her clitoris. She looked at Janet. Her friend was sitting impassively, but Lisa knew that similar thoughts were probably going through her mind.

'Hands up those of you who are virgins.' There was some giggling at Madam Stone's sudden command, but

179

no arms were raised. 'Come, now,' she said in a softer tone, 'don't be shy. It is important that we know.' Three hands were nervously raised, including that of the girl who had become the object of Lisa's desire. 'Good. Now perhaps we are getting somewhere. In future, if any of you do not answer mine or your other tutors' questions immediately and truthfully, you will be severely punished.'

'May I ask a question, miss, er, madam?' It was the oriental girl who spoke, her voice a lilting song to Lisa's ears.

'Ask,' replied Madam Stone abruptly.

'When you say virgins, do you mean with men?'

'That is correct. I take it that you have had experience with members of your own sex?'

'Yes, madam.'

'Do you like men?'

The young girl's face was becoming flushed. 'Oh yes, madam. It's just that I've never had the opportunity to, to make love with a man.' Her voice trailed off into a whisper and she looked down at the floor in embarrassment.

'The opportunity to do what?' Madam Stone's tone was mocking. 'Stand up, girl!' she barked. 'Now, repeat yourself, loudly, so that all the class can hear.'

The terrified girl stood at her desk. Lisa could plainly see that her tiny frame was shaking. 'I said that I've never had the chance to make love with a man,' she said in a slightly louder voice.

Madam Stone paced over to stand directly in front of the hapless girl. She towered over her and the young student was forced to bend her head right back just to look at her face. Her eyes were staring in terror but Madam Stone merely held her severe glare. Lisa couldn't help feeling sorry for the student. She wanted to wrap her arms around her and protect from this fearsome woman. 'You mean that you have never had the opportunity to be *fucked* by a man! Isn't that what you mean?' The girl nodded self-consciously. 'Speak up, girl!' commanded Madam Stone.

'Yes, madam,' she said quietly.

'Now say it – what haven't you have the chance to do?'

The girl spoke her reply slowly, in nervous monosyllables. 'Not had the chance to, to –'

'Say it!' commanded Madam Stone.

'Say it,' echoed Lisa to herself, willing the girl to end her torment.

'To be fucked.' As soon as the words left her mouth, the young girl buried her chin into her chest in shame, as though she had committed the most cardinal sin.

Madam Stone reached out with her hand and raised her face until she was looking directly into her eyes. 'That's right,' she said, her tone unusually tender. 'To be fucked by a big cock going into your virgin cunt.' She stressed each of the obscenities as she stroked the softness of her student's face. 'They are just words, nice words, and you must use them. What's your name?'

'Sammy-Lynn,' replied the girl, her voice a little more confident.

'Well, Sammy-Lynn, by the end of this first day you will no longer be a virgin – none of you will. Grantham Manor is no place for virgins.'

Suddenly the tension that had been building up in the classroom was swallowed up by the sound of laughter. Madam Stone smiled broadly and walked over to rest her hand on Lisa's shoulder. 'Oh, and Sammy-Lyn,' she continued, 'from the way this young lady has been looking at you I feel that you may have plenty of chances to enjoy other diversions.'

It was Lisa's turn to blush. She looked at Sammy-Lynn who grinned back at her, her large, brown eyes sparkling with delight.

'Now,' said Madam Stone as her voice once again took on an air of authority, 'everybody stand.' The students obeyed immediately, as did Lisa and Janet. 'Now, sit down if you have had fewer than five lovers.' The three virgins sat down, as well as about six others. Madam Stone looked at them for a moment, obviously making mental notes. 'Fewer than ten?' Most of the others sat down, leaving just two standing, apart from Lisa and

Janet. Madam Stone walked over to one of them, a tall, statuesque blonde with a slim figure which could have graced any catwalk. 'Your name?' she demanded.

'Kelly.'

'Kelly what?' snapped Madam Stone.

The girl looked visibly shaken by her sudden change in tone. 'Kelly, madam,' she replied in a meek voice. She spoke with a cultured American accent.

'That's better. You will stay behind after the class, Kelly, and be punished for your impertinence. Now, how many lovers have savoured this delightful body of yours?'

'Eighteen, madam,' said the girl gently. Madam Stone nodded and walked over to the other standing figure. She, too, was tall but very buxom and of apparent Mediterranean origins.

'And what is your name?'

'Serita, madam,' replied the girl, stressing the last word firmly. 'I've had twenty-six male lovers.'

'And females?'

'Probably about the same.'

Madam Stone grinned with satisfaction as she walked back to stand before the class. Lisa and Janet resumed their seats. 'Kelly, you may sit down. Serita, come to the front of the class.' The dark-haired student moved nervously through the rows of desks to stand next to her tutor. Her face was strong, her nose slightly too large, but her mouth was full. Her large, bra-free breasts forced her blazer apart and the striped tie lay suggestively between them. Her pleated skirt was a little too short and revealed the darkness of her stocking-tops and, despite her flat shoes, she was almost as tall as Madam Stone herself.

Madam Stone walked slowly around the standing figure, examining her as though she was a slave in an ancient marketplace. 'You clearly enjoy sex,' she said, presently. 'I wonder if we'll be able to teach you much.'

'My father, the Ambassador, thinks I am still a virgin, madam. It was he who suggested that I come here. I truly believe that it will be a waste of my time.'

'Really? Well, let us see what you can do, Serita.'

Madam Stone picked up a small handbell from a nearby table and rang it briskly. Almost immediately the door opened and Mike walked in, wearing nothing but a tiny, leather pouch which was already bulging in a ludicrous manner. The students gasped audibly at the sight of his slim but muscular body as he walked up to face the class. He stood still for a moment as though posing, with a grin that seemed to stretch from ear to ear. Serita eyed him cautiously, then her mouth opened slightly and she wet her lips with her tongue. He looked back at her, and Lisa could see that his bulge was growing by the second. For a moment she felt a little envious.

'Now, Serita,' said Madam Stone as she took a seat next to Lisa and Janet, 'show the class how you would satisfy a man like Mike.'

Serita looked across at her incredulously. 'You mean you want me to fuck him, here, in front of everybody?'

'Is there a problem with that?' said Madam Stone, as if it was the most natural thing in the world to have full sex before a group of goggle-eyed teenagers.

Serita shook her head. 'I can't, I can't,' she wailed. 'Sex is a private thing.'

Madam Stone stood up again. 'Go back to your seat, young lady,' she said in a clearly exasperated tone. 'You too will be punished after the class.' Mike watched with genuine disappointment showing on his face as the beautiful, uniform-clad girl returned to her desk through a gauntlet of chuckling colleagues. 'You have upset our handsome friend,' continued the tutor. 'You have been told already that you must never refuse anything. By the end of this week you will all have become proud of your sexuality and will delight in exhibiting your new-found prowess. But now we have a small problem. Mike is frustrated. He fully expected sex when he heard my bell. Whatever shall we do?'

She looked slowly round the class. Lisa smiled to herself at the thought of Mike being frustrated. She knew full well that he had spent most of the previous night in the company of one of the American couples.

'We could masturbate him, madam,' said a small voice from the back.

Madam Stone grinned. 'You mean to say we could give him a nice wank? No, I think Mike deserves more than that. What do you think, Lisa?'

She looked directly at Lisa, her eyes wide and taunting. Her meaning was clear. Lisa stood up and removed her jacket, then unbuttoned the front of her blouse. She quickly shook the garment from her shoulders to reveal her massive breasts and hard, erect nipples. She smiled proudly at the gasps of admiration from the group. She then unbuttoned the top of her trousers and eased the zip down, at the same time kicking off her shoes. She let the slacks fall to the floor and she was naked, save for a pair of black, hold-up stockings.

Determined to practise what she had learnt recently, she walked slowly around Mike and stared into his eyes. He looked down at her heaving breasts. 'God, I love your tits,' he whispered under his breath. She grinned and took hold of one of them and raised the nipple to his mouth. He sucked it greedily and took hold of her other heavy mound and gripped it tightly in his large hand. His other hand went to touch her bald pussy but she pushed it away and moved from him. She turned her back to him and faced the class, then moved backwards until she felt the bulge of his leather-covered crotch pressing against her bottom. He gripped her by the waist and forced himself even harder against her. She heard his heavy breathing and could feel the stiffness of his erection between her buttocks. Her pussy throbbed, and she could feel the lips opening in anticipation of the joys to come.

She took hold of his wrists and pulled his hands from her waist and then moved from him again. She turned her back to the class and looked at him mockingly. His cock was jutting forward and was pushing the leather pouch clear of his groin. She could see his hairy balls and a good few inches of his erection. 'Christ, Lisa,' he hissed through clenched teeth, 'I want you.'

'You'll have to wait,' she replied as she moved to stand behind him.

'I'm gonna come.'

'Don't you dare,' she growled. 'You're not going to deny the girls a good show.'

'Then let me fuck you! What's the matter with you?'

'All in good time.' She held on to his shoulders from behind and licked his back wetly. He shuddered. She pressed herself against him so that he could feel the wetness between her legs against his firm buttocks. She slipped her hands down and circled his waist, then caressed his groin lightly, taking care not to touch his ragingly hard erection. The entire class sat in total silence, scarcely daring to breathe. Lisa ran her tongue slowly down his backbone until she was crouching behind him with her face less than an inch from his bottom. She gripped the strands of leather that circled his waist and gradually eased the pouch down until his cock sprang free from its constraint and slapped against his belly. A chorus of girlish cheers echoed around the room.

She kissed each of his taut buttocks in turn, then ran her tongue over them to trace their shape. At the same time, she ran her hands up and down his strong thighs. Occasionally, she would allow her hand to lightly touch his heavy sac, then quickly move it away, teasing him mercilessly.

She noticed Madam Stone watching her every move closely. She was desperate to take him inside her, but she knew that she had something to prove, to show her tutor that she had learnt well. She stopped caressing Mike's thigh with one of her hands and pressed her own soaking pussy against it. She wet her fingers with her copious juices and put one to his anus, then eased it in gently. Mike groaned. She removed her finger and licked him between his buttocks. She savoured his scent and the taste of her own arousal.

'She's licking his bottom!' she heard a voice say.

'I wouldn't mind some of that,' someone else said. Lisa

185

made much of her actions in response, and rasped her tongue firmly up and down the hairy cleft.

'Oh, God, Lisa, you're gonna make me come, for pity's sake.'

She realised that she had teased him enough. She stood up and walked round to face him. She wiped her mouth on the back of her hand suggestively. He gazed at her, his eyes filled with overpowering lust. She looked down at his fierce erection. She wanted to engulf the monster in her mouth, but knew that he would stand no chance if she did. Instead, she walked over to where Sammy-Lynn was sitting and leant her elbows on her desk with her legs spread apart and her back arched so that her bottom was presented to Mike. Her breasts rested heavily on the coolness of the desk. She looked at him over her shoulder. 'Fuck me,' she breathed.

Mike moved over to her quickly, as though he was afraid that she might change her mind. Lisa turned her head to look directly into Sammy-Lynn's eyes as she waited for the inevitable. To her surprise, instead of the expected sensation of his cock touching her engorged pussy-lips she felt his tongue drawing wetly over her own bottom. Now he was teasing her! She couldn't believe it; he'd looked as though his cock was about to burst!

'Can you see what he's doing?' she whispered to Sammy-Lynn. The pretty little student nodded.

'He's licking your bum,' she said. She leant forward and whispered into Lisa's ear. 'I'd like to do that to you,' she said.

'You will, my darling. We'll have lots of fun together, I promise.' She felt Mike's tongue licking at the top of her cleft, then he eased it slowly down. He slipped it wetly over her anus and then began to lap against her soaked cunt. Then he moved away from her. She closed her eyes. 'For God's sake,' she said to herself, 'don't tease me any more.'

Her silent prayer was answered almost immediately. She felt the plum-shaped end of his cock slip easily into her oiled sheath. She groaned as the thickness of his long rod filled her completely and he held himself still for a moment with his groin pressed hard against her bottom. She could feel him throbbing inside her. He was clearly having trouble holding back.

She opened her eyes and gazed at Sammy-Lynn. The young girl moved her face closer and their lips met. Lisa pushed her tongue forward between Sammy-Lynn's pouting lips and wrapped her arms around her neck. They kissed passionately as Mike began to move in and out of Lisa's hot pussy. Lisa knew that she would come quickly; she was almost there already. She felt Sammy-Lynn circling her tongue around hers just as Mike started to pound furiously against her. She was so aroused that she could barely feel his big cock inside her. She tensed her upper thigh muscles and he fucked her even more rapidly. The sound of his groin slapping against her bottom filled her ears. She was coming, she was coming now, and it was going to be a good one. She felt the nerve-endings between her legs tingling and the build-up became unstoppable.

She heard Mike groan loudly and knew that, for the second time that day, her hot little pussy was being filled with a man's delicious cream. She stiffened her muscles and gripped his plunging rod tightly and held it deep inside her body. She could feel him throbbing as the sperm gushed from him. Suddenly, the sensation of final release tore at her loins, causing her to gasp into Sammy-Lynn's sucking mouth. Mike reached under her and rubbed her hard bud rapidly as her climax ripped through her lower body. She couldn't stand it any more.

She pushed his hand away and he eased his still substantial length from inside her. He leant his body against her, and she could feel the wetness of his wilting prick between her buttocks. She kissed Sammy-Lynn lightly on the lips. 'You wait until it's your turn,' she breathed.

'I want you to be there,' replied the bright-eyed virgin.

'I will be, I promise.'

* * *

187

After a few minutes Lisa was dressed and sitting on her chair as if nothing had happened. The atmosphere in the room, however, was electric. She noticed Serita looking at her coldly. She was obviously envious, no doubt wishing that she'd had the courage to perform before the entire class. The girl had learnt a salutary lesson already.

Sammy-Lynn was also gazing at her, but hers was a look of sheer desire. Lisa glanced under her desk. Her legs were wide open this time, and she was gently fingering herself through her tiny, white panties. The flimsy cotton was almost transparent with her wetness and the shape of her engorged sex-lips was clearly visible. Lisa looked around the room at the sea of flushed, excited faces. All eyes seemed to be fixed on her. She took a deep breath. Instead of detecting the musty aroma of old books, she was sure that the library was filled with the scent of sex. She tried to imagine the sight of more than twenty wet, excited pussies, and revelled in the knowledge that their arousal was down to her. And Mike, of course.

Her handsome lover had left the room, his duty done. Madam Stone sat in silence for some time, as if to allow the students to dwell on what they had just witnessed. Presently, however, she rose to her feet.

'Ladies,' she began, 'already you have learnt two important lessons. One, that the joy of having sex can be doubly pleasurable if witnessed by others and two, that the total lack of inhibitions can lead to the most delightful excesses. You saw Sammy-Lynn kiss Lisa passionately. I am certain that she wouldn't have dreamt of doing that before but, the fact that Lisa was, at the same time, being well and truly fucked made it seem the most natural thing to do.

'Mr Gee said that there are few rules here. There is one, however, that you must obey from now on. You must surrender yourself to your innermost desires and indulge in your every sexual fantasy. You must also share in the fantasies of others, and learn to experiment. As the old saying goes, you don't know if you like something until you've tried it.

'Never lock the doors to your rooms, especially when you are having sex. You will come to no harm, I promise, and you may occasionally get a nice surprise. It is a lovely feeling to be kneeling on a bed, sucking a lover's hard cock and suddenly finding yourself impaled from behind by someone you've never met before!'

The class erupted into laughter at this. Lisa looked across at Janet and grinned. They both knew from experience that this was something that was more than likely to happen.

Madam Stone held up her hands for silence. 'After lunch you will split up into four groups for your first lessons. Lisa and Janet here will each take a group. You have already met another of our tutors, Mike. He will take the third group and Paul, who I know you ladies will find equally attractive, will take the fourth.

'Before lunch, however, there is the matter of our three virgins. The loss of virginity is an extremely poignant event in a person's life so, for this time only, you will be allowed privacy if you so choose. In a moment I will summon a number of male staff. You may select the one you wish to relieve you of the burden of innocence and take him to your room. Now, I want the three of you to come to the front of the class.'

Lisa watched as the three students moved to stand next to their instructress. Sammy-Lynn stood confidently, with a broad grin on her face. The other two girls seemed more nervous. One of them, a chubby but attractive girl with short, brown hair and remarkably large breasts looked positively terrified. The other, a tall and willowy Asian girl simply stared into space.

Madam Stone moved to face them. 'Another rule of Grantham Manor is that nobody will be forced to do anything that they do not wish to.' She rested her hand on the tall girl's shoulder. 'Do you wish to lose your virginity?'

'Yes, madam,' the girl replied in a hushed voice.

Madam Stone stepped to one side. 'Tell the class,' she said. 'Tell them what you want to happen to you.'

The girl gulped visibly, then took a deep breath. 'I want to lose my virginity,' she said in a trembling voice. Madam Stone looked directly at her, the expression on her face indicating that she wanted to hear more. 'I want to be fucked, madam,' said the girl suddenly, blurting the words out.

'Excellent! You are learning quickly. And you?' She touched the chubby girl on the shoulder.

'I want to be fucked as well, madam,' she said, quickly. Her face was ashen, and Lisa formed the impression that she might faint at any moment.

'Are you sure?' said Madam stone tenderly.

'Oh, yes, madam. I'm nearly eighteen. It's about time!'

The class laughed loudly, but it was clear from the expression on the girl's face that she had meant every word. Madam Stone moved to stand beside Sammy-Lynn. 'And what about you,' she said as she stroked the lovely student's flawless cheek. 'Are you ready to give yourself to a man?'

'Oh, yes, madam,' said Sammy-Lynn excitedly. 'I want to be fucked and fucked and fucked!' She hugged herself tightly as she said the words, clearly revelling in their sound. Even Madam Stone laughed at her display of obvious enthusiasm. She picked up the bell again and rang it. All eyes turned to the door as the class fell into silence. After what must have seemed like an age to the three girls the door opened and six male staff members entered. They marched over to stand in a line before the virgin students. Each was very different, but all were handsome in their own way. They wore nothing apart from a pair of skin-tight, lycra shorts which did little to conceal the impressive shapes of their genitals. Lisa smiled to herself as she watched the young girls looking from one to the other as though they were selecting dresses in a clothes shop.

'You choose first,' said Madam Stone to the chubby girl. 'Touch the one you want.' The girl reached out and nervously touched the bare chest of the man standing directly in front of her. The man took hold of her hand

and immediately led her from the room. As she went through the door she turned to look back with a terrified expression at her colleagues, then shrugged her shoulders and was gone.

'Now, you.' It was the Asian girl's turn to choose. She took her time, moving slowly along the line and looking carefully into each handsome face. Then she walked back, this time blatantly examining the fronts of their shorts and beginning to smile. Finally, she stopped in front of one of the men and stared at his crotch. Lisa could see the attraction. He was a tall, muscular black man with a superbly defined erection that was threatening to burst through the thin lycra.

The student touched his massive chest and he took her hand in his. She turned to look at Madam Stone and mouthed the words 'thank you', then followed her prospective lover out of the room.

Now it was time for Sammy-Lynn to decide. As she stood in front of the four remaining men Lisa could see from their faces that they all desperately wanted to be chosen. She looked so tiny beside them, so vulnerable, and so beautiful. She looked from one to the other, clearly having great difficulty in making her selection.

'Hurry, Sammy-Lynn,' said Madam Stone. 'I wish to continue the class.'

'I have made my choice, madam.' Sammy-Lynn reached out and quickly touched the chests of all four men in turn. There were gasps from the other students as she turned to face Madam Stone. 'That is my choice,' she said, proudly, 'and I want Lisa to be there as well.'

Lisa looked across at Madam Stone, who nodded. Gleefully, Sammy-Lynn took the arms of two of the men and walked towards the door. Lisa and the other men followed, to rapturous applause from the rest of the class.

As Lisa followed Sammy-Lynn and the four, near-naked studs into the young girl's bedroom she realised that she would have to take control of the situation. After all, she was supposed to be the instructress.

The room was larger than the one she shared with Janet, and even more opulently furnished. It was dominated by a huge, circular bed, strewn with expensive cushions. Above the bed, angled to give the occupants a perfect view, was a giant mirror. Other wall mirrors had been strategically placed around the room for the same purpose. Sleeping would be the last thing a girl would do in a bed like this.

Sammy-Lynn stood in the centre of the room, close to the foot of the bed. Lisa noticed that for the first time she was looking a little apprehensive. Perhaps she was beginning to regret choosing four men to initiate her into the joys of sexual fulfilment. Each of them looked to be quite capable of satisfying any woman on his own. She stood with her hands clasped in front of her and her head bowed slightly to one side. Her eyes were nervously fixed on Lisa's.

Lisa walked over to her and slipped her arms around her waist. She kissed her lightly on the forehead. 'You are going to learn much in the next couple of hours, my sweet virgin,' she breathed.

The small girl gulped visibly, then forced a brave smile. 'Two hours? I thought – '

'That it would be all over in a matter of minutes? Even with one man, sex should last much, much longer than a few moments if a woman is to achieve complete satisfaction. And there is more to sex than merely fucking. The delights of arousal are just as important and enjoyable, if not more so.' She turned to look at the men. They were lined up like slaves in a medieval marketplace with their manly attributes displayed obscenely within the confines of their skin-tight shorts.

'Take those off,' she commanded, indicating the shorts with a brisk wave of her arm. The men obeyed immediately. Now they stood before the two excited girls naked. Lisa surveyed the row of bronzed, athletically built young men and licked her lips hungrily. Sammy-Lynn had chosen well, she thought to herself. Each of them sported a firm, rampant erection capable of pleasing the most discerning of women. She looked down at Sammy-Lynn. The young girl was staring, wide eyed, at the erotic display.

'Perhaps I should have only chosen one of them,' she said, her voice trembling.

'It's too late now,' whispered Lisa as she ran her hand lovingly through her student's long, black hair. 'You cannot tease a man to such a state of arousal and then let him down. That would be unforgiveable.'

'Will you do it with them as well?'

'Of course,' answered Lisa, 'but first, let me prepare you.'

Without waiting for permission, Lisa removed Sammy-Lynn's blazer. Then she unfastened the striped tie and slipped it from around her neck before letting it drop to the floor. She glanced at the men. Two of them were gently caressing their hard cocks as they watched. She was going to give them a show that they would never forget. She couldn't help but wonder if they would manage to hold back.

Sammy-Lynn stood impassively as Lisa slowly unbut-toned her crisp, white blouse and revealed the naked, olive-toned skin beneath. Unfastening the sleeves, she slipped the shirt from the girl's shoulders and gazed at her small, firm breasts and the buttons of her dark nipples. Lisa bent her head and took one of the nipples between her teeth and nipped it lightly. Sammy-Lynn gasped. Lisa did the same to the other, then drew most of the small breast into her mouth whilst circling the warm flesh with her wet tongue. Her pupil groaned with pleasure.

Still sucking her nipple, Lisa unhooked the short skirt and pushed it over Sammy-Lynn's narrow hips until it drifted down to the floor. She moved back and watched as the virgin stepped out of the skirt and kicked it to one side. Now, all she wore were black stockings and a sus-pender belt, small, flat shoes and a tiny pair of white panties which were still visibly soaked at the front. She stood in silence, compliantly awaiting her tutor's next move.

193

Lisa turned to the men. 'You,' she ordered as she pointed to one of them, 'take off her panties.' The man stepped forward immediately and crouched in front of Sammy-Lynn, his cock stretching enormously from his hairy groin. He hooked his thumbs under her panties and eased them slowly down to her ankles. Lisa saw him lick his lips as he gazed at her exposed crotch. He moved his head forward.

'Enough!' she barked. The man moved away quickly and resumed his place in line. Now it was Lisa's turn to reveal her charms. She removed her jacket and carefully folded it before placing it on a nearby chair. Then she took off her shirt and smiled as the men gasped in unison at the sight of her bared breasts.

'Oh, they are so beautiful,' breathed Sammy-Lynn. Lisa grinned proudly as she unzipped her trousers. She took them off quickly with her stockings and put them neatly on the chair with her jacket. There were no panties, of course. She was now as naked as the others, and equally aroused.

She took hold of Sammy-Lynn's hand and coaxed her to lie in the centre of the huge bed. She lay next to her and gently smoothed her hand over the waif-like form of her pupil, all the time gazing with genuine fondness into her watery, almond eyes. She bent her head and kissed her on the cheek, then put her lips to the tiny mouth. Sammy-Lynn responded immediately. She wrapped her arms around Lisa's body and pressed herself firmly against her as their tongues circled each other. She mewed softly as Lisa's probing fingers found the luscious wetness of her virgin pussy. She was soaking, and her juices were flowing from her to dampen the satin sheet beneath her writhing body. Lisa reluctantly resisted the temptation to worm her fingers deep inside the succulence of Sammy-Lynn's hot cunt; her virginity had to be taken by a nice, stiff cock. Instead, she moved herself downwards until her face was inches from the engorged sex-lips and her bottom was presented to the eager gaze of the four young men. She kissed the tops of Sammy-Lynn's thighs over and over

194

again whilst savouring the delicate scent of her arousal. The young girl was trembling, not with fear but with sheer lust.

Lisa moved her mouth closer to the glistening flesh. She blew gently, knowing the effect her hot breath would have. Sammy-Lynn moaned and opened her legs wide. 'Lick me, please lick me,' she pleased. Lisa put her forefinger to her mouth and wet it with her saliva, then traced the line of Sammy-Lynn's small opening. She blew again gently. 'Please, please,' begged her charge, opening her legs even wider.

Lisa moved her face forward and pushed out her tongue until the tip touched the fleshy sex-lips. Sammy-Lynn gasped loudly. Lisa circled her hot little pussy with her wet tongue, then drew the tip slowly up between the lips and traced the line of her opening until she touched the hard bud of her clitoris. Sammy-Lynn groaned as Lisa lapped the stiff little button. 'Oh, God,' she moaned, 'I love it, I love it!'

She gripped the hair on Lisa's head and pushed her face harder against her suppliant mound. Her juices soaked Lisa's face as she all but devoured the succulent puffy flesh. Her taste was exquisite. Lisa pushed her tongue deep inside her and touched the barrier of her virginity. She was nearly ready.

She licked her hard clitoris again, this time allowing the tip of her tongue to flutter over it rapidly. Suddenly, without warning her pupil came with a loud squeal of delight. She raised her bottom from the bed and pressed her pussy hard against Lisa's jaw as the orgasm took hold of her. Lisa licked and sucked her cunt expertly, knowing exactly how to draw every emotion, every sensation from her release. Sammy-Lynn gasped over and over again as wave after wave of pleasure tore through her thrusting crotch until, at last, her movements subsided and she fell back on the bed exhausted.

Lisa moved from the prone figure and stood by the side of the big bed. She wiped her mouth on the back of her hand. Sammy-Lynn simply gazed at her as she lay there with her legs still widely splayed. Her pussy-lips were parted in blatant invitation. She was ready.

Lisa turned to face the line of handsome men. Their erections were uniformly fierce, the gnarled flesh purple with lust. She moved over to stand before the first. He was a blond-haired man with Nordic features, and little more than Sammy-Lynn's age. He was also the best endowed of the group. Lisa took hold of his long, thick erection and led him to the bed. Sammy-Lynn looked nervously at his cock.

Still gripping his thickness tightly by the root, Lisa made him kneel between Sammy-Lynn's legs and guided the heavily veined shaft to its target. The wet sex-lips opened involuntarily like a tiny mouth. The time for teasing was past. Sammy-Lynn needed to be fucked.

Lisa put her free hand on the young man's firm bottom and pushed him forwards. She watched enviously as the huge, bulbous head of his cock parted the soft, virgin flesh. Sammy-Lynn suddenly jerked her body and gave out a little cry of pain. Her virginity was gone. Lisa bent over and kissed her pupil on the mouth, then released her grip of the thick stalk. She watched in fascination as the young man eased more of his length inside her, then withdrew until just the head was held within her tight grasp. He moved slowly forward again, this time sliding over six inches of hard cock into her succulent sheath, then eased back once more. Lisa looked at his face. He was grimacing, clearly having trouble holding back. He moved his hips forward again and eased the full length of his big cock into Sammy-Lynn's welcoming warmth. The young girl groaned with pleasure.

'Oh, shit!' the man hissed between clenched teeth. He pulled himself quickly from inside her and gripped his cock tightly, but it was too late for him. A spray of warm, creamy fluid jetted from the angry knob to soak Sammy-Lynn's body. The young man rubbed himself furiously as more and more semen streaked across her flawless, olive skin. Lisa ran her hands over Sammy-Lynn's breasts and stomach to massage the oily substance into her flesh.

Clearly, Sammy-Lynn had been right to choose more than one lover.

The young man who had been lucky enough to take her virginity moved reluctantly away to resume his place in the line. The expression on his face was a picture of self-annoyance. Lisa glared at him. 'You will be punished,' she said, tersely. Her words seemed to have the right effect. Although his head was bowed in shame, he was now grinning broadly.

She signalled to the next man to come forward. He was on the bed in an instant, and immediately plunged his stuff rod deep into Sammy-Lynn's pussy. She groaned with joy and wrapped her arms and legs around his rutting body. He plunged in and out of her rapidly, fucking her for all he was worth. 'Oh yes, oh yes!' she cried as her fingernails scraped the flesh of his buttocks, 'this is what it's all about!' His hips became a blur as he shagged her mercilessly and drove her small body across the bed until her head pressed into the pillows. Lisa saw her bite into his shoulder fiercely, then look up at the ceiling. 'Oh, God,' Sammy-Lynn wailed, 'look at that!'

Lisa looked up at the mirror to enjoy the reflected sight of the young man's bottom bouncing up and down on the barely visible form of her young charge. His groin slapped noisily against her thighs as he hammered in and out of her, clearly determined to make her come. He wasn't to be disappointed. With a loud yell, Sammy-Lynn threw back her head, then shook it from side to side as the tremors of release once again took hold of her senses. Her lover groaned and rammed his cock fully into her and clenched his buttocks tightly. He held himself still and gasped rhythmically, which told Lisa that he was filling Sammy-Lynn's cunt with his hot cream. 'I can feel it throbbing! I can feel it throbbing inside me!' she shouted happily. Her lover began moving again, albeit with less urgency, until he was done. He slipped from inside her and staggered from the bed to join his colleagues.

Lisa nodded to the remaining two men. They moved to the bed and Lisa made one of them lie on his back. She gripped his cock and then bent over him and put it into her mouth. She felt it throb between her sucking lips and tasted his saltiness.

Moving quickly from him in case her expert mouth should take him over the edge, she held his erection upright and motioned for Sammy-Lynn to squat across his groin. Her student lowered her body and greedily absorbed the thick stalk inside her ravaged pussy. Lisa had no need to tell the other man what to do. He moved to kneel with his hard rod inches from Sammy-Lynn's face. She reached up and took hold of it, her tiny hand barely circling his girth, then put it to her mouth. She sucked him cautiously at first then, having got the taste for it, took as much in her mouth as she could manage. At the same time, she moved her bottom up and down, fucking herself on her supine lover.

Lisa moved behind them and kissed her pupil's bottom. She watched for a moment, and thrilled to the sight of Sammy-Lynn's obscenely stretched sex-lips as they absorbed and reabsorbed the thick length, then bent forward and licked her anus. This was enough to give Sammy-Lynn her third orgasm. She pumped her body wildly up and down and knocked Lisa away from her with her near-manic thrusts. Her muffled cry of delight was masked by the groan of the other man as he filled her sucking mouth with his seed. Lisa moved quickly and made sure that Sammy-Lynn swallowed it all.

Sammy-Lynn fell forward on to her prone lover's body just as he came. His creamy fluid jetted from his throbbing cock and soaked her round little bottom as she rubbed her pussy against his hairy stomach. Once again, Lisa massaged the warm juice into her skin and thrilled to the touch of her firm buttocks.

At last the lovers fell apart and Lisa gazed down benignly at the exhausted student. 'And that, Sammy-Lynn,' she said, grandly, 'is the end of your first lesson.'

BOUND TO SUBMIT

Amanda Ware

Amanda Ware is a genuine miscreant, a writer with extensive personal knowledge of what it means to be a true submissive. In her hugely popular trilogy she leads the heroine, Caroline, through a succession of kinky trials during which she must surrender her will to a series of sophisticated masters. The first, *Bound to Obey*, set the standard by which all other studies of sluttish submission must be judged. In *Bound to Serve*, the sequel, Caroline is tricked into serving the cruel and manipulative Clive, who gives her to his former mistress for some harsh treatment. By the beginning of *Bound to Submit*, she has a new master, whom she marries in a bizarre ceremony of fetishism and depravity. The cruel Clive is never far away, however, and she finds it ever more difficult to resist his mesmeric influence.

The following extract is taken from *Bound to Submit*, the third book in the trilogy. At Caroline's wedding, she has been introduced to a photographer and a film-maker who want to use her as a model for images of bondage and submission. Both she and her new husband are excited by the idea, and she agrees. In this extract she finally discovers that the backer for the film is a dark figure from her past – can she hope to resist his advances?

Caroline felt fingers again working at the back of her head. She assumed the cameraman had arrived as the loosening of the hood had enabled her to hear muted sounds, enough to tell her that there were now two people in the room. She had been unable to hear what was being said and was very surprised that the hood was being removed. Perhaps they would replace it with a blindfold so that she could not identify the cameraman. She hoped that, whatever happened, those wonderfully strong fingers she had felt would continue their exploration of her breasts and clitoris. The hood fell free of her face and she was again able to see and hear. Should she turn around or would they rather she waited to be told what she must do?

'Caroline, you are lovelier than ever,' said a voice she thought she recognised, but she dismissed the idea as impossible. Her hands were still tied, but she pulled experimentally at the bindings, which held firm. Clive smiled at the small movement.

'Have you missed me, my dear?'

The question made her freeze. There could be no doubting the identity of the owner of that voice. The hint of a Scottish burr; the seductive tones that reminded her of this man's ability to control and dominate. She tried to twist around on the bed, but he moved further behind her.

'Lee?' she ventured, her voice rising in panic.

'Mr Esslyn had to leave us. He's gone to prepare the

contract that he wants me to sign. Caroline, I am the financial backer you've been told about. My darling, I am your new boss!'

Finding a measure of bravado in the fact that she could not see Clive's eyes, Caroline forced herself to remain calm.

'Clive, if you don't leave this room immediately, I am going to scream for help . . .'

'To whom, my dear?' Clive asked, moving in front of her and smiling at her swiftly lowered eyes. Gripping her chin, he forced her head up until she was looking at him. 'I repeat, to whom?'

'To Lee,' Caroline faltered, trembling as she felt the full force of that powerful gaze. 'Lee doesn't know about you, but I'll tell him . . .'

'Do you think Mr Esslyn is going to be interested in what you have to say? Without my financial backing, he won't be able to do his film. I think you'll find your pleas for help will fall on deaf ears,' Clive said, sitting beside her and again sliding his finger into her moistness.

'James . . .'

'James will only want to hear about how you asked Lee to contact me and ask me to come here,' Clive continued smoothly, rubbing his finger across her swollen clitoris. 'Mr Esslyn will say whatever I tell him to say.'

Caroline could only stare at him as the full force of the threat sank in. She knew Clive and he would not speak like this without the surety of the truth of what he was saying. She wished he would stop stroking her clitoris in such a way: it prevented her from thinking straight. Clive had lost none of his power to control and arouse her. She tried to fight against her own helplessness, but knew it to be a pointless battle. Clive extracted his finger and traced it around her lips smilingly, pushing it into her mouth and nodding his approval as she sucked on the intruder.

'That's my girl. I knew you'd see sense. Mr Esslyn says that I may audition you tonight.'

Clive got off the bed and Caroline struggled to stop herself from begging him to come back and touch her clitoris, to satisfy the huge craving within her. In any case, Clive returned quickly, holding something in his hands. Caroline could not prevent her eyes from roaming over his black-clad body. As always, he was impeccably dressed, the thin material of his sweater doing little to conceal the muscled hardness of his body.

'Before we start, I had better make sure that you are properly gagged and restrained. I don't want your screams irritating Mr Esslyn's tender conscience; besides which, I remember how well you like to be tied. Don't you remember, my darling?'

Caroline could only stare at him. She felt frightened, but in a way that only exacerbated the sexual feelings she had always had for this man. She wanted to open her mouth and scream for Lee to come, needing help to resist this man who had once more entered her life and again was taking control. Clive smiled as he watched her inner struggles.

'Can't do it, can you, Caroline?' he asked, as though reading her mind. 'We always had something good together and we will again.' As he spoke, Clive unfolded a wide piece of transparent plastic material. Moving behind her, he placed the plastic over her mouth and tied it firmly, before returning to kneel on the bed in front of her and bringing the ends forward, fastening them beneath her chin. Caroline was puzzled as there was quite a lot of the plastic lying in loose folds across her mouth. Surely she could easily scream through such a loose gag?

Spotting her baffled expression, Clive chuckled. 'Go ahead and try it, my darling. Open that lovely mouth and scream for your director.'

Caroline looked at him uncertainly, wondering what he was up to. Clive reached for both her nipples and twisted them. 'I said scream, my darling!'

As the pain hit her, Caroline opened her mouth to scream, only to find that she sucked in the plastic material which very effective muted her attempt to cry out, reducing it to nothing more than a murmur. The squeezing of her nipples became a caressing motion and the only sounds she was capable of making were moans of pleasure. Clive pushed her back until she was lying on her tethered wrists. Bending his head, he began to lick and suck at her clitoris until she was writhing with sexual excitement. Her ineffectual strugglings with her bound wrists were only adding to her arousal and it was not long before Clive tasted the increase in her juices which told of her satisfaction.

Lips wetly gleaming, Clive smiled as he raised his head and looked at her.

'The first of many, my darling. Now I think I will really tie you up before I begin your punishment.' His smile grew broader as her eyes widened. 'You didn't think I would let you get away with it, did you, darling? Running off and leaving me was not a very nice thing to do, you know, and for that you must be punished. I intend to make it a punishment you will always remember!'

Caroline was quivering with anticipation as Clive untied her wrists. She was unsure as to her feelings. The man she had never expected to see again was back and he seemed just as capable as he ever had been of controlling her emotionally and physically. She had tried to block out her memories of the time before she had met James, but one look from Clive's darkly fascinating eyes and she seemed to be lost. Everything that had happened between her and Clive seemed as if it had only occurred yesterday. She remembered how she had lived in his house and how she had done everything he asked of her. Now she was married to the man she loved, yet here she was obediently waiting for her previous Master's instructions. She still wanted Clive – as she always had. When he was with her, he had the power to make her to do whatever he wished. The prospect of her punishment at his hands merely made her feel aroused in the way she remembered so well. It was as though she had no choice, although she knew that was not really the case. If the door was opened and she was offered her freedom right now, she knew that she would stay. It was not disloyalty to James; it was something she could not and would not attempt to explain.

Still gagged, Caroline remained immobile with her back to Clive. She knew that he would tell her of his requirements when he was ready. Idly, she wondered about Lee. Had he planned this? She shuddered as she felt a movement; Clive had come to sit on the bed beside her. He stroked her shoulders and, had she been able, she would have begged him to fondle her breasts, those small, beautifully shaped breasts with the large nipples he liked so much. As if aware of her needs, his hands slipped along her arms and down to her waist, then gently stroked and smoothed her tanned thighs.

'California agrees with you, my darling,' he whispered. 'You are truly adorable.' There was a light chuckle as he continued to stroke her inner thighs, so desperately close to her swollen bud. 'You didn't really think that you had got away from me, did you? Surely you knew that I would come after you, my darling. We have unfinished business and you know I don't like to be in that position.'

His stroking fingers moved up to circle her breasts and she pushed them out for his caress. Chuckling again, he bent his head and sucked gently at both nipples. 'Oh, Caroline, I can read you like a book,' he continued, raising his head and looking at her intently. 'I want you to understand, my dear, that you are mine. You have been – shall we say – loaned out, and now I want you back.' Bending his head, he bit her shoulder, making her suck in her breath with surprise. Clive laughed as he saw that she had also sucked in folds of the plastic that covered her mouth. Smiling, he ran a finger across the top of the gag. 'Yes, I thought this would keep you quiet. You see, my dear, I have been planning this for some time. I am not telling you everything yet; it is too soon, but I will tell you that you are coming back to England. I have offered Lee the use of my newly acquired studios in Hertfordshire and, when filming has been completed, you are going to say goodbye to James and you are going to come back to live with me.'

Caroline's eyes opened wide and she moaned a protest. Ignoring her reaction, Clive retrieved the roll of thick black masking tape he had brought into the room. Seeing her look, he kissed the area that he had so recently bitten. 'I told you, my dear, that I have been planning this. Do you remember the last time I put this sort of tape on you?' Vigorously, Caroline shook her head. 'Oh, but I think you do, my darling. I taped your eyes and your mouth and your struggling limbs because I wanted to make you permanently mine. I'm sure you remember how Liam rescued you, don't you? And then I had to go to all those devious lengths to get you back. Surely you remember that?

Clive peeled off a piece of tape and cut it neatly to the required length. Silently, he taped the strip over the top of the gag, sealing it even more firmly in place. 'Now, I tell you what, my darling. I am going to get the implement with which I intend to punish you.' Firmly gripping her plastic-covered chin, Clive stared into her eyes. 'I am going to hurt you, Caroline, and it is no more than you deserve for running out on me. I am not going to tie you before I leave, although you may rest assured that on my return you will be very securely bound. I have put the tape on your gag, because I know that it cannot be removed without temporarily leaving a mark.

'Now listen to me very carefully, Caroline. On my return I am going to punish you as you deserve, but in the meantime, I am going to trust you. The door will not be locked and you will not be tied, so you have the choice before I return to take off your gag and run away. There is a robe that you can wear hanging in the wardrobe. If you stay, it will be an acknowledgement that you deserve your punishment and that you are willing to accept it. It will also be an acknowledgement that I am your Master and that you are my slave. You will be accepting that your return to England will be permanent.'

Releasing her chin, he bent his head and sucked at her nipples, slipping his fingers inside her warm moistness. Almost involuntarily, she arched her body towards him,

208

urging him to go on. She moaned with disappointment as he removed his fingers and raised his head.

'I am going to leave you now and I expect total obedience,' Clive said, his eyes boring into hers. 'You will not attempt to remove your gag and you will not attempt to leave.' He sucked his fingers, tasting her, and rose from the bed. 'After the punishment, if you have been a very good girl, I will · fuck you.' Smiling as if he had just bestowed a treasured gift, Clive walked to the door. He turned and remarked pleasantly, 'Oh, I almost forgot, Mrs Davies sends her love.'

Having delivered his parting shot, Clive went in search of Lee. He found the young director in his black and white study. The furniture was all in white leather, while the walls were panelled in shining black leather. As he entered, Clive could not withhold an admiring whistle. Lee looked up from the papers on his desk and looked grudgingly at the visitor. He did not like Clive but he could not ignore him, either. Clive prowled around the room like a slinky black panther, every movement a testament to subtle but undoubted power.

'Where's Caroline?' Lee asked as Clive draped himself across the white leather sofa with an elegant economy of movement that had to be admired.

Clive smiled as he extracted a long cigarette from a black monogrammed case. 'The lovely Caroline is at this moment fighting a mental battle that only I can win,' he said, lighting his cigarette with an elegant movement.

Lee frowned and rose to get himself a drink from the well stocked corner bar. As he filled his glass with a ruby red liquid, he tried to assert a little authority. 'I hope she is all right and that she will remain so,' he began, turning to survey his languid guest.

'What is your interest?' Clive asked in brittle tones.

'She is soon to be the star of my next picture. Obviously, that makes her very important to me, and . . .'

'And you fancy her,' Clive remarked baldly.

'I . . . well, yes, I like her, but even if I did fancy her, as you put it, ours is a purely business relationship.'

Very carefully, Clive stubbed out his cigarette in a black marble ashtray before moving to stand beside Lee. He put his hand on the younger's man's shoulder, not threateningly, but in an assertion of his control. 'I like you, Lee, and so I will be perfectly straight with you. Caroline used to belong to me and now I want her back. I am perfectly prepared to allow her to do your film, but after that she will return to my complete and absolute control.'

Lee looked at his backer, startled. He needed this man and his money and he was prepared to go along with Clive's duplicitous treatment of others, but there were limits. 'Clive, I will agree to your terms regarding the contract and I will go along with whatever you may want me to say to James, but kidnapping . . .'

Quite suddenly, Clive bent forward and gently kissed Lee on the lips. Raising his head, he looked the director in the eyes. 'My dear Lee, whoever said anything about kidnapping? Caroline will come to me of her own free will. At this very moment, she is sitting in an unlocked room with the knowledge that she is free to leave. Shortly, we will join her and you will see that, although she is untied, she will have made no attempt to remove her gag. She awaits me in the full knowledge that I am going to punish her, yet still she will not attempt to leave.'

Clive's kiss had taken Lee completely by surprise. He was shaken by it and unsure of how to deal with the mixed emotions that were surging through him. Before now, he had never had the least homosexual urging, and yet as he looked at Clive, he could appreciate the man's magnetism. He realised he had no doubt as to the veracity of Clive's words. Breaking away in a desperate attempt to regain his normally cool attitutde, Lee walked to the window.

'I don't want her marked. She appears naked in the film and it would not be suitable for continuity purposes if she had whip marks . . .'

'My dear Lee, who said anything about a whip?' Clive said, again settling himself on the sofa. 'Expertly applied, the cane is a much fiercer implement, but the marks will have faded prior to the commencement of filming.'

'What about James? What will he say when he sees her?'

'You will just have to confess that the tests involved a little punishment. He will understand that,' Clive assured him.

'What about Caroline? She will tell . . .'

'She will tell him nothing other than that which I order her to say,' Clive said, rising from the sofa and walking over to Lee. 'I can see that you still have doubts about the efficacy of my control. Do you have the financial contract?'

Flustered at Clive's closeness, Lee moved quickly to his desk and picked up the document. Silently, he handed it to Clive and watched as the other man quickly perused its contents. Without a word, Clive sat at the desk and signed and initialled the contract before returning it to Lee.

'Now we are partners in this endeavour, which I am sure will be very successful. Why don't we go and see our star?' Clive asked. As he spoke, Lee noticed that he held in his hands a thin willow cane. 'I've been wanting to test out this little item for some time. I selected it with Caroline in mind and I would be very pleased if you were present to witness her punishment. You will be able to see for yourself how very easily I can control her.'

Lee followed Clive to the door. His heart was beating unnaturally fast as he contemplated Clive's words and the punishment the man intended to mete out to his newest star. At the door, Clive turned to Lee. 'Who knows? You may develop a taste for this sort of activity and if it transpires that you would prefer to be on the receiving end – ' he paused ' – that can also be arranged.'

In the bedroom, Caroline was pacing the floor. So many times, her hands had risen to her face, ready to peel off the tape and remove the gag. Now that Clive was out of the room, she was able to think more clearly. Why should she stay? What was preventing her from simply removing the gag, putting on the robe and fleeing from the house?

She could phone James and he would come and get her. He would know how to deal with Clive. She sat on the bed and her hand moved to the phone, but she let it rest there, looking at herself in the mirrored doors of the wardrobes. She raised her hand to her face and touched the gag, running her fingers over the thick black tape holding it so firmly in place. Why didn't she just remove it?

Angry with herself, she dropped her hand to her lap and looked around. She rose quickly, crossed to the door and tried the handle. It opened easily, as she had known it would. Clive had no need to lie. He believed in his power over her, which was a better prevention to any disobedience that she might try than any lock could ever be. Frustrated, she closed the door and ran to the wardrobes. Opening one of the doors, she saw the towelling robe hanging there, just waiting to be pulled out and slipped over her nakedness. She knew the hopelessness of the situation even before she closed the wardrobe door.

Caroline returned to the bed and sat down, wishing that Clive had tied her and made it impossible for her to leave. By doing things this way, he was making it her choice. She would stay because she wanted to and she had no doubt that Clive would know how she was feeling and what she would do. She picked up the roll of tape and looked at it, imagining the feel of it around her wrists and ankles. How would he restrain her? She looked at the bed. There was an ornate brass headboard with matching corner posts at the end of the bed. She lay on her back and spread her arms and legs. Of course he would do it like that. She would be spreadeagled, her arms and legs firmly taped into position so that he could punish her in the way she knew he would choose. She shivered as she brought her hands down to her nipples, taking the erect teats in her hands and squeezing them. He would beat her inner thighs. That was where it would hurt the most. She moaned as she moved one hand down to her clitoris. She was gloriously wet and, as she ran her fingers over her slippery bud, she knew that she was submitting herself

212

voluntarily to her punishment; Clive's very willing little prisoner.

Flexing the cane in his strong hands, Clive stood in the open doorway and surveyed the prone girl. Turning triumphantly to Lee, he smiled. 'You see. Just as I told you. Do you need any further proof?'

Startled at his words, Caroline struggled upright into a sitting position. She whimpered as she saw Lee. Had he come to help her, and was that something she wanted? She watched as Lee walked over to the bed and sat beside her. His fingers went to her gagged mouth, smoothing the soft plastic before rubbing gently on the black tape. Caroline was startled by his words as his hands slipped to her breasts. 'A very clever way of gagging her, Clive. I applaud your choice. I trust she is to be restrained for the punishment?'

'Of course,' Clive agreed, walking over to the bed. 'I can't quite decide between the tape or ropes. Perhaps you would like to choose, Lee?'

Caroline could not believe this show of gentlemanly politeness. They were both acting as if it were the most normal thing in the world to survey a helplessly gagged girl, whilst discussing how she was to be presented for her punishment. Her hands moved to her face in annoyance, intending to rip off the gag and berate the two men. Swiftly, Clive bent over her, strong hands gripping her wrists.

'Now, now, my darling,' he chided her. 'You have been very good. We don't want you spoiling it, now do we?'

Now very much involved in what was going on, Lee helped Clive to push Caroline back down on the bed and held her while she struggled.

'Rope, I think, Clive,' Lee said, storing the scene before him away in his memory for possible later utilisation in his movie. 'You'll find plenty in that drawer over there,' he said, indicating a small cabinet. 'I'll hold her for you.'

Lee smiled at Caroline as he gripped her wrists in one hand whilst he kept her pinned to the bed with the other.

She struggled desperately, making ineffectual sounds behind her gag. She wanted Lee's hands to grip her breasts; wanted again to feel the hardness of his cock sliding into her vagina. Her frustration kept her struggling until Clive returned, holding several lengths of white silk rope.

Sitting on the bed, he spoke sharply to her, saying the words he knew she wanted to hear. 'Caroline! Stop struggling! You know it will only make matters worse. You are not going to escape because we are going to keep you here for as long as we choose.' As he fixed her with his mesmeric gaze, his voice became gentler, but no less authoritative. 'You will relax and let me tie you up. You will only hurt yourself if you do not. Your punishment will soon be over and then perhaps Lee and I will allow you a little pleasure. But first you have to be a very good girl, do you understand?'

Lee marvelled at the instantaneous quiet which resulted from Clive's words. He watched as Caroline allowed her wrists to be pulled outwards and securely tied to the headboard. Clive was very thorough, taking endless turns of rope around the intricate scrollwork of the headboard, pulling each turn tightly and securing the rope in a complicated series of knots. The same procedure was repeated at her ankles before Clive bound several lengths of rope around the girl's waist, securing each turn of rope around the mattress. When he was finished Caroline was only able to move her head but, not satisfied with this, Clive instructed her to close her eyes before sealing them shut with strips of tape. Standing back to admire Clive's handiwork, Lee wished he had a camera to record the picture that Caroline presented. She was very securely bound, gagged and blindfolded and at the mercy of two men, one of whom had the avowed intention of punishing her very severely. As he contemplated this, Lee glanced a little uncertainly at Clive, who measured the look and smiled.

'I appreciate your concern, Lee, but why don't you feel her cunt and gauge her reaction to all this bondage?'

Lee sat on the bed and slipped two fingers inside Caroline, only to find that she was dripping wet. Smiling in relief, he stood up.

'Let me demonstrate the advantage of having her blindfold,' Clive said as he tapped Caroline's thighs with the cane. She moaned and tried to move. As she discovered that she was truly helpless, her nipples hardened visibly and she moved her head from side to side. Clive bent down and squeezed her nipples, chuckling as he did so. 'You see, she doesn't know who it is that is touching her. If we remain silent during the punishment, she will not know which one of us gives her the pain and which the pleasure.'

Caroline whimpered and again tried unsuccessfully to ease her position. Clive bent his head and whispered in her ear, 'I would advise you not to struggle, my dear. You will only hurt yourself. The more you pull, the tighter the ropes will become.' He watched with pleasure as she opened her mouth to say something, but only succeeded in taking in a mouthful of plastic. 'Now don't be a silly girl. You must realise the helplessness of your position. You are our prisoner and there is no escape.'

As he said this, Clive probed her slit with three of his fingers, feeling her desperate attempts to writhe beneath him. He could not stop himself from taking one of her nipples into his mouth, while stroking and fondling the other. He was impossibly aroused and desired satisfaction just as much as Caroline. Almost impatiently he stood up, retrieving the cane. Without a word, he brought it down hard on Caroline's inner thighs, repeating the strokes without hesitation until a network of raised weals became apparent on the girl's skin. In between strokes, Clive was fondling her clitoris, feeling the increase in juices which told of her approaching climax.

Caroline pulled futilely at the ropes that bound her so securely. Each tug delineated her complete helplessness. The pain, at first intense and burning across the delicate skin of her inner thighs, changed inexorably to intense pleasure as she once again slipped easily into her role of Clive's slave. She knew she was where she wanted to be, fully aware that she could expect no mercy from her former Master. She acknowledged the delicious justice of her punishment and surrendered completely to Clive's dominance. She did not think about what was to happen and how she was going to deal with her new situation. All she could do was give herself up to the almost continuous orgasms that racked her body. In fact, she was reaching the stage of pleading mentally with Clive to finish the punishment and let her relax, but she knew that was all a part of the way he chose to exercise his control and mastery over her.

She tried to subdue her excitement by letting Clive's earlier words echo and re-echo around her brain: 'Mrs Davies sends her love. Mrs Davies sends her love'. The exhausting pleasure of yet another orgasm thrilling through her merged with images of Mrs Davies, Clive's housekeeper and the woman who had so enthusiastically kept Caroline prisoner at his behest. She remembered the beatings she had suffered at the woman's hand and also the pleasure she had enjoyed as those same skilful hands had manipulated her often bound body. Mrs Davies' features seemed to fill her mind; she opened her mouth to scream as yet another orgasm shook her. The plastic, now wet with her saliva, entered her mouth and she tried ineffectually to push it away with her tongue. Her head tossed and turned on the pillow as her body begged to be allowed some relaxation.

Seeing her exhaustion, Lee looked at Clive, who only shook his head and redoubled his efforts with the cane. She had not suffered enough. Grimly, Clive reflected on his own desperate attempts to find Caroline after she had left his house and not returned. How he had suffered when he thought he had lost her for ever. Now she was back in his clutches and when she had been punished enough, he would relent and let her body relax, but he would not let her go. First, she had to satisfy the raging need within him and then – temporarily at least – he would release her. In England she would return to him and when he needed to be absent on business, he would allow Mrs Davies to have the care and control of his little slave. He knew he could rely on his devoted housekeeper to impose a rigidly disciplined regime which would remind the girl of what being a slave was all about. He could hardly wait.

'Perfect!'

Clive walked towards Lee and grasped the proffered handcuffs. Returning to the bed, he looked down at Caroline. She was still gagged and bound, her thighs marked with cross-crossing stripes. Her head was turned to one side and he assumed that, in her exhausted state, she was probably asleep. He resisted the urge to peel the tape from her eyes, but it was too soon. He had not yet finished with her. Sitting on the bed, he gently rubbed a finger over her face, causing her merely to moan softly in her sleep. He traced the outline of her gag, noting with satisfaction the way the plastic now clung to her face, against skin wet with saliva and sweat. Reluctantly, he turned from his contemplation of the helpless girl and started to untie the knots at her wrists. With a start, Caroline awoke and turned her head frantically.

'Easy, my darling,' Clive said. 'I'm just going to untie you. The evening is still young and we haven't yet finished testing you.' He smiled as Caroline moaned. He knew she was tired and only wanted to sleep, but his desire for satisfaction was paramount. He released her ankles and then moved to sit beside her again. 'I'm going to remove your gag now, my darling, so I want you to be a very good girl. The punishment is over and now we shall have some fun.'

As he spoke, Clive unpeeled the tape before untying the gag. When her mouth was free, Caroline sucked in a gulp of air, relieved to feel a cool breeze on her face.

'Please will you remove the tape from my eyes?' she asked in a small voice.

217

Clive considered the request before shaking his head. 'I think not, my darling. I want your pleasure to be considerable and I think being blindfold will only increase that pleasure.'

Knowing better than to argue with Clive, Caroline lay still, luxuriating in the freedom from her restrictions. Clive bent down and kissed her, pushing his tongue between her unresisting lips. She lay still, accepting his kiss and, unbelievably, feeling faint stirrings of desire within her sated body. Almost involuntarily, her arms went around him. Her nipples were hardening with arousal once more as Clive continued to probe her mouth with his tongue, gently slipping his fingers into the moistness that told him she was again ready for him. Gently, he urged her into a kneeling position and, turning to Lee who had now removed his clothes, gestured for him to stand beside the bed.

Disengaging himself from Caroline's arms, Clive moved behind Lee. 'I want you to put your arms straight out in front of you, my darling,' he instructed, pleased at the instant obedience his voice was able to evoke. As instructed, Caroline stretched her arms out and Clive pushed Lee towards her. Putting his finger to his lips, he indicated that Lee should not speak. Clive gently grasped her hands and pulled them around Lee before snapping closed the handcuffs upon each of her wrists.

'Clive?' Caroline asked, a note of uncertainty in her voice.

'I'm here, my love,' Clive assured her, hurriedly divesting himself of his clothes. He felt relief as his erect cock was freed from any restraint, and gently pushed Caroline's head lower until Lee's hardness brushed her lips. 'You know what I like, my darling,' Clive said and, without further hesitation, Caroline opened her mouth, enabling Lee's cock to slide between her lips. With a gasp, Lee tangled one hand in her hair, holding her in position. With his free hand, he played with her small breasts, twisting the hard nipples alternately as she used her lips and tongue to suck and lick at him as his excitement grew.

Satisfied, Clive moved behind Caroline and knelt on the bed. He had lubricated his cock and now tested it against the tiny rosebud entry to the girl's anus. To his delight, he instantly slid inside, feeling her bear down to accommodate him. He grabbed her buttocks as he quickly climbed towards his orgasm, fuelled by the sight of that lovely blonde head bobbing up and down as she pleasured Lee.

Caroline knew she was approaching yet another climax and she welcomed it. The whole scene in which she was involved was tremendously exciting. Her hands were cuffed behind the naked male body of the man she was so enthusiastically pleasuring. Effectively gagged by the cock that filled her mouth, she could only guess as to which of the two men was in front of her and which behind. She arched her back and pushed her buttocks out as the thrusts deep within her rectum became stronger and more urgent. She tasted saltiness in her mouth as her efforts were rewarded, and she swallowed the offered semen. At the same time as the hand in her hair tightened, another stroked across her engorged clitoris, sending her into the paroxysms of orgasm. She did not know who it was that had so pleasured her. She only knew that, for the moment at least, she was content to stay where she was, a very happy and willing prisoner.

Caroline was awakened by a soft touch on her shoulder. She could not remember much about what had happened, apart from the sexual enjoyment she had received and knew she had given.

'Stay perfectly still, my darling. I am just going to take the tape off.' She was aware of growing brightness of light as Clive gradually removed the strips from her eyes. After the session with the two men, one of them had unlocked one of the handcuffs and pulled her hands away from the body around which her arms had been imprisoned. Her hands had been brought together in front of her and the open handcuff relocked on to her wrist.

'You are taking no chances with me,' she had said very softly, feeling lips brush her forehead.

'You got away from me once before, my darling. I do not intend to repeat my mistake,' Clive had responded and, accepting the inevitable, she had settled back on the bed.

Now, as the remaining tape was peeled from her eyes, she blinked in the unaccustomed light. Clive bent over her. 'I think we had better get you showered, my love. You smell disgustingly of sex!' Laughing, he pulled her off the bed. She held her hands out in mute appeal; he shook his head firmly. 'I'm sorry, Caroline, you are my prisoner and until I have to let you go that remains the position and don't tell me that you don't enjoy it!'

Caroline looked at Clive and knew that he spoke the truth. Was there a part of this evening that she had not enjoyed? Tremulously, she smiled at him, confirming his assumption.

'Come on then. Into the shower with you!' Clive ordered.

Once in the shower, Clive was gentleness itself, soaping her and allowing her to do the same to him. As his fingers curled around her breasts, she responded to his touch with a growing sexual need. 'Tomorrow, we are going to spend the day together . . .'

'No!' Caroline was as startled by her reaction as Clive. He stared intently at her, his black eyes seeming to fill her vision as they both stood immobile under the warm water.

'I . . . I mean, I can't . . .' Caroline faltered. 'James . . .'

Clive ignored all her protestations subsequent to that one word which had lodged in his brain. Now, he reached out and gripped her by the arms. 'No? You dare to use that word to me! Have you learnt nothing? Was your punishment not sufficient? Listen to me, my dear, and listen well. You are my slave and as such there is no room in your vocabulary for that word!'

Suddenly, he bent his head and kissed her fiercely, forcing her lips apart as he jammed his tongue into her mouth. Caroline made a small sound of protest and struggled against him, causing him to grab the chain between her cuffed wrists and wrap an arm firmly across her shoulders, immobolising her. She could not help moving against him as her arousal grew. The kiss was so intense that she could hardly breathe, but she returned it with a passion which almost equalled his own. Suddenly he released her and grabbed a flannel from the side of the soap dish.

'If you can't say what I want to hear you say, you had better be quiet!' Clive growled, pushing the cloth into her open mouth. Grabbing her again, he roughly massaged her clitoris as the water continued to cascade over them both. He forced her cuffed hands over his head and stared at her. 'You are mine, Caroline, as you have always been since the first day I set eyes on you. Tell me that you're mine!'

She whimpered into her makeshift gag and tried to shake her head. Clive redoubled his efforts with her clitoris and she felt her knees weaken at the approaching orgasm. As she reached the peak, Clive pulled her hands roughly from around his neck and pushed her against the wall of the shower cubicle. She felt him behind her, penetrating her anus again and pounding into her as she climaxed. His fingers gripped her nipples, intensifying the strength of her orgasm. At the height of his fury, Clive pumped his semen into her rectum. His fingers clawed at the gag in her mouth. 'You are my slave, Caroline! Say it! Say it!'

Weakly, she nodded. 'Yes, Clive, I am your slave.'

'And you always have been?' he gasped.

'Yes, I always have been,' she whispered, wondering in her confusion what on earth she was going to do now.

Having achieved his aim, Clive dried her gently. As he removed the cuffs, he bent his head and gently kissed both of her wrists.

'Caroline, I have missed you so very much,' he said, cradling her head.

Caroline felt a surge of confusion. She loved James, she

was sure of that, but how was it that Clive was able to make her feel as he did? Clive dried her hair and she was amazed at his gentleness. This man was capable of such contrasting emotions. After the violence of their scene in the shower, he was now behaving with such compassion. As she watched him, Caroline felt a sexual awareness that could not be denied. She decided to forget her confusion and just enjoy the moment. She watched as Clive rolled a black stocking over her foot and smoothed it up her leg, before repeating the process on her other leg. He produced a black leather suspender belt, which he slipped around her waist before fastening the stockings to the belt. Caroline shivered with anticipatory sexual excitement as Clive pushed her feet into black high-heeled shoes. Smiling at her, he got to his feet and stood back to admire her. Turning, he retrieved some white silk rope from the bedside table and knelt before Caroline.

'We have to get you ready for bed, my love,' Clive said. 'I do not want you trying to escape while I am asleep.'

Both of them knew she was not about to try any such thing, but Caroline surrendered to pleasurable feelings as Clive placed her feet together. Running a caressing hand across her shoes, he tied her ankles tightly. When he had bound her knees together, he helped her to stand. His expression as his eyes travelled over her made her clitoris pulse, her wetness telling her that she was yet again very aroused. Crossing to the wardrobe, Clive extracted a garment and returned to her. He held out a floor-length transparent plastic coat and helped her to slip her arms into the sleeves. Once she had done that, he buttoned the coat and she realised that it fitted her exactly. She shivered as the cold plastic enfolded her body. Clive put his arms around her.

'I had it specially made for you, Caroline. I knew I would get you back.' Caroline relaxed as his embrace warmed the plastic, which was already beginning to adhere to her body. 'Do you like it, my darling?'

Caroline nodded. She hoped that this was the prelude to another session. She was a little disappointed when

Clive released her and eased her hands behind her back. As he tied her wrists tightly together, he whispered to her, 'Patience, my darling, patience.'

Caroline smiled. Yet again he knew exactly what she was thinking. Clive bound her elbows together, before tying more rope around her arms, allowing her erect nipples to remain visible through the turns of hemp. He paused in his work to squeeze those nipples, making her knees buckle so that she almost fell. Laughing softly, Clive eased her on to the bed. With a rustle of plastic, he pushed the coat apart where the buttons ended and slipped a finger into her wetness. Caroline groaned and leant back on her bound arms.

'You are such a delicious little slave,' Clive said, his cock dripping with the fluid of his own excitement. 'How could I ever have let you go?' He bent his head as he removed his finger. Caroline screamed with delight as his tongue probed into her. Making small tutting noises, Clive raised his head. 'Too much noise, I think.'

'No, please! Clive, I'll be quiet!' Caroline pleaded as Clive moved to the bedside table and returned with two squares of matching plastic.

'My dear, what did I tell you about that word?'

Before Caroline could say anything further, one of the squares had been folded and tied across her mouth. She made protesting noises as the gag was knotted behind her head. The second square of material was similarly folded and tied across her eyes. Clive stood back to survey the effect, stroking his cock as he did so. This was everything he had waited and planned for ever since she had left him. She writhed on the bed, fighting her bonds more as a means to give herself added pleasure than from a genuine desire to escape.

He fell on her and pushed her roughly over on to her side. She moaned with pleasure as she felt the hardness of his cock against her buttocks. The coat was pulled up and that hardness probed her anus yet again as she bore down to help him ease his cock further into her. He gripped her plastic-covered breasts as his climax mounted, feeling the

223

ropes that bound her and ensured her helplessness. Suddenly, he was pumping his semen into her bound body as she struggled against him. Putting one hand between her legs he felt the hard little bud, triggering an almost instananeous orgasm. He felt the increase in her juices and hugged her closely, revelling in the feel of her plastic-covered body, so helplessly bound. Whatever it took, he knew that he would do everything in his power to keep her with him and to carry through his original plan to make her his permanent slave.

THE SCHOOLING
OF STELLA

Yolanda Celbridge

Yolanda Celbridge is our most prolific author, with ten books to her name and a few more in the pipeline. They have so far fallen into two distinct groups, both devoted to the joys of bottom punishment. The Maldona series is an extraordinary trilogy of erotic fantasy novels revolving around the complicated Rulebook and the physical upbraiding of miscreants according to its strictures. The trilogy begins in southern Spain with the perverse society of women that is *The House of Maldona*; it continues in the Aegean Sea as Jana, leader of the Order of Maldona, takes the most nubile and obedient of her slaves on a quest for adventure in *The Island of Maldona*; and concludes in *The Castle of Maldona*, in which Jana and her lover travel to a Balkan castle run along similar lines to Maldona – except that it involves some men with very curious physical attributes.

Yolanda's other books involve an 'erotic Baedecker of the UK', to use her own phrase. Novels such as *Memoirs of a Cornish Governess* and its sequels *The Governess at St Agatha's* and *The Governess Abroad*, *The Correction of an Essex Maid*, *Private Memoirs of a Kentish Headmistress* and *Miss Rattan's Lesson* are set in a pre-war world of corsets and chastisements, in which the essence of ladylike comportment can only be instilled through the unsparing use of disciplinary implements. *The Schooling of Stella* continues in this vein, relocating the action to Scotland's sternest training college, and its sequel, *The Submission of Stella*, is due to be published in February 1999. Yolanda has also promised us a masterpiece of medical erotica in November 1998, *The Discipline of Nurse Riding*. As we're big fans of medical paraphernalia, we think this will be one to look out for.

The following extract is taken from *The Schooling of Stella*. Those who have read Yolanda's work before will know what to expect. Anyone else has a pleasant surprise in store. Stella is new to Kernece and has not quite got the hang of the rules yet – but this is not necessarily such a bad thing.

Stella found that something Morag had said preyed on her. It was at ablution, before her caning in Miss Dancer's study. She had spoken of Jakes, that he 'needed' women, yet despised them. How did he need them, and what did he do to assuage his need? Was it something to do with biology; with the power of the pea vine, as Stella saw in her dreams and which made her *masturbate* so much? She used that word to herself now, for she had seen it in textbooks and now understood what it meant. But it still made her shiver. The other thing made her shiver even more: a hard penis, actually put inside a lady's place! The very thought made her wet, yet shocked and terrified. She had tasted Jamie's cream, and that was one thing, it was sweet and lovely. The thought of the cream spurting inside her naked place was frightening, yet wickedly tempting. Was that what Jakes did with the women of Kernece? And with how many? All? Morag, even? Stella's head spun, and she resolved to educate herself in this mystery. Above all, she wanted to know why the beautiful Jakes despised women. Was it because they took his seed from him? She thought it would be a useful task to teach him not to despise women.

Her drowsy thoughts of Jakes were dispelled early in the morning after her submission to Morag, by a shattering whistle that made her jump, and a shriek of 'drudge!' from the distance. She was surprised at the speed with which the dorm awoke as one. The girls, slipperless and clad only in nighties, rushed to the door. Buffy, Muffy

229

and Tuffy scampered gaily in the lead. She was confused: Rousing Bell had not yet sounded, and it was only half-light outside.

'Come on, Stella!' urged Alberta. 'You don't want to miss breakfast! It's the Bull! Last one to get to her study has to be her drudge, for as long as she wants!'

But Stella was still drowsy, the lovely glowing smart of her flogged backside making her lapse again into her daydream. When she finally shook herself out of bed and padded to the doorway, the rest of the dorm was already stumbling back to bed. She followed the corridor against the stream, glumly aware that she would be last to arrive, and hence the Bull's drudge. She was right. The Bull stood at her door, waiting with a grim smile as Stella walked evenly.

'Ah, Shawn, the new squit and Matron's girly! I thought it might be you, you lazy slut! Into my study, drudge!'

Stella obeyed. The Bull's study was a spacious bedsitting chamber, with, surprisingly, its own ablutions, and a rather dramatic view over the Parph. Its white walls were decorated with photographs of young men in military uniform, and one of a strikingly handsome young woman: the Bull herself. In the photograph, she was brandishing one or other implements of sporting prowess or, Stella noticed with a shiver, instruments of correction. The furniture was almost mannish in its relaxed, leathery comfort, and a good fire burned in the grate, with a pungent sweetish aroma that Stella surmised was peat moss.

'Heard about your little trick with the good old pot perm! Very smart. I remember cousin Stackenham doing that to me a while back, but I whacked his bum for it, the rotter! With his own sword! So you're in the Blue Army – rather gave the game away with that little stunt. I suppose you think you're special, whacking that idiot Charity on the bum, I don't doubt. Well, we'll soon see about *that*.'

Stella wanted to disagree, but the Bull went on merrily, 'You are my drudge for as long as I want, Shawn. You can miss breakfast – you'll trough with me – and classes too, on my say-so. Now take off that nightie, and put these things on. I've plenty of cleaning and jobs for you, and I expect you'll be hopelessly slow. We'll see if you can make tea.' She pointed towards a little kitchen alcove, with a sink and gas ring.

Stella remembered that her first class was actually a free period, with which her timetable was plentifully studded, and which was meant to be spent studying in the Library, her free afternoons being intended for sports. She did not think anyone would notice her absence. The Bull handed her a bundle of clothing and told her again to strip off her nightie. Nervously, Stella lifted her nightie until her mink was bare, but hesitated as the garment reached her breasts. To be naked in ablutions was one thing, but it seemed somehow improper to be naked in another person's private room. The Bull snorted at her to hurry up, and said she was a mossy little slut, though her tone was not unkind. She took Stella's nightie and sniffed it, making a face.

'Pooh! You stink, drudge! I suppose I should scrub you, but you'll work up a good lather at drudgery, and anyway your uniform's been worn by plenty of other drudges. Although you might find it a tight fit. Those bubbies are a bit grand for a new squit! And that bum ... Well, I'd say she needs a good tanning for being such a whopper, but I see that's been attended to.'

Stella did not understand what being a new squit had to do with possessing a large croup, but unfolded the unfamiliar garments. Uniform! It was certainly a strange one, and smelled odd. She held the things up, and saw that they would indeed be a tight fit.

'Pretty, ain't it?' said the Bull. 'Number eight kit, not many of them in College. I annexed this from the Purser, because I like to see a drudge dressed properly.'

Stella began to put on her uniform, and found it a squeeze. She had expected a drudge's kit to be more coarse smock of rough cotton, but this was more like a frilly maid's uniform at some exotic London banquet. The fabric was deliciously thin, and she had a black blouse, short frilly black skirt, white stockings, suspender belt and petticoat, high-heeled poppy shoes and – to her amazement – a poppy corset! The ensemble was topped by a frilly white maid's cap, and Stella was both surprised and tickled to find that all the garments were made of thin, silky rubber! She had rarely worn white stockings, and never ones made of rubber.

She first put on her corset, and the Bull insisted on knotting it for her. Stella gasped at the tight constraint which she felt pushing up her already welling 'bubbies' and forcing the tops of her buttocks out. She wanted to look at herself in the glass, as it felt so tight and naughty! She slipped on the rest of her things; they squeezed her too, though not as tightly as her corset. Her blouse was open quite deep, showing her breasts pressed hard together like two ripe fleshy melons. There was no brassière, and she observed to the Bull that there were no knickers either. The Bull grinned and snorted that a drudge should not wear knickers, as it made her bum easier to lick, and gestured towards a rather frightening tawse which hung above her bed.

'A girl's like a horse: needs a lick on the crupper from time to time, to keep her at it,' said the Bull thoughtfully, as though to herself.

'We'll bathe before tea, drudge,' she said, not looking at Stella. It was as though Stella could have been anyone at all. The Bull used the royal 'we', meaning herself.

'Put the kettle on for tea, and we'll have toast with that. Meantime you can heat some water and scrub my back.'

As the dawn glimmered outside, Stella busied herself at her tasks. She felt oddly excited that the Bull treated her as a drudge, not even as a person. Stella felt nothing more than an animal – a horse with a big crupper! – and as the water boiled she imagined herself a captive of the proud Isbisters: paraded naked, and hearing her crupper and bubbies arrogantly discussed as though she were nothing more than a beast of burden. Jamie would be there, of course, idly flicking her body with the tip of his sword . . .

When the water was ready for the Bull's ablutions,

Stella filled the sink and fetched sponge and soap and towel. She was already proud of her efficiency as a drudge, and thought her new role far more exciting than lessons, or the dreadful breakfast of stewed tea and 'vommo'. The Bull was sucking on a mouthful of Parph apples from a big bucket that stood beside her gas ring. As she swallowed the bitter juice, she spat the stones and gobbets of juice and flesh on the floor. Stella guessed she would have to clean this up on her hands and knees. She hoped it would be on hands and knees, skirt high, with a lick to the bum from that juicy tawse to encourage her! She grinned at her wondrous naughtiness, and indicated to the Bull that her ablutions were ready.

Then, to Stella's surprise, the Bull slipped off her quilted nightgown and stood naked in front of her drudge. She wore a nonchalant expression, as though she were quite alone. First, she positioned herself in a squat on the commode, and noisily did her business. When she airily waved her hand, Stella was proud that she had anticipated the command, and was ready with white tissue paper. Then the Bull rose, and placed herself at the sink, handing the soap and sponge for Stella to scrub her back. Stella bent to her task, and did not stop at the Bull's back.

She was entranced by the beauty of the Bull's body: a lithe, ripely muscled frame that had not an ounce of fat, but swelled as fully and as handsomely as Stella's own breasts and buttocks. Her creamy skin was beautifully enhanced by the mane of silky auburn hair that caressed her back and breasts. The Bull stood akimbo, allowing Stella to sponge her most intimate places, then suddenly turning so that she might do her front. Stella did so, taking her time at scrubbing the wondrous breasts, with their big plum-red nipples twice the size of the Parph apples which the Bull kept chewing and spitting. Stella was pleased that at her washing, the nipples became deliciously tense, and the Bull's face turned just a tiny bit red! She passed down the firm belly, soaping a rich lather, then scrubbed the strong horsewoman's legs, and surprisingly dainty feet.

'Make sure you get all the jam from between my toes,' said the Bull rather crudely. Stella had the occasion to kneel and her skirt rode up to reveal her bare nates as she paid particular attention to the feet.

'Now, drudge, you deserve a lick or two on the bum,' said the Bull, 'as you seem to have forgotten somewhere.'

She pointed at her lady's place, adorned by a mink of superb, silky lushness that seemed to extend halfway up her belly, almost to the sweet dimple of her belly-button! Gulping, Stella went to work with her sponge. The Bull casually parted her thighs and held the cheeks of her bum open, so that Stella could wash the lips of her fount, and her anus bud too. She saw that the Bull's fount was glistening slightly, as though her attentions made her excited. Stella found that her own fount was just a little bit moist at the thrill of her 'drudgery'. The Bull's damsel was very big and Stella found her fascinating, resisting the urge to put the sponge down and touch the nubbin with her naked finger. It was like a crimson thimble, standing sweetly between the fleshy folds of her fount lips, and Stella was sure it was just a little hard.

'You've a good pair of jugs, drudge,' said the Bull suddenly, with a bird's-eye view of Stella's upthrust bosom. 'I think you'll go for Kernece Football. I bet Miss Harker's noticed you too, starkers in the showers.'

Stella replied diplomatically that Miss Harker did like to chat with her when she was showering. The Bull snorted that she was not in the least surprised.

'She hasn't bagged you yet, for her team?' she said anxiously, and Stella said she was unaware of any bagging.

'Good. Then we'll bag you for ours. First game tomorrow afternoon! I don't care if you have free periods or not, just rearrange them and tell them we said so.'

Stella did have the afternoon free for games. As she was towelling the Bull dry, she asked what Kernece Football actually was. The Bull roared with laughter.

'You'll find out! It's in the appendix of your Rulebook, you mossy slut! I dare say you haven't got that far yet.' Stella said that was true.

234

'Well, Kernece Football is tough. Are you tough, drudge?'

Stella moved towards the tea-kettle, and said proudly that she had been Captain of Netball, which caused the Bull to gaffaw even more.

'For one thing,' she said, 'in Kernece Football, there is no ball, not as such. And precious few rules, either, short of a prohibition on murder.'

Stella gulped, and served the breakfast, being permitted a cup of tea and piece of buttered toast herself, which she had to eat standing up while the Bull lolled in her arm-chair. Her quilted robe fell carelessly open to show her fine legs and the strands of her wet mink-hair curling on her soft thigh-skin. Stella thought her a picture of indolence.

After her breakfast, the Bull carelessly threw crumbs and crusts on the floor, which was of bare burnished boards adorned with thick hearthrugs, and told Stella to get on with cleaning the floor while she dressed. Stella looked for cleaning things, and had been right: there was a bucket, dustpan and cloth, but no mop. She smiled and got down on her knees with a bucket of cold water, and began to brush. When she had swept away the crumbs, she went to work with the bucket and cloth, throwing herself into the task with vigour. She paused when she saw the Bull standing over her, in uniform now, and holding her tawse.

She wore the same poppy jacket, but her skirt was not the long blue one Stella had seen at Matron's. She had a pleated and very short skirt, which showed her superb legs in bright silk stockings. These stockings, like her blouse, were a leaf green which formed a piquant contrast to her jacket. Stella was suddenly envious of a senior's privileges, and especially of a Prefect's. She had lovely shoes, too, in a darker shade of green. The Bull casually flicked her bare bum with the tawse, and told her to work harder, then sat down with her legs over her chair and lit a cigarette. She puffed contemptuously and flicked cigarette ash right in the place that Stella had washed, so that she was obliged to do it again. Stella knew she was being teased, or humiliated, and did not mind! Especially when the Bull delivered a proper stinging tawse-lash to her naked croup, which made her jump, and the frilly skirt slither across her bare skin, while the lace-ends of her corset bounced and tickled the tops of her fesses. She found that quite nice, and rubbed her bottom with exaggerated gestures to please the Bull.

'Ouch, Miss!' she cried each time the tawse struck her nates. 'My bum smarts so. You are awfully cruel!'

The Bull smiled each time she said this, and usually rewarded her with another cut from her lash, so that Stella found herself cleaning over and over in the place near the Bull's chair, where she was in easy reach of the tawse.

'Yes, I am, am I not?' she said pleasantly, dropping the royal 'we' in her enthusiasm. 'Runs in the family. The Stackenhams have always loved discipline, my girl. Pater used to tell me about flogging the men in South Africa before Ladysmith; and Grandmama, who was Russian, wouldn't be outdone. She told us that when she was little, *her* Pater would have the serfs stripped naked and flogged with the knout while they were having supper. She said it was awfully thrilling to see a naked man, or woman, writhing under the lash while they were eating their borscht. Perhaps that is why she used to serve borscht so much.'

She rewarded Stella with another, seemingly effortless lash. It caught her right at the cleft of the buttocks and hurt abominably, so that Stella shuddered and overturned her bucket. Her bum really glowed now, and she was trembling with mingled fear and pleasure, because she knew what was to happen. It occured to her that she might have overturned the bucket accidentally on purpose.

The Bull rose to her full height, and towered over her crouching drudge. The talk of flogging seemed to excite her, and her face glowed.

'Well!' she cried, stepping over the puddle of water, 'We should make you lick that up, but we're in a good mood, so we'll be lenient. Over the chair with you, drudge, and skirt well up for a proper tanning! A good dozen on that lovely crimson bare of yours will teach you manners!'

Stella meekly obeyed, her heart pounding, for she was not displeased. She buried her nose in the chair cushions, smelling the warmth from the Bull's own bottom, and stretched her fesses in the air as high as she could. The Bull noticed.

'My, anyone would think you were begging for it,' she said. 'Most drudges squeal and squall something rotten.'

'I am obedient, Miss,' said Stella softly. 'If I have earned a flogging, then flogged I must be. Would you like me to make you some borscht to eat as you lash my bum?'

She grinned to herself at her impudence, and was rewarded with a strangled 'Well!' from the Bull. 'That's insolence, and not so dumb!' she exclaimed angrily. 'For that, slut, you'll get *two* dozen. And one for luck! Keep count!' Stella said nothing, but waited.

The first lash was harsher than all the others, but not as hard as Morag's cat-o'-nine-tails. Though the stroke made her buttocks squirm quite tensely, Stella knew she could take it. Even this early in the morning! The second and third strokes came in quick succession, and then the Bull paused. Stella had to admire the woman; the strokes seemed to come with a fluid, graceful ease that did not make her gasp or pant.

'I'm enjoying this,' chuckled the Bull. 'Golly, I'll make you dance, you stupid drudge!'

'Do you flog many girls, Miss?' asked Stella in a voice whose calmness took the Bull somewhat aback.

'Why, yes,' she said. 'I've reddened oodles of bare bums, and I love every minute of it. Yours is special, though: she's already well poppy, and I shall make you into a true Poppilian!'

'I should like that very much, Miss,' murmured Stella. 'So I can be proud when the other girls see me at ablution.'

'Hmmph!' cried the Bull, and recommenced the

beating, as Stella counted in a hushed voice. The strokes really were hard; the Bull had not lectured her about flinching or squirming, so flinch and squirm Stella did. She could not help herself, and wondered if two dozen were too much, but then at the tenth or eleventh she reached that wonderful serene plateau again. She became one with her flaming bottom, and seemed to float on air, her pain a distant warm event taking place outside her for her own pleasure. She exaggerated her squirming, hoping it would please and excite the Bull – a sign of her willing submission.

At the fifteenth, Stella could not stop herself from giving a long, low 'Mmmm' of pure joy as a particularly hard cut jolted her with a spasm of searing pain. The seeping moisture in her fount became a trickle that wetted the tops of her thighs. The Bull paused again.

'You are a tough one!' she said. 'I could have sworn that was a cry of pleasure! Are you enjoying it, drudge?'

'Oh, no, Miss,' cried Stella. 'It stings most horribly! My poor bare bottom! You hurt her so!' The Bull laughed.

'*I'm* enjoying it,' she said. 'I love seeing a girly squirm and cry. I am so happy with my lot. Wouldn't you just *love* to be me?'

Stella did not answer, and her silence seemed to upset the Bull, for her strokes became faster and faster. Stella was emboldened, her slit now slippery with her juices, and she began to moan, 'Oh, yes, *yes* . . .'

'You *are* taking pleasure!' the Bull exclaimed, as though thunderstruck.

'Have you never heard of subs and doms, Miss?' said Stella almost contemptuously. 'Well, you are a dom, you take pleasure in flogging –'

'Yes!' cried the Bull, a little too hastily. 'Always have, always will. Why, Pater entrusts me with beating the serving maids at Stackenham Hall . . .'

'So that is why I'm dressed thus!' said Stella. 'It stands to reason there must be those of . . . a different persuasion. Have you never been flogged yourself?'

'Of course, when I was a new squit. But chance treated me well. I hated it!'

'Are you sure?'

'I like doing it. I like seeing a girly's bare crupper well squirming. I like seeing yours squirm.'

'Gosh,' said Stella, 'hurry up and finish, Miss, so I can rub my bum! She's really smarting so beautifully. And if it gives you pleasure, why, I cannot *stop* myself squirming.'

'You are a strange one,' said the Bull as she brought the flogging to a tumultuous end, with Stella allowing her fesses to dance in an exaggerated sensuous rhythm, a ballet of pain. When it was over, she stood and rubbed herself, not bothering to smooth down her skirt, so that the Bull had a clear view of her shining wet thighs and fount. There was a puzzled expression on the Bull's face. Stella now stared her out, directly in the eyes, until the Bull blushed and averted her gaze. Stella took the tawse from her limp hand.

'In answer to your question, Miss: no, I wouldn't like to be you. But you would like to be me, wouldn't you? A girly new squit again, just for a moment. Admit it.'

The Bull bit her lip, then smiled – shyly!

'I'd never thought . . . Well, you took such pleasure. I don't know . . . Oh, hang it, anything for a giggle!'

Her smile turned to a grin, and she lifted her skirt, revealing her deep poppy knickers. 'It will be just like old times, before chance elevated me . . .'

'It is no giggle, Miss,' said Stella gravely, throwing the tawse aside. 'Take your blouse off.'

'Is that needed? I mean, my knickers, yes, but – '

'Of course I'll have your knickers, Miss,' said Stella severely. 'But you weren't afraid to be unrobed when I was just a drudge, washing you. The blouse, please.'

Slowly, the Bull unbuttoned her blouse, and her full ripe breasts spilled out so lovely and bare that Stella had to restrain herself from kissing the big dark nipples that stood so round and erect at their softly curving tips. She took the blouse and went to the kitchen where she found the bucket of Parph apples. She soaked the blouse at the

239

sink, then emptied the entire contents of the bucket into the blouse, whch she knotted tightly to make a cruelly knobbed truncheon. She swung it experimentally, and felt unsure; it was so heavy and so hard. Yet she had to *teach* the Bull . . .

'Now, crouch on the rug, Miss Bulford,' she ordered curtly, 'with your thighs spread and your bum in the air. Feel free to bite the carpet if you need to.'

'How . . . how many?' gasped the Bull, paling as she saw Stella's weapon. Stella put her siltetto heel on the crouching woman's neck.

'As many as you like,' she said. 'For you like flogging, Miss, so you are going to flog yourself!'

She handed the weapon to the Bull. She ordered her to begin beating herself on the bare buttocks, with all her force, until she decided she could take no more.

'*I* decide?' wailed the Bull. 'That isn't fair!'

'We'll see how tough you are,' Stella sneered. 'Begin!'

The Bull groaned, and lifted the weapon, then smacked it with pleasing force on her bared high nates, making herself flinch. She repeated this three or four times, until her flinching became a delicious squirming of real discomfort.

'Oh, it *hurts*, Miss!' she wailed. Stella ground her heel into the Bull's neck and ordered her to beat herself *much* harder.

'You like it, don't you?' she whispered.

'No! No! Oh! It's harder than Jakes's whip! Oh cruel chance! Oh!'

'You can always stop if you wish,' said Stella, pretending to yawn, but pondering the mention of Jakes. Languidly, she reached for the Bull's Rulebook which lay on her desk, and opened it at the appendix.

'I'll just inform myself about Kernece Football while you get on with things,' she said, pretending to be bored. 'I might as well use the time constructively.'

In truth, her fount was flowing very copiously with hot oil as she saw the delicious blush that now suffused the Bull's magnificent bare buttocks. And to her delight, she saw a glistening on her vicim's thigh-skin; the Bull too was flowing with fount-juice! As the flogging continued, the Bull's strokes became harsher and harsher, her wriggling and mewling more frantic. Stella found the section on Kernece Football in very small print, and what she read almost made her drop the book.

'Oh!' the Bull cried. 'It's worse – I mean it's better than Knobkerry Night! You wicked mossy bitch! I must . . .'

And with that, Stella saw the Bull's hand feverishly clamp her fount and begin to rub her damsel. She watched, tremendously excited – almost beyond control, as the Bull masturbated in time with her flogging. Her bottom was now a beautifully deep crimson. Then Stella herself lost control, and sighed as her fingers found her own engorged, throbbing damsel, which she flicked and rubbed until her whole body glowed with spasming pleasure.

'So that's what you want,' she said faintly, and roughly took the truncheon from the Bull's flogging hand.

'Don't make me stop, I beg you!' gasped the Bull.

'I am just starting,' replied Stella. 'Turn over, and press your knees up against your bubbies so that I can see your bum and thighs.'

When the Bull was on her back, and in this position, Stella roughly squatted right on top of the Bull's face, with her thighs spread wide and her damsel positioned above the other woman's mouth.

'Now tongue me while you diddle yourself, bitch!' she blurted. 'I won't be left out.'

She gasped with joy as she felt a hot wet tongue flicker against her throbbing nubbin. She began to beat the bared buttocks and thighs that the Bull stretched before her, laying her whole weight on the woman's head and holding the weapon with both hands. Raising her arms above her head to their full length, she dealt blow after severe blow as the Bull continued to masturbate, her hips writhing in a sensuous dance and her fount gleaming with her copious fluid. Stella could feel her own flow anointing the Bull's

241

tongue and lips, and knew that her liquid was so copious that the Bull's chin and shoulder must be quite soaked.

She could scarcely control her own writhing as she came to her plateau and knew that soon she would orgasm. She laid the truncheon suddenly aside, and bent over, drawing her knees in so that her thighs tightly cradled the Bull's wet cheeks, and placed her own mouth on the Bull's glistening swollen fount lips. She gently removed the flicking fingers and replaced them with her own tongue, licking the Bull's swollen hard nubbin until it seemed so big she could take it between her lips. She did, chewing and gently biting the stiff limb as though it were a Parph apple. The Bull's moans became a howl: her love juices drenched Stella's mouth as both women cried out and spasmed in their ecstasy.

'Well!' said the Bull, getting unsteadily to her feet, 'I suppose my bum's all crimson like some mossy new squit's.'

'Yes, she is, Miss,' said Stella, smoothing down her skirt. 'And she is lovely. Did you like being me?'

'Hmmph!' snorted the Bull. 'Like doesn't come into it. Chance brought you to me, and permitted you to bewitch me for a moment. The Whip of Chance if everything at Kernece.'

'Surely, fate . . .' Stella began.

'You haven't properly studied your Rulebook!' sneered the Bull. Her bare breasts bobbed sweetly in her agitation, as she forgot her lovely nudity. 'Everything here is decided by lot! To be a Prefect, to be sent to the Remove . . . even the Headmistress herself is decided by drawing lots. Of course they can be influenced in many ways, especially if Clapton favours you. She is Mistress of the Lots just now, and even that rank is decided by lot.'

Stella blurted that she wanted to know about Jakes's whip, and the Bull reared up, telling her a slut of a new squit should not ask questions. Then, just as suddenly, her face softened and Stella saw sadness behind her hauteur.

'You'll find out,' she said gently. 'Oh, you'll find out.'

Stella asked if there were any more tasks for her, and the Bull said that she could go to her lessons. She added, though, that Stella was remiss in not properly polishing the floor, and the curtains needed to be washed, and . . .

'Oh, there are so many things to do!' she cried, blushing. For a moment, Stella saw a sweet, innocent girlish face beneath the handsome features of the Head Prefect. 'Just remember, Stella Shawn,' she added – shyly, 'when I whistle for a drudge, the last girl to present herself gets the task. Be sure that when I whistle, you walk slowly. Now, I'll see you tomorrow for Kernece Football.' Her tone was again brisk and haughty.

'It sounds awfully tough, Miss,' said Stella uncertainly.

'Oh, it is. And it'll be worse for you.' Her gloating sneer told Stella that she was now the Bull once more. '*You* are going to be the ball.'

CHAINS OF SHAME

Brigitte Markham

Brigitte Markham has written only one book for Nexus, but it's a masterpiece of darkly bizarre eroticism and we hope that she'll write a few more. *Chains of Shame* introduced us to innocent but cheeky teenagers Laura and Helen on holiday in Corfu. They stay with Helen's aunt, Angela, who has a novel agenda for them – she wants to oversee their sexual awakening. She finds them keen to learn and to experiment with the darker side of love, and sends them to the private island of the perverse Mr Tostides, where their introduction to the sophisticated rituals of submission and domination can remain uninterrupted. Mr Tostides has more than the girls' education in mind, however.

In the following extract the girls have realised just how far Mr Tostides is willing to go in order to dominate them completely. They are to be sold at auction, and must prove their sexual worth to the buyers in what proves to be a night to remember.

Donna came for the girls many hours later. Laura felt filthy and very tired. They were released from the pens and led, shackled in a line, back to the almost deserted seraglio and into the shower room. As they were lined up facing the bar in the middle of the room, Donna stood behind her victims.

'Bend over the bar, lean on your elbows and part your legs as wide as possible,' she said.

The metal was cold against the base of her stomach. Laura wondered what the hell was happening now, and then slim fingers began stroking her upraised bottom and thighs. She was so tired, and now her legs, after standing so long, had to be almost straight to meet Donna's orders. The fingers caressed, now greasy, inside her body and over her mound. Laura felt herself grow wet. She looked round. The maid smiled the warm, knowing, slightly envious smile of someone who had shared, vicariously, her seduction and deflowering. Laura's vagina opened, her own dampness mixing with the grease, and her anal ring relaxed around the two fingers impaling her.

Something narrow and flexible was pushed deep into her bottom, and was held in place by a hardness somehow inside the muscle ring. She wriggled; it felt funny. A very thin, flexible tube slid into her pee-hole; deep into a place nothing had touched before. She opened her mouth to exclaim.

'Silence.'

The lash whipped her shoulders. The tube in the front

was also locked. Fluid poured into her bowels, filling her, churning and rushing. Her belly felt tight and a little hand tested the growing bulge above the bar. Now liquid flooded her bladder. Cramps started. The fluids seemed to boil and bubble, scouring at her tissues. Her muscles tried to expel the liquid, but the bungs obviously had valves to prevent that happening. A hand in the small of her back held her down. Another flood whooshed into her vagina.

Laura felt as if she would burst. Tears pricked her eyes. Just in time, she was pulled to her feet, pushed away, and made to squat over a gully beside her friends. She closed her eyes, ashamed and frightened. She felt someone remove the tubes, and her body emptied in a violent paroxysm. Laura remembered the last time her inside had been cleaned like this, and Penny telling her something about enemas and douches and how some people got their kicks from them. A hose of warm water cleaned them down. She couldn't imagine how this could be a turn-on. Laura returned to the bar and resumed the humiliating position. The process was repeated. New fluids poured in; different fluids that caressed, soothed and warmed. Her internal organs felt stimulated and, when these were in turn expelled, she suddenly felt lighter and refreshed.

Under the shower that followed, the maid employed her body to wash Laura's body. Coiling like a snake, breast to breast, nipple to nipple, shaven sex to shaven sex, she covered Laura with soap. She made love to Laura, giving all the reassurance she could to the young Welsh girl. Laura relaxed a little and began to find the stimulation disconcertingly intense. Her lips and clitoris felt swollen beyond this mild arousal, and her rings became noticeable – especially those in her sex.

Towelled dry, Laura was taken to the tables, still manacled. An application of burning cream to her mound and armpits cleared any regrowing hairs. She was painted and hung with chains. A new touch, designed to enforce her feeling of bondage, came in the form of a fine chain that ran tightly from the back of her collar, between her lips, over her tongue and back again. It made an effective gag.

Laura was made to stand, and new chains of polished steel joined wrist to wrist, ankle to ankle, and both shackles together. Laura caught sight of herself in the mirror. A stranger, with kholed, dilated eyes, stared back. A stranger draped in fine silver chains, with scarlet nipples and pudenda, and hennaed geometric patterns on her hands, feet, breasts and shoulders. This exotic stranger had no personality, no past and no future. She lived only in the present – a slave – an object to be bought and sold. Laura shivered with that revelation. With her scarlet nipples standing proudly erect, and her intimate lips swollen, the slave she saw was obviously aroused.

They were taken to a large, silent space with three spotlighted platforms. Laura guessed it was the great hall. Beyond each platform was darkness. Laura, lifted by strong male arms, mounted the first platform. Donna told her to kneel, buttocks on ankles and hands behind head. The chain running between wrists and ankles made this pose awkward, and she had to open her thighs wide to achieve it – which was no doubt the intension. A hand towel, and a bowl of what looked like pink cream, were placed by her side. When she looked round, Helen and Penny were, as she expected, in the same position, equally exposed, their breasts thrusting proudly.

Donna stood in the light. 'You will each be told to take up certain positions during the inspection. Do not hesitate, do not speak – even to answer questions from your prospective buyers. I will be on hand to answer and to ensure you obey, and our clients expect to see evidence of your discipline.'

She withdrew into the darkness. Laura heard people coming in. They hovered just beyond the pools of light, hesitating, waiting for a brave soul to take a lead. They talked in low voices. Half-blinded, Laura searched the shadows for Jack and Peter, but neither appeared. Tostides swept in and cajoled his guests.

'Look at them, and inspect the goods. They'll do anything you want. Touch them, test them, make sure they're worth the money I'm sure you are prepared to pay.'

He strode into the light, straight up to Penny, and began stroking her breasts.

'Come on down, feel these firm tits. Look at these superb nipples. She's aching for it, this one. Likes a bit of pain, good with men and women, under thirty, experienced and well trained.'

The sales pitch worked. People in cocktail dresses and suits surrounded Penny. Hands reached out, stroking and poking. They made Penny bend forward and hands invaded her pussy and bottom, greased with the contents of the bowl. Laura watched as the fingers worked rhythmically and Penny began to move, helplessly aroused.

Another group began to coalesce around Laura. Hands began stroking, poking and nipping. A woman ordered Laura to open her mouth wide, and she looked inside, checking her teeth. She entered Laura's tight sheath and rubbed the treacherous bump. She grew wet and ashamed. Someone twisted her nipples hard. She gasped.

'Bend over, let's see her arse.' The voice was upper-class British, the gender male. Hands spread her cleft and a greased finger poked inside. 'She's nice and tight. Pity she's not a virgin.'

'I prefer my women freshly broken in.' That was a Latin American male.

Another male, sounding like an escapee from a gangster movie, asked for a demonstration. 'Show us how she reacts to the crop.' Fire exploded across her buttocks.

The unknown female spoke. 'Have her tits been cropped yet?'

Donna replied, with a certain distaste that made Laura wonder if she retained some affection for her. 'No, not yet, but I'm sure she would bear it well.'

Two brutally hard fingers thrust into her pussy, and a thumb went into her anus. Laura gasped again. They withdrew and a hand slapped her bottom hard. This person said nothing. For the next few minutes she was ordered to stand, bend, shake her breasts and touch her toes. Hands slapped her breasts and pinched her calves and arms, checking muscle tone, resilience and obedience.

A gong rang out. Suddenly she was alone. Lights lit up the crowd for the bidding but it was still hard to see with the spotlights straight on her face. A man stood in front of her, facing the crowd, gavel in hand and a lectern to bang it on laden with a large book and a pen.

'Ladies and gentlemen, you have had the opportunity to check the goods – now for business. Before we begin, let me remind you that payment must be made in cash dollars by midnight tonight.' He cleared his throat.

'The first lot this evening is Helen, an eighteen-year-old with long brown hair. She exhibits some dominant tendencies, but has shown herself to be an apt pupil and is used to discipline. Have we a bidder to start us off?'

'One hundred.' Laura wondered who was bidding

'One fifty.'

Slowly the bids increased, and Peter's voice regularly led them. Eventually, Peter bid two thousand, and so secured Helen's purchase. Helen was taken away, crying with relief.

'Lot two is Penny. A twenty-nine-year-old with advanced masochistic tendencies. Do I hear five hundred?'

The bidding seemed to go on for ages, with three voices dominating the action: Jack, Tostides, and another man with a strong East European accent. The price rose, fifteen thousand, seventeen, twenty, twenty-five. It was so much more than Helen's price that Laura began to suspect that the auction had been arranged in Peter's favour. Then she began to suspect something worse: that the auction was rigged against Jack, Penny and herself. The East European went silent. Jack bid fifty-five thousand dollars. It was an unbelievable sum. The bidding seemed to have stopped. The gavel came down once, twice.

'One hundred thousand.' Tostides boomed out his bid.

The auctioneer looked towards Jack. 'Do you wish to go further?' There was a pause, and whispering ran round the room. There was not a whisper from Jack.

'Lot two, then, for one hundred thousand, to Mr Tostides.' Penny cried out. Laura's heart sank. It was all a con; a dirty, despicable, evil trick. Laura looked to Penny;

her head had fallen forward and she was muttering. In tears she was led away.

'Lot three. A most charming eighteen-year-old, Laura. Laura has shown a remarkable aptitude for discpline and, although no longer a virgin, she is virtually unused.'

Quaking, Laura listened to her fate. She had a sinking feeling. Again the bidding went high, all the way to one hundred thousand, but this time the winner was the East European. Jack, despite a bid of ninety thousand dollars, could not compete. Stunned and cheated, Laura joined Penny in the slave pens again. Helen was nowhere to be seen. At least she had got away.

Laura was starving and light-headed. Since the enemas they'd been given nothing to eat or drink. Penny stood alongside, her hands likewise bound with silk cords behind her back. They were joined by a thin chain between their nose rings but were otherwise free to move. Not to see, however, for they were blindfolded.

It was odd, Laura thought, to be wearing panties again. Not that they were normal panties, of course, but tight, almost transparent, white elasticated panties that pressed her sex against the pair of subtly moving love balls. In turn, the balls moved against another set in her rectum. She felt swollen and very wet, and her nipples pushed hard against the tight binding of a strapless latex bra a couple of sizes too small.

A door opened. She felt a breath of warm, excited air on her cheek and heard laughter and shouting. A feast was in full swing and the diners waited for their dessert and entertainment – Laura and Penny.

Donna tapped her bottom with a whip and hissed in their ears, 'You're on. Your owner wants to see how you'll perform.'

Laura had the sensation of bodies moving out of their way, heard chatter and giggles and the wet, sucking sounds of sex nearby. The air smelled of spices and wine, cigar smoke and incense. Her foot squashed something, like a grape, and hands stroked her as she passed.

'Halt!' Donna had regained her powerful voice since the shower room.

The whip tapped her bottom. She edged forward until her thighs bumped into polished wood. The whip tapped her hips. She shifted right and bumped into Penny.

'Climb up and sit.'

She turned towards Penny, wary of the chain's pull on her nose. Hands guided her, cupping her bottom and breasts, stroking her thighs and sex. It was awkward with tied hands, but the table was low. She wondered which way she faced; probably towards the dais and Tostides. The balls in her body moved against each other, their eccentric weight stimulating, arousing.

'Further back, until I tell you to stop.'

They had to trust Donna. Bumping each other, they shuffled backwards until their feet were on the table top. Laura noticed that the noise had dropped away to a background chatter. Her ankles were tied together, crossed to keep her knees open, and then her wrists were released, but only to be tied to her ankles. She was sitting tucked up, her weight over and around the balls, compressing a pelvic area already filled with the heavy globes. The chain between their nose rings was removed.

A gong rang. Tostides spoke over the diminishing bustle of sound.

'Friends, the competitors are ready and the first bets have been placed. Before we begin, I'll go through the rules. The competitors will be put through a number of trials, each one designed to induce orgasm. The first girl to be exhausted loses. It is now eight. If they both last until midnight, the General and I will intervene. Donna, let the fun begin!'

Donna stood back and called clearly, 'You will rock back and forth.' Donna's hand pushed Laura from behind.

'Aahh, uh, ahhh.' Laura couldn't keep quiet. Shock and bubbles of sensation burbled around her hips as the balls moved and rolled, now pressing her clitoris and already swollen lips as she went forward, then her anus as she went back. She felt Penny moving with her and heard her gasps and groans. God, how long could she endure this? Her breasts, catching the mood, swelled against the confines of the bra. Her nipples ached.

All around voices cheered and called bets. 'One hundred for the blonde.' 'Fifty the black hair.' 'Blondie'll come first. Come on!'

Laura gritted her teeth, but the hand pushed her on, and with every forward roll her body felt fuller, more compressed, closer to an uncontrollable explosion. Her breathing became rough, her mouth open. Her body trembled, the pressure building. Her clit felt as if it would pierce the panties.

A female voice called out from close by, 'Look at her sex lips. They're fat as slugs!'

She felt fingers between her legs, tugging at the crotch, and suddenly the panties split away from her mound. Her lips flowered. Fingers sealed her entrance, keeping the balls in and rubbing her stiff, hard, long bud. Donna kept her rocking, denying her the reflex desire to rub the hand. She gasped, groaned from the depths of her throat, and started to come. Hands pinned her to the table by the shoulders, and held her knees apart. She shook with the intensity of her orgasm, guts cramping and her head shaking.

Someone called out the score. 'One each.'

Laura felt Penny shaking beside her and a wave of disgust swept her rational mind. Why couldn't she stop her body from enjoying this? A tear of frustration trickled. She had to hold out, had to. She felt sharp metal against her hip. She squealed but no harm came. She felt hands picking at her blindfold and suddenly light flooded in. She blinked and looked round. The stage on which they were displayed was in the middle of the room. All around her, the audience sat watching avidly. In front of her, Tostides and Gorski looked down, the former worried, the latter very obviously enjoying himself. She looked at Penny. They smiled at each other.

Donna and a new woman stripped away their bras. The

256

stranger wore only a corset and stockings, exposing her naked sex and full, heavy, dark-brown-tipped breasts. The Princess and the Contessa stood to either side, crops in their hands. Laura remembered Tostides' words about women being crueler than men. He had determined to show her just how cruel they could be.

'Cup your breasts, elbows back and arch your backs.'

They were going to crop her little breasts! An extraordinary feeling swept through Laura – a combination of fear and anticipation. This was the test Penny had long since passed, the ultimate test of resolve and discipline, and Laura would not fail. She sensed an expectant silence spread around as the details of this test filtered through the audience. To her left, enthroned above the mass, Tostides and Gorski sat watching. She caught the Greeks' eye and steeled her resolve.

'Three strokes above, three below, and three on the button. Begin.'

Laura set her jaw and placed her palms under her firm, peachy mounds. They felt harder than normal. She locked eyes with Penny in mutual support and encouragement. Neither pair of eyes more than flickered as the crops descended with wicked snaps; only gasps and a tightening of expression betrayed the pain.

'Two.' They each breathed slowly out and in.

'Three.' Laura winced momentarily. Penny's breasts were marked by three distinct horizontal red lines. Her own smaller models had one broad bar across them.

'Hold them up with your nipples. Higher!'

Laura took a tight grip on her hard, already tingling nipples with three fingers, using the rings for extra purchase. This time she gasped audibly after each stroke to the undersides. Penny's breasts shook violently.

'Hands behind heads, chests out!'

Donna leant between them and removed their nipple rings, hooking them on to their earrings for safe keeping. Laura felt the tension rise as the pain in her breasts diffused and spread, the redness covering her thrusting, shaking boobs.

Penny grunted, groaned, shook her head and closed her eyes as the crop snapped across the top of her nubs. Laura tensed her whole body and tried to force the pain to disperse. The next stroke caught the underside of her halo, shaking her breasts, sending a quiver through her body. She wanted to knead her poor breasts, but that would be a sign of weakness. The last strokes sent each girl rocking backwards and doubling, the crops stinging the very tips of their breasts, but they forced themselves back upright and grinned to each other. The crowd began to cheer.

There was no time to enjoy their triumph. The blindfolds were replaced. Unseen hands dragged Laura a short way backwards. She had been aware of space behind, between her and the crowd, but there had been no opportunity to investigate what might be there. They held her upright, and raised her arms. She felt leather rings close tight on her wrists, and then her ankles were jerked apart and restrained.

Donna spoke quietly in her ear: 'Gorski wants to see how you respond under the whip. Bear up!' Laura wondered if this commentary was supposed to help. She felt Donna kneel and remove the rings from her belly. 'Just a precaution. I'll hang them on your earrings. Oh, and by the way, if you drop the balls, you'll get double.'

Laura gritted her teeth and tightened her internal muscles. Here we go again!

The air whistled, and she jerked as the knots of lash flickered and snapped over her buttocks. This was just like that day in the foyer; not too painful, but just bearable. Was it only the day before last? She heard Penny's gasp from nearby.

'Unmph!' A second lash splattered across her belly. The lashes established a rhythm, alternately striking front and back. Tiny tongues of fire danced on her thighs, between her outstretched legs and breasts. Her flesh was on fire, burning, and heat spread. She whimpered, and her hips began to move, seeking the next stroke. She felt wet, and the balls in her vagina moved. She gripped them, increasing the pleasure they gave. Suddenly, the lashes came from below, licking upwards, stinging her thighs, snatching at her lips, seeking her knot. She heard Penny cry, and moaned herself. Her body yearned for another such onslaught on her throbbing, aching pussy. They left her for a few moments, shaking, trying to hold the balls in as she chased the lash. Whoosh! Tendrils of fire flickered; she bucked, pleading for orgasm, but she held on to those heavy balls.

After all that, Donna removed the balls as she sagged on her bonds. Donna took them slowly, creating aftershocks in her belly. Laura speculated, with a head drugged with pleasure, what was coming next. She became aware of two bodies – one in front, the other behind – by their hands, and then their cocks rubbing against her. One mouth nipped her breasts, the other her neck. She heard Penny gasp, and then the hands behind gripped her buttocks.

'Ooh, oh, ooh.' His stem eased inside, pushing her in turn against the man in front. The thick cock forced its way in, corking her.

'Aah, ah, ah.' The second penis surged bluntly against her bruised pussy lips, battering them aside, and he lodged himself. Neither moved except to rub her breasts and hips. Instead, and against her will, Laura found her hips moving against them, her internal muscles gripping and relaxing. They held her still between them for a long time as her next orgasm grew. Abruptly, they left her, gasping, open, empty.

She heard movement, and another pair of men took up the same positions. She knew they were different because their bellies also touched her. Her buttocks were gripped hard, wringing a cry, and then both thrust together. It was easier this time for both were already lubricated. She guessed they had come from Penny. Immobile, they held her and again her muscles sought pleasure. They held her longer, and her breathing became more rapid. She was on the verge of orgasm. Her blindfold was whipped off and she found herself staring, wild-eyed, into Tostides' face.

Laura screamed with disgust but her body refused to stop. They jerked out and Tostides stood, pumping on his cock as she shook, her hips straining uncontrollably. His sperm splattered over her belly, striking her clit. Another shower poured over her buttocks, and she came, helplessly.

Donna finished putting the rings back in place. Laura's body was tiring, and she hardly registered the operation even though her delicate flesh was swollen and tender. Donna stroked Laura's bottom and explained in a low voice:

'Time to lie down. You're going to be our dessert bowls. Don't worry – this will take a long time. Try and relax.'

Slaves approached with trolleys laden with every kind of fruit, warming dishes and jugs, ice cream and wafers, brochette and choux pastries. Bottles of champagne nestled in ice buckets and there were bowls of nuts, yoghurt, dried fruit, Turkish delight, honey and creamy puddings. The smell of chocolate drifted into the air, mingling with the scent of sex and exotic oils surrounding the table.

They were spreadeagled on the table, their heads level with each other's hips, their bottoms raised on cushions. The hoard descended. Hands raised Laura's sex and opened it wide. A jug of thick cream was poured. Laura gasped. It was cool and slow. The woman in the corset crouched over her chest and lowered her shaven, wet, very open sex on to Laura's left breast. She used her fingers to spread herself even wider and began to consume the swollen mound. Soaking, rubbing back and forth, she opened wider until the cone almost disappeared. Laura felt wet warmth and clutching muscles, and saw the woman's eyes close in pleasure. Having smeared her left breast, the woman repeated the process on her right breast, and then moved up to smother Laura's face in honey. Laura gasped, opened her mouth and stuck her tongue into the soft, wide, hot hole.

Something first pushed into her vagina and moved around in the cream. The sex crawled away, she looked down. Leila was eating the banana that protruded from her warming, melting, creamy sheath. Ladles full of warm runny, dark chocolate were poured over her breasts and guests bent to dip fruit and wafers, scooping up the sauce, seeking to savour the mélange of cocoa and female arousal. Honey poured into her navel, and almonds dropped on top. One man dipped his head and ate them, cleaning her out with his tongue. She was told to open her mouth, and a spoonful of vanilla ice cream filled it, shockingly cold.

'No swallowing, now, that's for our use,' someone said.

The woman kissed her, licking out the fine vanilla, and then a penis entered. She licked his chill flesh, swallowing the food. Tongues licked at the chocolate, nibbling. Fingers, slices of fruit and biscuits dipped into her sex to be eaten with relish. Men entered her refilled creaminess, and then fed her or their friends with their dripping cocks. Ice cubes melted on her nipples, and more warm chocolate poured, setting quickly. The Princess climbed above her and coated her black-furred sex and buttocks in the chocolate from Laura's breasts before demanding to be licked clean.

Only men now employed Laura's mouth. She was filled with cock; thick, short, long, circumcised, flaccid, erect, hairy, smooth. She licked and sucked without discrimination. Some men thrust, others kept still. Some spurted inside, others in her hair or across her face and breasts. Others came directly from Penny tasting of come and cream, or from slave girls fragrant with musk. Only half her senses were aware of the men, because hands worked below. Subtle, cunning, female fingers pierced and pulled, spread and caressed. These fingers were oily, slippery, sometimes feathery, smacking, nipping and rubbing. They avoided her clitoris, building the tension again, seeking the strongest reaction.

261

Champagne fountained over her face and breasts and filled her vagina, triggering a gentle orgasm. They started again, with more coating and fillings, more enterings and eatings. Laura undulated and moaned, jumping when ice cream burnt her breasts or sent shocks through her womb, sucking chocolated-coated cocks or clits, chasing the tongues that tasted her mouth.

Suddenly, as she climbed gently to another peak, the diners climbed away. Her heavy limbs were released and for a few moments, she was lying alone as a frame was mounted above her. She remembered to look at the clock, and saw with relief that it was after ten. The frame was very simple: a box as long as her trunk, with padded upper surfaces. They took her ankles and bound them, thighs parted and vertical, feet high, her hips tipped up. Her arms were bound to the uprights beside her head. Penny was tied in reverse over the frame, head to toe.

Large syringes, like her mother used for icing cakes, pressed into Penny's and Laura's relaxed anal rings. As she felt her own rectum fill, Laura saw the plunger forcing cream inside Penny. On and on, the cool cream went in until the plunger was fully depressed. The syringe was removed. A tiny white drop oozed from Penny. Laura felt the cream melting inside her. She was full and she realised a man was above her, his thighs hairy and naked, his penis long, hard and red. She wondered idly if it had been in her mouth. She looked down. Another man stood ready to enter her. He was shorter, and his cock sprouted thickly out of a dark, sticky bush of hair.

The man bumped his plum against Penny's oozing anus, coating the tip in cream, and then took hold of Penny's hips just as Laura felt a steadying contact on her thighs. She tried to relax her knot, to let him enter, but he drove hard. Her eyes popped open to see Penny's sex stretching around the long penis above. Laura grunted, moaned, and cream spurted from Penny as her rectum filled, splashing down. The cock in her bottom pushed, fat against her squidginess. Her sore tissues clutched, the crown popped through. Laura felt every bump and vein as he began to pump, just as the cock above pounded Penny.

Hands invaded her sex, forcing fingers against her clitoris and between her lips, playing, rubbing. Other fingers began to pinch and roll her nipples. Laura closed her eyes, wallowing. A new feeling, a realisation, seeped into her head. These people had no love for her; they only wanted to use her, to enjoy her body. In return, they were helping her to enjoy herself, to come, and come, and come again. It was too much. Yes, she pleaded, yes, do it, do it, fuck me.

'Release their hands and give them a drink,' someone said.

Laura shook her head. Things were getting weird. Something thick, much thicker than a penis, pushed into her bottom. She looked up to see a black phallus, complete with balls, buried in Penny's bottom.

Donna's voice whispered, 'Well done, nearly eleven. Keep going.' Then she raised her voice. 'Just to make sure they don't slack – and to give us a break – Laura and Penny will now play with themselves. If either appears not to be trying, can I have a couple of volunteers to wield the whips?'

Laura almost welcomed the sight of her tormentor-in-chief, Leila, standing ready with a long switch. Her great bush was smeared with chocolate and cream, her breasts heaved, diamond-tipped with excitement. The Contessa's soaking, pouting sex hovered closer to deal with Penny. Laura stroked her fingers over her stick, hard, tight breasts and sore nipples, testing their state. They were deeply aroused. She licked her lips and tried to ignore the audience, closing her eyes. Laura reflected on the vicissitudes of life; for weeks she had been wanting to touch herself, weeks when any such touch was totally forbidden and punishable. Now she had been ordered to do just that; to do the thing she had always been told was wrong; the thing she did in secret, ashamed of her lusts and the fantasies that fed them. But to do it here, in public? So difficult, so embarrassing, so shaming.

'Eyes open,' said the Contessa.

Penny's fingers were seeking her own ravaged sex, delicately teasing the rings from the traces of honey and cream, before dipping into the dark, deep red. Laura took a deep breath and caught sight of a twitching whip. She promised herself that this was different, a one-off, never to be repeated. Laura spread her lips wide and began, as she liked to do, to stroke the smooth central groove with a single forefinger. It wasn't working. She needed to close her eyes, to picture Helen as she used to do, or Jack. Penny dug deep, scooping her fingers in, hooking and rubbing. A drop of musk dripped from Penny, strong, sexual, and landed on her lips. She tasted the essence of the moment. Her hips twitched. Her clitoris, untouched, leapt, and her fingers entered her deeper than ever before, her other hand spreading herself wider, as wide as ever she had stretched. Laura abandoned shame. It left her gasping. She played games with her button, and twitched her nipples, even though they hurt, to add a delicious spice of pain. Above, Penny gripped her sex hard and moaned. Laura's stomach knotted, and snapped.

The frame had gone and women surrounded her, tongues and fingers searching, stroking, plunging the phallus in and out. Laura found herself kneeling, open, leaning back against soft breasts, her ears and neck being nibbled, kissed and licked. They looped fine cords through her labial rings and tied them around her thighs, opening her completely. Donna inserted a thin pipette just inside the tiniest opening, and nipped the small bulb, forcing a warm jet of liquid inside. An itching heat spread, below, but almost at the surface, of her vulva. Feathers tickled her open, exposed body, her anus, vagina, clitoris and nipples. They held her arms above her head and feathers played, twirling in the soft hollow at the base of her spine. Another tickled her navel, and she felt a new tightening around her nipples. Collars of gold, sprung to bite, accentuated already intense arousal. Her blood thrummed and boiled. Mouths kissed her, and then she was bent forward, her bottom high, hands held out in front, and she felt the sting of Leila's whip, criss-crossing, setting her buttocks on fire.

Her head, floppy because all energy was devoted to reacting to pleasure, was raised and held against a downy mound. She knew, by the softness of voice and touch, that the women still toyed with her, and the thick hard column that penetrated her bottom again was not flesh. She licked and sucked and kissed. Her sore, hot bum heaved at the smooth thighs and belly that plundered her innards. The itch in her bladder grew. The heat of her bottom spread inwards with every thrust of the dry, hard phallus. Her head filled with the taste of the sex she drank from, driving her to a frenzy.

Laura became detached, her body lost in sensation, her mind escaping the fleshy bonds. She imagined she was hovering above the table, looking down on her slender, weak body as it twisted and bucked, fully conscious of every passing sensation. She was amazed at the size of the phallus that pierced her bottom; appalled, yet thrilled, by the colourful streaks of chocolate, cream, yoghurt, sperm and honey covering her body; but curiously unconcerned by the throbbing, gold clamped, purpose, distended nipples on top of her conical and hard breasts.

She watched her body reach another orgasm, slower now, but intense and protracted. The woman with the corset who had coated her breasts, held her own swollen veined breast to Laura's mouth. Laura sucked on the velvety teat, knowing in a dark corner what she did, but excited beyond reason. She suckled the nipple, and her detached self moaned in the depths of her debauchery.

They let Laura lie back, stroking her thighs apart and releasing her labial rings. These women, these implacable, terrible wonderful women, whipped her open again with minute lashes, frothing her to renewed fury. Ice melted on her swollen, bruised tissues, thrilling tired nerves. Then the men gathered. Her hands were tied to her collar, and they took her, men and women, again and again, in every way possible.

Laura's jaw ached with constant fellating, constant drinking of sperm, and her thighs trembled. She had come so many times. Still Donna told her to keep going, promising it would all be over soon. Sperm splashed her thighs, and a tongue lapped it greedily. She was laid back on the long, deep shaft in her bottom. Hands gripped her breasts, twisting. A new penis entered her slit. No doubt it would be a long time coming. Laura could no longer tense a muscle. A dark, hirsute female sex hovered over her mouth. Leila had returned. The man thrust into her belly, his cock rubbing against the other through the walls of her womb. Leila lowered her hot, pungent, flesh mound. Laura reached with tired tongue and lips, entering the dense, damp, musky forest. Her arms were still held above her head. Tongues ranged over her flanks and lapped her armpits to wipe away her sweat. Leila ground down, shifting to present her secret, dilated anus to the mouth she knew would lavish the praise she desired.

Laura pierced the ring of Leila's anus while she felt the penis in her bottom begin to pump. The cock in her belly drove deep. Leila shifted forward, driving her long, thick labia into Laura's mouth. Laura did not mean to do it, but as the second man pumped, her armpit was bitten, a nipple was twisted, and her nose was nipped by Leila's anus, she climaxed, and bit hard on the soft flesh. Leila screamed and rubbed down, smothering, drenching.

Dimly, distantly, Donna cradled her head. 'Drink this, you've done it, both of you. You've beaten the bastard!'

The liquid was thick, warm, almost fiery. God, she was tired, so tired. Laura reached out her hand and touched Penny's fingers, to show how proud she was, to congratulate her friend, but she could not think clearly or even make her fingers grip. Her eyes closed, heavy eyelids refusing to stay open. A thick fog flowed through her veins. Laura tried to speak, to complain, but nothing seemed to matter any more.

SISTERS OF SEVERCY

Jean Aveline

Jean Aveline's first novel for Nexus, *Sisters of Severcy*, is in our opinion one of the finest SM novels written to date. It is original, highly arousing and strikingly well written, and we hope that Jean will go on to write many more novels of a similar calibre for us.

The villa at Severcy is a place of extremes. Here, innocence and love vie with experience and cruelty as young Isabelle is led into perversion by Robert, the handsome Englishman who visits the villa one summer. As Isabelle is introduced to the dark pleasures of Severcy, so her sister aids in the sensual education of Charlotte, Robert's bride in England. In the following extract, which we feel makes a fitting end to the collection, Isabelle's initiation into the pleasures of the flesh lacks only one final ritual before it is complete.

I sabelle sat on a chair in Alain's bedroom facing a full-length mirror. Maria was fussing with Isabelle's hair, a clutch of pins held in her teeth. The maid had used gold braid to plait a dozen strands or more. Now she was twisting and coiling the strands so that they formed a harmonious whole, neatly compacted against Isabelle's scalp. Maria had already spent almost two hours painting an intricate series of interlinking geometric patterns on to Isabelle's naked body. She had laboured with the dark pigment and a small brush until every part of her charge was ornamented in this way. Isabelle had been forced to lie down, to stand, to raise her arms, part her legs, lift her breasts, hold her hair clear of her neck, open the cheeks of her behind and generally endure the itchiness of the brush and the coarseness of the ground plant that formed the pigment. As the paint dried, so it lost much of its colour, becoming dark grey, matt and scratchy to the touch.

As Maria put the finishing touches to her hair, Isabelle looked through the glass doors that led to the Mexican room. This was not strictly a room but a sprawling, iron-framed conservatory that pushed out from the side of the villa into the surrounding gardens. She could see cacti growing from yellow sand and large, smooth boulders. It was the first time that she had been in Alain's bedroom and it was entirely ordinary apart from this view, this astonishing glimpse of another continent. She expected to see exotic birds and strange animals but nothing moved

271

except for the occasional wisp of cloud visible through the glazed roof.

When Maria had finished Isabelle's hair she went to a wardrobe and took out a long, thin, rather battered cardboard box. It was the kind of box that might contain canes made for the schoolroom. The maid set it on the dressing table and opened it. Reaching her hand inside Maria brought out nothing more dangerous than a handful of long, brightly coloured feathers. These she arranged in Isabelle's hair, pushing the shafts into the compacted plaits and carefully fixing each with pins. When she had finished, Isabelle turned to face the mirror and saw that they formed a sort of head-dress. The feathers drooped at the ends, each finishing in what appeared to be an eye, dark blue and shimmering. The filaments were so soft that the eyes seemed to float above her as she moved her head. The effect, when seen with her painted body, was to turn her into something unrecognisable; she looked savage yet beautiful, as she imagined a jaguar or a leopard to be, but more exotic still than those creatures.

Maria began to oil her skin. The dark, greyish pigment was long dry and the oil soaked into it, reviving its colour so that it became a brilliant indigo. The patterns seemed to swirl before her eyes as Isabelle looked at them. Maria had her stand so that she could oil her back and behind and the length of her legs. She took sandals from the dressing table and dropped them on the floor obliging Isabelle to step into them. They were made of a coarsely woven fibrous material and had cords that Maria wound round her ankles and the lower part of her calves to secure them. The final item was a gold mask, the metal beaten thin and burnished. It was fashioned after the image of a beautiful boy and, though it was perfect and unscratched, it had the feeling of something ancient. Maria slipped it over her head and attached it with leather bands, which she fed beneath the plaits so that they were invisible.

'I need to tie your hands, mademoiselle,' said Maria.

Isabelle put her hands behind her back and the maid lashed them together with the same material that had been

272

used to make the sandals. When this was done Maria walked over to the glazed, double doors and opened them. A blast of hot air swept into the bedroom. Isabelle stepped forward and was about to pass through the doors when Maria suddenly stopped her as if something had been forgotten.

'Excuse me, mademoiselle, there is one more thing.'

The maid dropped to her knees and reached for Isabelle's sex. She took the labia and pulled, stretching each lip repeatedly, with little regard for Isabelle's comfort, until they stood out conspicuously pink against the darkly painted skin.

Satisfied, Maria stood and led Isabelle into the Mexican room. The heat that had swept into the bedroom now surrounded Isabelle, pressing like a giant hand against her throat, making it hard for her to breathe. From time to time she was forced to dip her head to avoid the cacti, at least those which branched and spread like trees. Most seemed to grow straight up in thick green columns or squatted as malevolent spheres, armed with great spines as sharp as needles. It was unnerving to walk among them naked and bound, and with her vision restricted by the mask. At one point she heard a series of cries coming from ahead of them. The voice was a woman's and added to the sharpness in the air.

Quite soon, Alain came into view. He was seated in a cane chair wearing the loose trousers, open white cotton shirt and felt hat of a plantation owner. Behind him, and dwarfing him, were the remnants of a stone building that Isabelle recognised as a pyramid, or at least part of a pyramid. The original structure must have been vast. What was presented here was a single corner, ragged where it would have joined the remainder of the building, but otherwise surprisingly well preserved. The sharp, square, inclined edge of the pyramid was clearly visible and the stones were crisply dressed to fit tightly, one to the other. At the front of the ruin were broad steps that led up the inclined face but which finished abruptly in a broken line at a height of about five metres. Later, Alain would tell her that this structure had nearly sunk the ship that carried it back from the New World. It was the reason for the Mexican room, the only addition made to the villa since the time of Alain's grandfather.

In front of the pyramid and next to the place where Alain was sitting, was a table made of the same stone. Sprawled on this was the naked figure of a woman. Although the figure faced away from her, Isabelle was sure that it was Anna; no other woman in the villa had such a body, firm and athletic, yet yielding and soft in its offering.

Alain appeared to be in a kind of reverie, and so quiet were the footfalls of the two women in the sand that he only noticed them when they were almost upon him. It must have been the sound of Maria's starched, black dress rustling that caught his attention. His eyes widened as he turned and looked at Isabelle. For the first time, she saw him take an unreserved interest in her, an interest untainted by irony. He rose from his chair and when she halted, walked around her, taking in every detail, reaching out and touching her at intervals as if touching something extraordinary, something that might disappear like a mirage. When his eyes met hers though, they looked straight through her. Isabelle realised that it wasn't she herself that merited such attention, but only her surface: the surface of indigo and gold that had been applied by Maria, but which he had designed himself. She realised that it was his own dream that interested and aroused him; she was simply the carrier, the canvas on which the image had its representation.

'Turn around, Anna,' he said in a hushed voice.

The woman on the stone table turned. She smiled at the vision.

'What do you see?' he asked.

'A spirit.'

'Yes. A spirit of the desert. Or a goddess.'

His hand touched the cords that bound Isabelle's wrists as he walked around her for the hundredth time. Beads of sweat were running down her back, converging in the depressions on either side of her spine and running on into the valley of her gleaming, oiled behind. He ran the back of his hand upward, from her waist to her neck, and she shivered. His hand came away covered in a mixture of oil and perspiration but the pigment stayed pristine. Isabelle could feel his desire as a resonance in the dry, furnace air. She wanted him to take her when she was like this, invisible behind her mask. It would be like sex in the dark, the way it had sometimes been with Anne-Marie. Isabelle was disposed to pleasure at the moment. It was the heat and the place, and it was Anna gazing at her with dark, gleaming eyes. It was also the man behind her with all of his power, and it was the promise she had given to him, the promise of herself.

At that moment Anna shifted her position slightly and for the first time Isabelle could see between the girl's legs. Her sex was inflamed and the lips were fuller than usual, but it was not this which caught Isabelle's attention. Standing from Anna's left thigh, the back of which was pressed to the surface of the table, was a cluster of cactus spines. They stood vertically from the swell of flesh which curved inwards to meet her sex. The spines were at least six inches long and as thin as needles. Isabelle looked at the girl's face but saw nothing there to betray any discomfort; instead she saw a perverse satisfaction and pride.

'Remove her mask, Maria,' Alain said abruptly.

It took a few moments for the maid to accomplish this. When she had, Isabelle looked no less exotic. The geometric patterns covered and transformed her face as surely as they covered and transformed her body.

Alain went over to Anna. He must have seen Isabelle tense as she glimpsed the spines. Now he ran his hands over the top of them, brushing them so they vibrated. Anna started to close her legs reflexively, but checked herself, stretched them wider instead and offering herself fully.

'Use your mouth on her sex,' he told Isabelle.

Isabelle knelt before the girl and pressed her lips to the heat of that inflamed place. Anna tasted of the sea and Isabelle sucked deep. Above her head, she knew that Alain

275

was manipulating the spines. She could hear Anna's groans and feel the spasms that passed through her body. Whether it was pain or pleasure she did not know.

'More spines,' Alain said to Maria and the maid hurried away.

Isabelle continued to work her tongue and Anna lifted her belly, rotating it slowly. Since Isabelle's hands were still tied, she could not steady the girl, only follow her as she moved. From time to time she would suck in the flesh around Anna's little bud and pull it into her mouth, nipping and licking, until Anna bucked. When Maria returned, she handed the spines to Alain who went to stand at the other end of the table, out of Isabelle's field of view. Whatever he did there had a strong effect. Soon, Anna was writhing around, and Alain told Isabelle to pause for a moment, so she sat back on her heels. Looking up, she saw Anna supporting herself on her elbows and reaching to kiss Alain who stood above her. As she kissed him, he pushed one of the spines into the flesh of her breast, piercing her just below the nipple. For as long as she kissed him, he maintained the pressure on the spine. Isabelle watched with a fascinated horror. This spine was not the only one that impaled her. Two small forests grew from the area around her nipples.

When the girl's lips withdrew from her master, so he released the spine. The girl's face was flushed and sweating with excitement. She glaced at Isabelle as if to persuade Alain to have the kneeling girl begin again at her sex. He said nothing. Instead, he took another spine and laid it on the down slope of Anna's breast, pressing hard enough to indent the skin but not enough to break it. Anna looked from the spine to Isabelle. Her expression was a compound of desire and greed, mixed with a little madness. As Isabelle watched, the girl reached for Alain with her lips again and he pushed the spine home. Anna groaned and rolled her shoulders voluptuously, kissing for a long time as he twisted the spine in his fingers.

Twice more Isabelle watched this procedure and then Alain told her to use her tongue again. Anna moaned from the moment that Isabelle's lips touched her and she continued to moan until, many climaxes later, Alain told Isabelle to stop. This time, when Isabelle sat back she saw that Anna's body was a complete arch. Her head hung down from her shoulders as she supported herself on her elbows, and her breasts and belly were uppermost, pushed out. Alain smiled at Isabelle.

'She has told you of Don Luis?'

Isabelle nodded.

'It was one of his games. I play it to please her. A great advantage is that the spine leave no scars so the procedure can be repeated over and over again.'

Anna raised her head and gave each of them an unusually shy smile, thanking them in a quiet voice.

Alain took the mask from the chair where Maria had laid it. He looked at it carefully, perhaps seeing his reflection in the polished surface; he then carried it to Isabelle. He slipped it over her face and attached it himself this time.

'The bag, Maria,' he said when he was finished. This evidently meant something to the maid because she immediately turned and hurried back to the bedroom. He offered his hand to Anna, who rose shakily and seated herself on one of the chairs. For the first time, Isabelle could see that there were a number of iron rings embedded in the surface of the table, which might be used to secure a person. With Anna there had clearly been no need. As Isabelle looked at the girl, a rivulet of sweat ran from her breast, slid across her belly and pooled between her thighs. Isabelle wanted to lick her again and she wanted to suck on those pierced breasts. She wanted to taste the salt and excitement. She wanted to know what else had happened in the desert in Mexico, the real desert. The sight of the spines brought crueller thoughts to the surface, impulses that centred on the dun-coloured nipples, spared by Alain as yet. Isabelle forced herself to look away, fearful of her own cruelty.

When Maria returned she was carrying a small, red, leather bag scuffed with use.

'Take her into the pyramid and get her ready,' Alain told the maid. 'Leave the bag, I will need it later.'

Maria set the bag down on the stone table while Isabelle looked at Alain mutely.

'A small surgical procedure,' he explained in response to the unspoken question.

Before Isabelle could ask more, Maria took her arm and led her to the overbearing, alien structure with its impossibly large blocks of stone and its savage reliefs. At the side of the building, invisible from the table, was an iron door. Maria paused when they reached it and produced a key from her pocket. Isabelle felt herself pulling away from the maid against her will. Alain's word had provoked in her a cold terror, and she was suddenly shaking. When the door was opened and the shadowed interior gaped before them, Maria tried to lead the bound girl inside, but Isabelle couldn't move; when Maria tugged at her arm, Isabelle dug in her heels.

Finally, Alain came over to them. 'Don't disappoint me in this, Isabelle,' he said.

'What will you do?' she asked in a trembling voice.

'Nothing that you cannot bear,' he replied. 'I expect your submission in this, as in all things, without consultation or negotiation. Robert has already agreed it. Shall I put him to the inconvenience of coming here? Or would you rather leave?'

Isabelle bowed her head and, after a moment's further hesitation, walked slowly into the pyramid. Maria was already inside and lit an oil lamp as Isabelle entered. The space was small, no more than a few metres square. The walls, floor and ceiling with covered with tiles that gleamed in the light of the lamp. The same grotesque motifs that she had seen carved on the stones outside were repeated on their surfaces.

In the middle of the room was a leather couch, glaringly European and out of place in this setting. Beside the couch was a glass cabinet filled with jars and bowls and neatly arranged surgical instruments. Maria stepped behind Isabelle as the girl gazed about herself in horror.

The bleak, sterile surfaces were designed for easy cleaning, for the efficient removal of body fluids, for the eradication of evidence perhaps, evidence of the most intimate crimes. Fingers picked at the cords that bound Isabelle's hands as she tortured herself with images of the worst kind.

'Sit on the couch please, mademoiselle,' the maid said coolly.

Isabelle did as she was bid, lying back when Maria pressed on her shoulders. The surface of the couch was slick against her back and smelt new, as if it had never been used before.

Maria was taking a series of objects from the inside of the cabinet and setting them out on an enamelled metal tray. There were sounds; sounds of metal, sounds of glass, gurglings, murmurs from the maid. In her anxiety, all that Isabelle felt able to move were her eyes, and she cared not to look. Even so, her ears unerringly identified those many small sounds. The metal sounds were the sharpening of a knife. The gurgling came from alcohol being decanted, and the scent was overpowering. The murmurs were sounds of pleasure; the maid was anticipating her actions, enjoying them already.

Isabelle's knuckle whitened on the edges of the couch as she tried to keep herself still, keep herself from fleeing. She was aware of Alain pacing back and forth before the opened iron door, like a guard. Occasionally he would glance into the room – or cell – and briefly examine her naked, offered body.

For a moment the maid came to stand before her, looking down at her sex. In Maria's hand was a glass dish and in the dish a white paste that she worked vigorously with a fine, steel spatula. She then returned to the cabinet and there were new sounds and smells.

'Why don't you tie me?' groaned Isabelle.

The maid appeared at her shoulder, still working on the paste, although it was thicker now and tinged with brown.

'There is no need, mademoiselle. The procedure is nothing. No worse than having your ears pierced.'

'Pierced?' asked Isabelle.

Maria seemed to realise that she had said more than she should and turned away from the naked girl. That is the way that Alain found them a few minutes later when he entered the room. His bulk made the space seem impossibly crowded and claustrophobic.

'Is it ready?' he asked, glancing at the paste.

The maid nodded.

'Has she been cleaned?'

'Not yet, monsieur.'

Alain took up one of the dishes. 'Alcohol,' he said, confirming what Isabelle had already guessed. He took a ball of fresh lint from the metal tray and soaked it in the clear liquid. 'It will sting.'

He pushed open her thighs and ran the lint around the whole area of her sex. When the liquid touched the pinkness of her nether lips it did indeed sting, and she tensed as if she had been slapped.

'It is said to dispel bad humours that might be carried in the air,' he told her. 'We want no infection.'

His insistent application of the alcohol brought a stream of tears from Isabelle's eyes. When he was satisfied that the area was clean he stepped back and allowed Marie to apply the paste.

'An extract of the leaves of the cocoa tree,' he told her.

There was more alcohol in the paste; Isabelle could feel it evaporating as the girl smeared it carefully on the lips about her clitoris. Then a cold numbness seeped into her flesh, radiating in a slow wave from the coated area.

Alain stroked her legs thoughtfully as they waited for the anaesthetic to take full effect. Maria busied herself with the task of removing a series of needles from a small leather pouch, laying them out on the table of Isabelle's belly. That belly was tense and still as Isabelle regarded the shining steel implements with a frozen horror.

Alain examined several of the needles for size and sharpness, laying them experimentally against the lips that were to be pierced. Finally he chose one of the larger ones and handed it to Maria. She dropped it into a bowl of alcohol and methodically removed the others from Isabelle's belly. Alain made Isabelle edge down the couch until her behind was poised on the very edge and her feet were pressed to the sides of her hips.

Then, when all was ready, Maria came to stand between Isabelle's widespread thighs. At a nod from Alain, she pulled at the lips of Isabelle's sex, as she had done in the bedroom, but this time she concentrated on the area around the clitoris, stretching out the membranes as far as they would go. Isabelle, unable to help herself, began to wriggle.

'If you don't keep absolutely still this will injure you,' Maria told her.

Isabelle looked down to see the needle approaching her sex and an apologetic but determined look on Maria's face. Isabelle froze in horror as Maria lay the needle horizontally on her belly directly in line with that part of her lips that overlay her clitoris. She could hardly believe her eyes as Maria drove the spine through her flesh in a single clean motion. There was no pain, only a numb tearing sensation, but still Isabelle screamed. She screamed for her body which was longer as God had made it.

Alain smiled. 'Such drama,' he murmured, 'and over such a tiny thing. Later you will have cause to scream.'

Isabelle gazed at him in a state close to shock. He stroked her face gently as Maria tidied away the various instruments and jars.

'Leave the needle in place for now,' Alain said, turning to the maid. 'And bring her outside when you are ready.'

When Isabelle was calmer, and this took some time, Maria took her once more into the openness of the Mexican room.

'On the altar I think, Isabelle,' said Alain.

She hadn't thought of it as an altar before and hesitated before approaching. Alain took her arm and guided her forward. She felt his large hands on her waist and suddenly she was lifted as if she were a child and carried through the air. He deposited her lightly on the table and stepped back. Her sex was level with his eyes now. He

281

would see clearly that she was wet and he would know that what he had done to her had excited as much as it had terrified. He told her to open her legs wide and she edged her feet sideways. When the nether lips split apart, a tremor of excitement passed through her body. She opened herself until the tendons of her thighs were visible as hard rods running from knee to sex. The cheeks of her behind tightened and also parted. Her second opening was revealed and the circling vortex of indigo drew the eye.

Alain told Maria to open the red bag and lay out its contents. A number of the items that Maria arranged neatly on the uneven stone surface between Isabelle's feet were familiar to her; there were silk ties, cuffs, a number of leather straps, a small whip and some of the smooth, black rods that she had seen in the chest in Robert's bedroom. As familiar as they were, she could not look at these items without a tightening of her throat and a butterfly tingling in her belly. Besides these things there were a number of glass jars, some containing liquids, other creams. In a small open wooden box gleamed a collection of gold rings.

Isabelle felt a hand on her ankle at that moment and looked down. Alain was stroking her foot as he gazed at the various objects, perhaps deciding which he would use.

'Secure her legs, Maria,' he said.

The woman took two of the leather cuffs and buckled them around Isabelle's ankles. The cuffs had metal eyes and Maria slipped silk ties through each, knotting them. The ties were rather short and Isabelle was obliged to open her legs still further so that she could be secured.

Alain picked up one of the jars and removed its glass stopper. From it came an unfamiliar, chemical smell. He passed the jar to Maria.

'Rub it into her breasts and between her legs,' he said.

The smell grew stronger as Maria dipped her fingers into the jar. She started at Isabelle's breasts, rubbing in the cream with circular motions of her hand. At first there was a sensation of heat and then cold as the cream began to work. Her nipples became very erect as Alain watched. It felt as if someone were blowing on them and pulling on them at the same time. It was very arousing. A tingling spread from these sensitive places to her surrounding skin, to her neck and to her stomach. There was an irritation too, and a desire to scratch herself.

Maria's hands went to Isabelle's sex. She worked across the whole area of the smooth hairless mound and inside too, across and under the thin membranes, carefully avoiding the needle. Here the effect was much stronger: a simultaneous burning and cooling; a feeling that a thousand tiny tongues were licking her, rough and rasping; a sensation of air rushing over the membranes. Her belly flooded with excitement and she took a series of deep breaths.

Alain came to stand before her. 'Bend right over,' he said.

She bent from the waist, her head hanging vertically so that her hair lay on the stone between her legs. In this position her behind was the highest point of her body and the parted cheeks could be seen, even from the front, where Alain now stood. He ran a hand up the outside of one thigh to the hips that flared from the narrowness of her waist like an exotic, darkly patterned flower. Her bound hands rested in the small of her back, the fingers clasping and unclasping as the cream worked its magic.

Alain picked up one of the black rods. It was of a kind that was narrower in the middle than at the ends. He dipped it into the cream and passed it to Maria telling her to push it into Isabelle's behind. When the maid had it pressed to the whorl of tightly closed muscle above Isabelle's sex, Alain lifted Isabelle's chin until she looked directly at him. Against the gold of the mask, the darkness of her eyes was especially fine.

'Open yourself,' he told her.

Her eyes slid away.

'Open,' he repeated, 'and look at me.'

He clearly wanted to see her reaction as the rod penetrated her and the cream affected those sensitive tissues.

283

It was not easy for Isabelle to comply. She remained stubbornly tight despite her best efforts to relax.

'I can't,' she groaned.

'Play with her sex, Maria.'

The woman's thumb pushed into the wide, wet opening and her fingers rubbed along the inside of Isabelle's nether lips. Alain watched as the girl's eyes sparked with arousal. Maria worked around the little opening to her urethra, not touching it directly, not over-stimulating it, but drawing feelings from deep in Isabelle's belly to that place and teasing her with them. All the time that she did this the rod was pressed to her anus, nudging and demanding entry, demanding that Isabelle should want it. Finally Isabelle gave a deep groan of pleasure and opened. The rod slipped in as if finding its true home. Maria pumped back and forth until the passage was easy and the rod slipped in silkily, as it should in a girl's behind. Alain watched all of this in Isabelle's eyes, seeing every part of the drama unfold. Then, satisfied, he told her to stand. The rod was visible between her legs, protruding obscenely. It was held in place by muscles feeble with desire but it was still secure because of the tapered middle. It burnt her, cooled her and stirred her as Robert's sex had in the library.

Alain stepped back and admired this thing that he had created, part woman, part dream. He turned to Anna. 'I must ask for the pleasure of your mouth,' he said.

Anna, composed now, smiled. 'It is yours,' she murmured.

Alain seated himself in one of the cane chairs and Anna rose from hers to kneel in the hot sand before him. He parted his legs and she edged forward so as to undo his trousers. His sex was already hard when it emerged and Isabelle could not help but stare. It was unusually thick, at least as thick as her wrist although no longer than normal. Anna's lips were fully stretched as she took it into her mouth, and her cheeks distended as if she was trying to swallow an apple whole.

'Use the needle,' Alain told Maria. 'You know what to do.'

Isabelle gasped in surprise. 'No,' she said, though the word was muffled by the mask.

The needle had missed her clitoris by the tiniest fraction, as Maria knew that it would, and when she had released the pulled-out lips they shrank back, pressing the shaft of the needle tight against that nexus of sensitive nerves. Now that the anaesthetic effect of the paste was wearing off, the needle hurt but also stirred. Maria took the end and slowly turned the instrument that impaled Isabelle so intimately. The friction on the bud was so subtle, so tantalising, so surprising in the pleasure that it gave, that Isabelle pushed out her belly to feel more. It was by this means that Isabelle was brought to the edge of climax. Alain watched Isabelle intently as Anna used her lips and fingers on his sex. From time to time he would give instructions. He would have Maria apply more cream to the girl, to her breasts so that the heat was increased, to the inside of her thighs, to the join between sex and anus. He would have Maria twist or pump the rod in Isabelle's behind until she was gasping. When she was too close to a climax he had Maria pull the needle outwards so there was no pressure on her bud, only a burning where it pierced her. In this way he prolonged and heightened the process until Isabelle begged for release, begged to be allowed to climax. When she was frantic with need he told Maria to step back and they watched Isabelle as she twisted in her bonds. Sweat poured from her body and her groans were delicious in their despair.

'You have my permission to climax,' he told her. 'You have only to move, to dance for us, if you want that pleasure.'

Isabelle found that when she did move she could stimulate herself. As the muscles of her thighs contracted and relaxed so they forced the needle back and forth across her bud. If she twisted in a slow, primitive sort of dance the stimulation was strong. She watched Alain as she did this and saw his arousal. She danced for him like a slave

285

girl for a sultan. She raised and lowered her pelvis, opening her legs, stretching out her sex, and all the time the needle moved against her. Wetness ran from her sex on to her thighs. The rod in her behind slipped in and out, riding on the taper, falling slowly as she opened the ring of muscle, rising as she tightened and squeezed it back in. There was great pleasure in seeing Alain's eyes narrowing as they swept across her, a sense of her power, a satisfaction that she could move him to feelings other than anger, could make him gasp as she ground her pelvis faster and began to groan in the depths of her need. He delayed his own climax several times, pushing Anna's lips away, so that he could continue to watch Isabelle. Anna's eyes, as they feasted on the vision of gold and indigo, were black with desire, and Isabelle performed for her too. Alain toyed with the spines that pierced Anna's breasts, firing Isabelle's crueller impulses. When he pushed the kneeling girl's head to his sex for the final time he began to pluck the spines from Anna's breasts, slowly. Each time that he did, she moaned.

Isabelle's climax was strong, as strong as anything she had ever felt with Robert. As she writhed in a final paroxysm, so Alain climaxed and Anna drank his seed.

Afterwards, all was still, except for the breathing of Alain and Isabelle which synchronised as they regarded each other. She saw nothing monstrous in his features now, not as she once had.

'Untie her, Maria,' he said, as soon as he was able to speak.

The maid complied, picking at the ties around Isabelle's feet until they fell away, then bade her turn around so that she could free her hands. Since he said nothing about the rod in her behind or the needle at her sex neither woman touched them.

'Lie down,' he said to Isabelle. 'Rest for a moment.'

Carefully, so as not to injure herself, she settled to her knees on the stone surface and lowered her body with a sigh. She was exhausted in such a heat and sprawled on her back, yawning, stretching out her legs which were heavy with the exercise.

'Go to her, Anna; hold her, treat her as a sister.'

Isabelle smiled to hear this, remembering her confessions in the study. Alain knew all of her desires.

Maria cleared the table, packing the various items into the red bag. Anna looked on as the maid fussed, smiling to see her friend. As the girl climbed on to the table, Isabelle took her hand and squeezed it. Anna responded with a light kiss to her shoulder.

'Her mask?' she asked, looking over her shoulder at Alain.

'Remove it if you wish.'

This was not so easy since Anna didn't know how it was fastened. She pulled Isabelle's hair by mistake two or three times and they giggled, Anna to see Isabelle jump and Isabelle to hear the girl's overly profuse apologies. When the mask was free, Anna handed it to Maria and then lay her head on Isabelle's breasts. They cradled each other and rocked back and forth in a barely perceptible motion like lovers reunited after a long absence.

'Fetch water and a sponge please, Maria.'

When the maid returned with a large copper bowl, Isabelle was lying on her back with her eyes closed and Anna was stroking her gently. Her hand ran slowly from Isabelle's neck downwards across her breasts and belly, seeking out all the sensitive places but not to arouse, only to soothe and bestow affection. When the hand returned to her neck, Isabelle took it and pressed her lips to it. Anna allowed this and then slipped her fingers into Isabelle's mouth so that she could suck. Maria watched this for a moment, envious perhaps, and then went over to Alain. She sponged his face and washed his sex.

As Maria finished, so Alain rose and went to stand over the two girls. Anna was lying on her side with her back to him as he approached. Her behind was very full when seen in this position. He took her ankle and pushed the leg upwards so that the taut, shining cheeks opened and her sexual parts could be seen. He was hard again and he pushed into her sex. She groaned and looked over her shoulder but his eyes were not on her, they had themselves fixed on Isabelle. Anna reached her hand down her back, arching to grasp his sex and make a tight ring about the shaft with her fingers. He groaned and looked at the girl. Perhaps it was this tightness that made him think of her anus, as he withdrew and pushed at her narrower opening. She held her cheeks apart with the hand that had grasped him so that it was easier for his entry. Even so, his thickness made her gasp and he had to halt when he was no more than half embedded. Isabelle, realising the difficulty, used her hand to lift the girl's leg high. Perhaps the sense of being opened in this way helped Anna to open her behind. Certainly Alain was finally able to push in until his belly rested on her cheeks. Isabelle sucked at Anna's breasts, nipping the brown tips with a sharp, quick motion that made Anna groan. Soon, Alain was able to move freely and settled into a steady motion. Anna closed her eyes and withdrew into herself. Every muscle in her body went slack. Only her throat seemed to work and she emitted a great, low moan. Isabelle let the girl's leg down and lay on her back. She was very aroused and began touching herself as Alain watched. She pinched up her nipples and ran her hand across her belly.

'Let me see you,' he said.

Isabelle opened her legs wide and pulled them up to her chest. Nothing was hidden then. As he looked at the rod in her behind, she clenched with the sudden thought that he might take her there and he saw it jerk. She saw how that aroused him and she began to clench and unclench, exciting herself in that way. He moved back and forth more quickly and Anna's moans became groans. Her neck contracted and her head arched back. Alain took hold of her hair using it to pull her on to his sex. Isabelle touched the rod in her behind and looked into his eyes. It was an invitation. She used the other hand at her sex, taking the needle in two fingers, one either side of the lips and pulling upwards. She pulled until it hurt and then pulled further until her bud was exposed. She didn't touch it, but the pulling made her feelings very strong and her mouth opened wide.

'Climax,' he told her in a choked voice, 'I want to see you break open with the pleasure.'

She used the needle to caress herself. She took the rod in her hand and began to twist it. Alain was pounding into Anna ruthlessly now. Isabelle's legs opened unnaturally wide and her knees came to rest on the table beside her breasts. She quivered from head to toe. Great juddering waves of excitement coursed through her. Her eyes didn't leave his until the climax took her by storm and she burnt and broke and wept and screamed. His own climax began as he watched her and he tore into Anna's behind in a frenzy.

Before Isabelle was allowed to rise from the table, Alain told Maria to remove the needle. Isabelle winced as it slipped from her. Alain went through the little wooden box that she'd seen earlier and chose one of the gold rings for her. It was small, too small even to fit over Isabelle's little finger, but when Maria slipped it through the punctured labia it felt like one of the heavy iron rings she had been tied to. The maid closed the ring with her fingers and it lay gleaming at Isabelle's sex like a golden pearl in an oyster.

'It is only temporary. We will find you something else when the wounds are healed.'

Isabelle examined it proudly, laying her fingers on the skin of her stomach and pulling so that it moved. It felt as if she were being held at that sensitive place, as if two fingers were lightly pinching her.

'It will help you to remember what you are,' Alain said, 'and it will be useful for tying you.'

He held out his hand and she took it. As she rose from the table the ring pushed against her bud and there was a stab of pleasure. He saw her eyes widen and knew it.

'Go to Robert,' he told her. 'He will want you when you are like this.'

Robert did indeed want Isabelle when he saw what Alain and Maria had made of her. He took her into the gardens, having her walk in front of him so that he could admire her transformation. The head-dress of feathers made her seem taller and emphasised the length of slenderness of her legs and even more like a beast of the imagination, dangerous and seductive. The gold circlet at her sex fascinated him and he had her stop a number of times so that he could toy with it and excite her that way. He took her to the lake and made love to her there, on the green banks and among the plants that grew at the water's edge. She crouched like a leopard in the shallow water among the reeds while he sodomised her. The salve in her bowels took his breath away as he entered her, making him use her roughly.

Afterwards, as they lay on the green velvet of the gently sloping bank, he told her that they would be leaving for London the next day; news of a ship had arrived that very afternoon. His words were casual, delivered as she lay on her belly and his hand delved, once more, into the space between her legs. When he was ready, he took her again, but for once, her mind wasn't with him. All that she could think of was that her farewells hadn't been said.